FIRE ON THE RIO GRANDE:

The First American Revolution

by Kevin H. and Karen C. Evans

Cover designed by Laura Givens
Map by Brook West.

This book is a work of fiction. Names, characters, places, and incidents either are products of the author's imagination or are used fictitiously. Any resemblance to actual persons, living or dead, events, or locales is entirely coincidental.

Kevin H. and Karen C. Evans
Visit my website at https://tyrca9.wixsite.com/kevinandkarenevans

Printed in the United States of America

First Printing: April 2020
1632, Inc.

eBook ISBN-13 978-1-948818-79-7
Trade Paperback ISBN-13 978-1-948818-80-3

This is dedicated to family, close friends, and others that have believed that we were writers, and that someday, something real would actually appear.

CONTENTS

by Kevin H. and Karen C. Evans

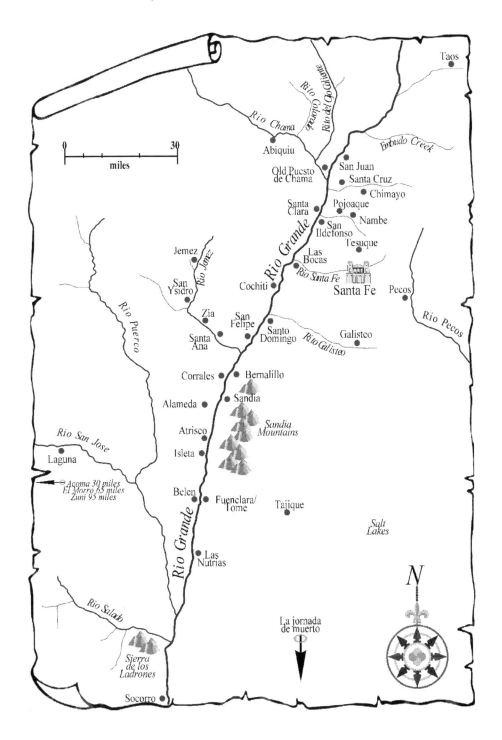

Taos

Rio del Ojo Caliente

Rio Colorado

Rio Chama

Embudo Creek

0 — 30
miles

Abiquiu

Old Puesto
de Chama

San Juan
Santa Cruz
Chimayo

Santa
Clara

Pojoaque
Nambe

San
Ildefonso

Tesuque

Jemez

Rio Jemez

Las
Bocas

San
Ysidro

Cochiti

Rio Santa Fe

Santa Fe

Pecos

Rio Grande

Rio Pecos

Zia

San
Felipe

Santo
Domingo

Rio Galisteo

Galisteo

Rio Puerco

Santa
Ana

Corrales

Bernalillo

Alameda

Sandia

Rio San Jose

Atrisco

Sandia
Mountains

Isleta

Laguna

Acoma 30 miles
El Morro 65 miles
Zuni 95 miles

Belen

Fuenclara/
Tome

Tajique

Salt
Lakes

Las
Nutrias

Rio Grande

Rio Salado

La jornada
de muerto

N

Sierra
de los
Ladrones

Socorro

PROLOGUE

Siege at Bernalillo Chapel
September 1634

Teniente de Bances shouted, and seventy muskets choked out smoke with the musket balls at the barred gates of the small mission church near the village of Bernalillo in the Territory of Nuevo Mexico Adentro. It wasn't every day that Spanish soldiers were sent to attack a church. Usually a church was a refuge, inviolate. But these particular Spaniards, barricaded inside this church, had offended both the Governor General and Father President, and so there was nobody else to plead their case. There was nothing for it but for de Bances to follow orders.

The Teniente clenched his teeth and shouted again. The soldiers sweated in the afternoon sun, and another round of musket balls hit the gates, sending wood splinters and chunks of adobe flying. No sign on surrender. This was going to take all day.

Teniente de Bances resisted the urge to wipe sweat out of his eyes. It was also running down his back under his uniform. In Burgos, his home, he didn't remember getting this hot. This new land, that it took him close to a year to travel to, was not making any effort to make him comfortable.

* * *

Inside the church, dust filtered into the air as another blast of musketry rattled the rafters. But the thick adobe walls and massive doors shrugged off the impact of the projectiles. Father Philip The Steadfast, member of the Society of Jesus, secretary to the personal secretary of the Governor General of New Mexico, looked sadly at the thirty or forty people crouched behind him. Many were bruised and bleeding from the beatings they had suffered in the prison in Santa Fe. Father Philip had organized and led the raid and now was caught in this church with the twenty or so men, and a handful of women and children, who were near the church when the conquistadors arrived.

He was the only blond in this congregation because he'd been born in the lowlands, now known as Holland. He was about thirty-five but looked older. The burning desert of Nuevo Mexico had aged him in the past two years he'd lived there.

More than seventy of the Governor's conquistadors were formed out in the plaza, their avowed purpose to execute every last person inside the church and recapture the Indio leadership that Father Philip had rescued. This old mission chapel had been built thirty-five or forty years earlier, when the Bernal family arrived. It was pink adobe over a frame of hardened oak, with the requisite double towers at the front and the standard arrangement of rows of benches on either side of the center aisle. Father Philip felt momentarily encouraged that the benches were built in the sturdy Colonial style instead of the spindly furniture that had become fashion in the court in Madrid. These benches were sturdy enough to make a great barrier at the door.

The floor was glazed tile, and the overhead rafters weren't covered; one could see the red tiles of the roof in the gloom above. On the side wall, near the nave, was a ladder that led up to the trap door in the wall. That led to the towers. It was supposed to be for the bell ringer, but there were no bells here. They were expensive.

Raymundo, his personal manservant, poked his head out of the door in the upper wall that led to the tower. "Father, they brought up a battering ram. It looks like they intend to smash the door off its hinges." Raymundo, a fifteen-year-old Indio lad, was devoted to Father Philip. He had worked with the priest since the man arrived two years earlier. Today, he was in the only tower still sporting a roof to spy outside. He had ten-year-old Marcos up there with him. They were waiting for a signal from allies.

The walls were a couple of feet thick, but the church had not been built to hold out in a siege. How was he going to save his people? Father Philip turned to the nearest man--he thought his name was Jose. "Get everyone back from the doors. Get the internal barricade finished." Father Philip hadn't spent much time outside Santa Fe, so he didn't know the people of Bernalillo well.

Jose was a young Spaniard who had been born in Santa Fe. He had helped with the raid the night before. He said "Yes, Father" and hurried off. There were two more young men from the raiding party, piling benches against the door.

Then Father Philip called up to the tower. "Raymundo, get down here with that thing you found."

Jose herded the women, children, and captives towards the front of the chapel, all the way up to the nave. Philip hoped they would get help soon.

by Kevin H. and Karen C. Evans

Raymundo came into sight from the hatch to the tower. He climbed down the ladder and met his cousin, Mateo, who was lugging something the size of a large man's leg. It was an Abus Gun, a bulky metal gun barrel mounted on a wooden stock and supported with a mono-pod in the front. Where his Indio manservant had come up with the monstrosity remained a mystery, but Father Philip suspected that it was an ancient trophy from some family's service against the Ottomans on the far side of the Mediterranean Sea.

When Raymundo and Mateo arrived, Father Philip put one last bench on the barricade. "How many shots do you have for that thing?"

Raymundo, a head shorter than Father Philip, brushed his straight black hair from his eyes and looked for a clear spot on the floor to put his monopod. He didn't look up when he answered, "Three."

Father Philip sounded more upset than he meant to. The muskets hadn't fired again, but the assault on the door boomed over and over. "Three? What are you going to do when you run out of those fist-sized bullets?"

Raymundo grinned and pointed to the pile of loot next to the ladder. "Friend Blue-eyes, I have an entire cask of musket balls. Eight or ten of them will fill the barrel nicely, and at least we have enough powder. I wonder what Father Tómas was thinking, storing powder underneath the vestry?"

The heavy wooden doors boomed. Father Philip crouched down again behind the pile of planks, kegs, and the finely finished pew that was reserved for the Bernal family. "Hurry, Raymundo. They outnumber us, they are better armed and armored than we are, and the doors are giving away. Perhaps the Lord will provide, but I fear we are doomed."

CHAPTER 1

Chapel, Palacio of the Governors, Santa Fe
February 1634

T his was the Provence of New Mexico, al Dentro, which meant The Interior. There was the Camino Real, the royal road that led from Mexico City to El Paso, the pass. And then it led from El Paso to Santa Fe. Of course, this royal road was a dirt track for most of its length.

The title of palace may have sounded grand, but that was not the case in Santa Fe. The town was laid out in a grid pattern around a central plaza, just as dictated by the Colonization Board, with the palacio on one side and other official buildings around the square. But when it was built, the first Governor General felt that the specified palacio was not grand enough or large enough. So he built it across one whole side of the plaza, blocking one of the regular streets. He had wanted it to show the local Indios the glory and majesty of Spain. But from the outside, the single-story pink adobe building with the small unglazed windows looked like what it was, a pathetic attempt at majesty.

It was unseasonably warm for February, and most of the snow around the plaza was melting. The sun above shone in an impossibly blue sky, and the trees around town, most of them native juniper, were all thick with yellow pollen. Weather aside, today was a great and marvelous day because mail had arrived from Mexico City. Word had been sent by swift couriers when the mail expedition reached Isleta, which allowed the notables time to arrive in Santa Fe.

All of the notables had assembled, seated on the benches of the chapel. The Governor General and his staff, with the Father President and his aides, were behind a table placed in front of the nave. The rest of the gathering was representatives from all the land-grant families of the province. They sat in the chapel, which was the largest room in the palacio. Here in the Provence of New Mexico, al Dentro, they were so far away, not only from Mexico City, but from Spain, that they only received mail sporadically, maybe once or twice a year. So they were all eager for news, gossip, anything interesting. Each piece of mail, no matter who it was addressed to, would be meticulously read aloud by the Father President's clerk, Pedro.

Father Philip was the only Jesuit present, because he was the only Jesuit in New Mexico al Dentro. He had been here two years, working as he did as the clerk to Father Juan, secretary for the Governor General. The only reason he was there for the mail was to hand Father Juan the next piece to be read.

Letters to the Governor General and the Father President were read first, followed by news for the land-grant families. Father Philip was low on the precedence, even though he probably had more mail than anyone else. He always had an enormous amount of correspondence. The Society of Jesus so firmly believed in communication that some uncharitable types compared the Jesuits to a gaggle of old women gossiping in the marketplace. Because of that fact, the clerks always held his letters to the last.

Nevertheless, the Jesuit had anticipated this package of letters for months. Seven months ago, in the last group of letters to arrive in Santa Fe, several of his colleagues from the order had mentioned a strange new happening in Germany. It was something about a whole town from the future appearing in one day. These people from the future, called uptimers by many, were rumored to know things that will have happened over the three hundred sixty-six years of the future. Philip was very curious what else he would learn about these uptimers.

The morning wore to noon, and Pedro kept reading. Servants were in and out of the chapel with wine or fanning their betters to keep the flies at bay; not that there were many flies this early in the season, but if the servants were there fanning, they would hear the news as well.

Finally, around noon, Pedro turned and handed something to Father Juan, who gestured to Father Philip. "Father, this is your stack. The messenger said they needed a separate bag just for your mail. It's like those Jesuits don't do anything but write to you. It's all letters, not a package in the lot. The others at least get something sent from home: lace, or food, for example."

Father Philip just laughed as he took the bag. "Don't worry about me, Father Juan. First of all, I have nobody at home to send me packages. And with the amount of time it takes to get things from Europe to here, I don't think any food they could send would be very edible. And if it was something to drink it would be stolen along the way, I'm sure."

They both looked in the bag, and Father Philip chose a thick roll of parchment. "Here, Pedro. Start with this one." He chose it because it looked most likely to have something interesting for everybody.

Pedro opened the ribbon and seal with a flourish, and all those with drowsy eyes were pulled back to attention. "Father Philip," he said as he handed a stack of papers to the Father, "this appears to contain some extra pages. And it says they are copies from something called an En-cy-clopedia. They have been hand-copied so that you would have the most accurate prediction of the future in our province."

Father Philip took the papers from the clerk and briefly looked through them. He said, "Indeed, Father President, these are all a series of articles related to Spanish colonies in the Americas. But these articles are said to be from the future."

The Father President, Xavier Bautista, held out his hand, and Father Philip handed over the roll. After a brief examination, he handed the papers back to Father Philip. "Interesting. What do they pertain to? I don't understand."

Philip looked over the papers again. "As you remember, Father President, I received news of this German city, Grantville, in our last bundle of correspondence. Last I had heard, it had not been decided whether it should be visited by the Inquisition for witchcraft. Does your order say anything more of that situation?"

The Father President frowned. "I do seem to remember a mention of it in one of my letters, but I paid it little heed. After all, it's in the Germanies. What could it matter to us here?"

Father Philip bowed slightly in reverence to the Father President. "The note in this stack says that the decision has not been finalized, and there is some dissent as to the final solution. As it stands, Grantville is still as it was, and the war in Europe proceeds much as it has done for years. The Pope will not make this decision in haste."

The Father President nodded. "I am certain you are right, Father Philip. What do these papers include?"

Father Philip skimmed the pages, but instead of having Pedro read them all, he handed different pages to different people, and everyone gathered around to see. Every man who got a piece of foolscap looked through the bit he received. The first thing everybody looked for was their name, but the articles were very vague about individual people.

The head of one of the families jumped to his feet. "That Portuguese upstart, Duke of Albuquerque, has given my land to someone else! This is outrageous!"

Another land-grant noble hurried over. "When does that happen, Ferdinand?"

"Hmm, let me see. It says it will happen in 1660. That's less than thirty years from now. I see that he waits until I am dead and buried. I am already approaching fifty. Who knows how long I will last."

When few names were found, everybody looked to see where to dig for gold. Most of the residents left Spain in hopes of finding gold. This area, discovered by Coronado, had been found when he was in search of the Seven Cities of Cibola, the cities of gold. But there were no cities, just small villages of Pueblo Indios, built of adobe on the mesas. And they had no gold. And so far, almost none had been discovered in this northern wilderness.

But no reference to gold was mentioned, or even silver. The most valuable substance discovered so far were big salt pans, which were scraped up, and the salt was sold back to Mexico. The farming was very good, and the cattle ranching was extraordinary, but none of that was worth any money in Mexico City. All that New Spain wanted was the salt and the native slaves that were sent back to die in the mines.

It took several minutes for the articles to be perused. Father Philip was enjoying the description of a new medical technique described by his counterpart in Venice when his superior, Father Juan, the Secretary to the Governor General, screeched. "This can't be right! We were told it would never happen again."

Everything else was forgotten as all gathered around the distraught little man. Governor General Francisco de la Mora Ceballos asked, "Father Juan, what's the problem? Did something horrible happen to me?"

Father Juan looked up from the paper. "Sir, it isn't you. It's another Pueblo revolt. Not until 1680, but they will succeed. They drive us out and burn the city."

Everyone fell silent as Father Juan read them the entire article aloud. It was clear that in forty-five years, all the natives would unite and drive the Spaniards completely out of New Mexico al Dentro. Hundreds would be killed, and everybody else would be exiled.

When Father Juan finished, Father Philip noticed how quiet everyone had become. He wondered if he could hear a pin drop. He had to admit, though, that it was frightening. The idea that they could be driven out touched some of the deepest fears of the colonists. There were only about two thousand Spaniards living in all of New Mexico al Dentro, compared to almost thirty thousand native Indios.

The Governor General said, "Give me that article and any others that may relate to the revolt. I've read the records of Oñate. I will not have a revolt in my tenure. We will decide in council how we're going to stop this."

The articles were gathered and handed to Father Juan, and the Governor General left with a rattle of his sword.

Thirty-six years earlier.
An encampment near San Juan, Provence of New Mexico al Dentro, New Spain.
December 1598

Don Juan de Oñate y Salazar, Governor General of the new colony, sat at his camp table fuming with anger, then slammed his fist. The tray with wine and cups tumbled to the floor. He

jumped to his feet and began to pace. "Those fools! Intemperate foolish natives, what did they think would happen? Those rebels in Acoma killed my envoy and all of his party. My nephew! The only survivors leapt from the top of the cliff and were saved by landing in the sand. Of course, we stormed their Mesa fortress, and now we must impose a punishment so terrible that they will never again rebel."

The tent was silent, and all the soldiers, aides and servants waited for the sentence. Oñate sighed and sat back down, then nodded at the scribe nearby. "Very well, write this down. I decree that every man over the age of twenty-five shall have his foot cut off. Every last person from that village must serve twenty years of personal service to the crown. Make them build their cursed village on the valley floor and burn to the ground that village on top of the Mesa."

The Governor General's Teniente said, "You might as well just call them slaves, sir. That's what they'll be after all."

Oñate smiled grimly. "No, Teniente, they are condemned prisoners serving lawful sentence. Remember, the Viceroy told us that there was to be no slavery in New Spain."

Santa Fe, Palacio Chapel
February 1634

After the Governor General departed, the Father President looked at Father Philip. His gaze was appraising, as if he were deciding if he could trust the Jesuit. "How much credence do you place in this Encyclopedia?"

Father Philip shrugged. "How is one to judge, your grace? Many of my order are amazed at the artifacts they've already discovered in this Grantville. These uptimers seem to be miracle workers. They really could be from the future, and nobody has yet to find that they are running any kind of falsity. There are more than three thousand of the uptimers, and it would be difficult to maintain that kind of fraud for almost three years. And besides, as to the revolt, how much could the natives do? They are divided. They have five separate languages and at least twenty villages along the great river, broken into family and tribal groups. And you know how they are constantly in conflict with each other."

The Father President nodded thoughtfully. "That is so. We have not had so much as a whiff of revolt for more than thirty years."

Father Philip smiled. "I'm sure it continues because of your skillful political maneuvering, Father President. I don't think we have anything to worry about. As my grandmother always told me, less said, sooner mended, right?"

When the Father President left in a flourish of robes, he had a brooding look in his eyes. The others in the chapel left in ones and twos until Father Philip and Pedro were alone. With a little help from Raymundo, Father Philip was able to carry his correspondence to his scriptorium. It was a tiny cell in the palacio, which was also where he slept. It was covered with papers from top to bottom. He had a small table where he sat to write letters. The only place to put the new mail was on his bed.

Father Philip looked at the pile of letters he hadn't touched yet and settled contentedly into his chair. Finally, he was alone with his sack of letters. That was delightful and would keep him occupied for days to come. But he couldn't help think that there was trouble ahead. The Governor General and the Father President were both angry.

Socorro, Facing the Jornado del Muerto, Journey of Death
March 1634

Captain Fernando Gonzalez shifted in his saddle, working his upper body as he tried to settle the armored breastplate more comfortably on his frame. Steel refused to grow to fit the man, and over the years the captain's gut had become more and more imposing. Without finding a comfortable spot, he motioned to one of his men. "How many do we have left and how much are they carrying?"

Teniente Marcos Doñato came up to the Captain, making his salute. "We have about seventy men left, about half of what we started with in the Jemez mountains. Their burdens have increased correspondingly. Each one of the natives is now carrying about one hundred and twenty pounds of salt. The ones we have left are the strong ones, that is, the ones who have not yet been ripped by the salt and had their skin cracked off their bodies."

Gonzalez nodded. He knew what killed the natives: if it wasn't the direct burden of the salt, it was from inhaling the salt dust. "Doñato, sometimes I think we get as much for the slaves as we do for the salt. The Franciscans say we do this to save their souls. I don't care about souls. I just want to get rich and go home."

Doñato shrugged again. "Captain, who cares about their souls? Anyway, they probably won't survive until Mexico City to be saved."

Gonzalez grinned. "Well, at least we get to visit Mexico City, don't we? I have wanted this since I arrived in this godforsaken territory.

Doñato laughed. "I know a little cantina on the south side of town. I'll take you there when we arrive."

Jemez Mountains
July 1631

A man stood at the mouth of a small canyon in the mountains above the Jemez pueblo. There were many canyons and arroyos here, but this one small canyon was different. It ran at such an angle that the sun never shone directly on the floor of the canyon. And in that canyon there was a cave formed by water dripping through limestone. It opened up areas inside the mountain and filled other places with jagged teeth of stalactites and stalagmites.

It is the cave that Teopixqui hoped for. He was accompanied only by one servant, Quimtchin, as the others had died in a fire some months past. Teopixqui refused to think of it as a failure; he chose to consider his calling as a priest to be more important than any other concern. The fact that the Ironskins in the south took offense at his religious practice was merely a setback.

Teopixqui, a proud priest of a Nahuatl death cult, was dressed mostly in face paint and feathers, a fine-woven loin cloth covering his lower parts, and he wore a headdress of tall feathers which fluttered above his hawk-nosed face. His feathered cloak, used only for formal occasions, was folded and stowed in Quimtchin's pack. He had a belt hung with the wicked macuahuitl, a weapon sometimes used as a ceremonial blade and other times as a weapon of attack. Teopixqui was quite proficient at swinging the wooden sword, embedded with deadly teeth fashioned from glassy obsidian. His head was shaved, and he wore sandals. He was tall, almost six feet, and well muscled. And his face had the lines of permanent frown.

He had heard rumor that the Ironskins were weak here in the north and outnumbered by indigenous people. He heard that a village near here was wiped out by the lung fever. He heard many things.

This cave in this small, unremarkable canyon was going to become a secret haven for worshipers of the darkness. The cave looked difficult to enter and was screened by an old juniper tree and some rabbit brush.

Teopixqui pointed to the cave and glared at Quimtchin. His servant was small, from one of the conquered Indio villages near Mexico City. Quimtchin had been with him for years and now was looking old and bent, with gray hair and wrinkled skin. But Teopixqui didn't care. "You must crawl in and then tell me if this is sufficient. Don't be gone too long or I will cover the entrance and leave you there."

The man bowed, but it looked more like a cringe. A small smile touched the corner of Teopixqui's mouth, but he said nothing.

Quimtchin dug dirt away from the dark hole with his hands and then crawled inside. It was only large enough for him to enter on hands and knees. The sides of the opening touched

Quimtchin's ribs as he wriggled through.

While he was gone, Teopixqui sat on a bolder and examined the sky. Not much of it was visible in this narrow canyon, but he could see white clouds piling higher and higher. There was already a huge cumulus cloud slightly north of him. The sun was hot and oppressive, with building humidity. Teopixqui breathed in the moisture-laden air and sighed, nostalgic for the jungles of his boyhood. It was the first time he had enjoyed this climate. The dry air up here hurt his nose and throat and dried out his skin. His eyes would sometimes feel so dry that they would crack if he blinked too often.

He resented the sun. The things that he worshiped were afraid of the sky eye and pooled in the depths. Teopixqui was certain that if they got deep enough in this crack in the earth, they would find creatures that worshiped darkness and breathed out poisonous fumes.

A voice came weakly from the small cave. "Master, this cave will do. But I can't reach the ledge near the entrance to pull myself out."

For a moment, the priest thought about leaving the man to starve within sight of daylight. That thought made him smile, and as his lips stretched over his teeth, they became visible. They had each been filed to sharp points.

"Master?"

The voice broke his reverie, and Teopixqui frowned. If he left the man there, he would have to do his own digging and even build the fire and prepare food tonight. And as all of that was beneath his dignity, he decided to keep this servant for a while longer. "Let me look. There may be a way to get you out."

It felt somewhat degrading, but he knew there were no other eyes to see. He lifted off his headdress and set it on a juniper branch, then knelt in the dust and stuck his head into the cave. It took a moment for his eyes to adjust. When he could make out details, he saw a ledge a couple of feet in front of him, which seemed to drop off into the infinity of darkness. He moved farther in and looked over the ledge. Quimtchin stood down about five feet. It was obvious from the marks in the dust that the man had fallen over the ledge. "I see you. What else have you found?"

Quimtchin limped to the right, and pointed. "There is another cave entrance there that I can walk through. The ceiling is high, out of sight in the darkness. And it goes flat for a long way."

Teopixqui lay on his stomach and stretched his arm over the edge. "Can you reach my hand?"

Quimtchin limped back to the ledge and stretched up. He was a very short man, and the hump on his back prevented him from reaching too high, but he was able to grasp the priest's hand. Teopixqui started crawling back, hauling his servant up the stony wall. He could hear whimpers and groans but didn't let go or stop until his servant was on his stomach over the edge. Then he let go and backed out of the hole. He was still adjusting his clothing when Quimtchin crawled out.

The servant had a lump on his head and a scrape down one leg. That was causing the limp. Teopixqui turned and headed down the slope, knowing that Quimtchin would follow. And slowly, Quimtchin did.

Santa Fe, Outside the Garrison
March 1634

Don Miguel Quezada examined the young Teniente in front of him. They got younger every year, which seemed to accentuate the pain in Don Miguel's back and left knee. He was past forty.

This was a new arrival, one of thirty soldiers who came with the caravan of supplies and mail ~~delivery~~. This one was, what, twenty or twenty-one? And a prime example of the haughty Spanish noblemen who had helped conquer half the world.

This Teniente may have been a little different, though. He didn't have that defeated look so many sent north carried with them. Don Miguel asked, "What is your name, son?"

The young man threw back his shoulders, and with fire in his grey eyes answered, "I am Teniente Raum Santiago Angel de Bances."

The old captain smiled slowly. "I know your family. Is there not an inherited knighthood that goes with that name?"

The young man looked decidedly embarrassed. "Sir, my father told me not to use the title. He said it was just a carpet knighthood, and until I had earned a real knighthood, I wouldn't differ from the court parasites in Madrid. My father selected New Mexico specifically for me; he said it would test my soul."

Don Miguel looked the young man over one more time. He definitely had Hidalgo features, with hair brown, but not black like the Moors. And his attitude was that of humility in the face of pride. "Teniente, if you keep talking like that you may even impress me. Nevertheless, you are here so that I can tell you about your duty and the locations and dangers of your duty. The first thing you have to know is that you only have one chance in two of surviving past your first year here. Outside of the Valley of the Rio Grande there are two related tribes of natives. One tribe is called the

Apache, the other we call the Navajo. If either tribe captures you, they will kill you very slowly. So don't wander far on your own.

"Here in the Rio Grande valley we have a very different danger. We call it the War of the Two Majesties. That's really where you need to watch your step."

Raum learned that the Governor's office and the high officials of the Church were in constant competition over the work they got from the natives. Each side wanted all of their labor for themselves. And each side was in a fierce struggle to exclude the other side from profit.

The old officer continued. "By law and by decree of both the King and the Pope, natives are not to be abused or enslaved. If there is a single thing in New Mexico that is less observed than these laws and decrees, such a thing is beyond the imagination of anyone in the world. Both the Governor General and the Father President want to control the natives. The Governor General sees the natives as placid beasts of burden that are not quite human. And the Father President is notching his belt for the number of souls he's saved.

"The land for the colonists, which includes us in the Army, has been divided up under the system call Encomendia. That means you get a land-grant that you are not allowed to live on. You must live in town. At least that's the law. Not too many people pay attention to it. They all want to pretend they're great lords and ladies of noble houses, so they have built large haciendas with their land-grant grants. In reality, most of them are low born peasants who came out here in desperation, trying to escape from poverty in Mexico City."

The young Teniente stood silent under this instruction. He'd already heard this in Spain before he left, as well as during his instructions in Mexico City. But it was the prerogative of the garrison commander to tell him whatever he wanted.

Don Miguel was really rolling on his narrative now. "The other factor of life here is called Repartimiento. People in charge have decreed that the Indios must pay for their own conversion and servitude. This decree allows us to take what we want from the villages. Most of the families with land-grants interpret this as the right to take everything and leave the natives nothing. You can't do anything about it, so don't waste your efforts. Complaining will get you put in prison or executed.

"As to the Army, we have only about four hundred of us total. If you are thinking about battles involving many thousands on both sides, this is not the place for that. The only people who could put thousands of people in to a battle are the Indios, and if they ever figure that out, our army will be like a candle in a hurricane. The one thing that makes this manageable is the fact that they all hate each other more than they hate us.

"Now don't expect too much of our soldiers. This isn't Spain, or even Mexico City. For the most part, they are the dregs of the Continent. Almost all of them were given the choice between execution or serving in the Army here in New Mexico. They are thieves, liars, promise breakers, arsonists, debtors, and rapists. Almost all of them would just as soon kill you as look at you. Take any army in the world and mark its moral character down as far as you dare, and that would be better than what we have here."

Teniente Bances interrupted. "Sir, aren't there any redeeming qualities of the Army? How can we accomplish our orders?"

Don Miguel stood with his mouth open for a second, and the Teniente could see that he'd seriously interrupted the flow. Bances blushed and averted his eyes as the older Captain got himself back into the tirade.

"As to the bulk of the common colonists, they came up here to get rich and go home. The only really valuable things are the labor of the natives and the salt from the salt pans we have dug out of the ground. There is no gold. I don't want you out there trying to find it; the Apaches and the Navajo will kill you, and you will never go home to your family.

Tribute from the villages provides a significant portion of the food everybody needs, and drafts of young men from the villages are sent every year to Mexico City but they never come back.

"Stay away from the native women; the difference in culture is so extreme as to be outside of comprehension. You can end up an honored guest or as half a dozen pieces scattered across the countryside.

"To sum it all up, you need eyes in the back of your head and a firm hand, because without them this land will eat you alive. You are so far away from the center of Spain, that nothing, and I mean nothing at all, is the same. Dismissed. Go find your quarters."

Teniente de Bances snapped a salute, turned on his heel, and marched smartly out of the office.

Father Phillip's Scriptorium
March 1634

Father Phillip was writing a letter. There was a ray of sunshine peeping in his small window, high on the wall opposite him. It was a pleasant morning, and he was enjoying writing, when there was a knock on his door. With a little effort, he stood up from the wooden chair and opened the door, surprised to see a young Teniente standing respectfully at attention. "Come in, Teniente. It's de Bances, right? I remember you from the day you arrived. How are you liking Nuevo Mexico?"

The Teniente stepped stiffly into the small cubicle. It was as full of paper as he had ever seen a room. He stood, still stiff, in front of Father Phillip's desk. "Father, I have been told that you received some news in your latest letter about a possible future for Nuevo Mexico. Would it be all right if I read some of it?"

Father Phillip smiled, then stood up and cleared the books and papers from the only other chair in the room. "Certainly, my boy. I would be delighted to share them with you. What part are you interested in?"

De Bances raised his eyebrows. "How much is there ?"

Father Phillip laughed. "I've gotten so many letters that they put mine in a separate bag. I had more than one friend send me word of the miracle village that appeared, entirely populated by non-Germans. So each sent me a different part of the story. I have a passage on the war going on now in central Europe. I have an article about Mexico, which is the name of Nuevo España. I have an article about North American Indians. And then there's the article about the history of Nuevo Mexico al Dentro. That's the one that everyone wanted to see. That's the one they all thought they would find their name in."

De Bances ducked his head a little, appearing embarrassed. "The truth, Father, is that I want to read it all. Maybe not today, but before I left home almost two years ago, I was an avid reader. I loved almost any book I could find. It's one of the reasons my father sent me out here. He was worried that my brains would dry up, as Cervantes writes."

Father Phillip laughed and sat back down at his desk, and shifted piles of paper before retrieving one. "My son, I understand the affliction. Here, start with this article on the Thirty Years' War. It applies to our lives here."

Outside the Plaza, Taos
March 1634

Father Santiago the Diligent was a short, angry little man. In his friar's robes, he paced back and forth by the gates. It was a typical Pueblo village, except that instead of being on top of a mesa, the people built their adobe complex here on the high plains. The houses were built close together, most of them sharing walls with other homes. There were at least three levels, accessed by ladders, and a large circular area with a ladder leading underground to their kiva.

When the soldiers arrived, Teniente Ramirez dismounted from his horse and saluted. Father Santiago was in a foul mood. He snapped, "So good of you to come, Teniente. I have been expecting you for three days. How many men do you have?"

Teniente Ramirez bowed slightly. He had been admonished by the Father President to treat Father Santiago delicately. "Gentle Father, I have thirty-five fully armed and armored men. They are all good sons of the church and are here in obedience to their priest."

Father Santiago nodded and turned toward the open village gate. "Begin here. I want every last mask and doll and every other item of pagan regalia destroyed. I want them burned right here in the middle of the Plaza. Understand me, Teniente. I will not tolerate the pagan rituals of these Indios. The Father President has decreed that there will be no heresy in New Mexico, and I intend to see that his decrees are obeyed to the letter. Burn them all, and if they protest kill a few just to show we are serious."

Teniente bowed again, and turned to his Sergeant. "Have them dismount. They know what to look for. It is not a new task." They stormed into the village, each with a lit torch.

Canyon south of Santa Fe
October 1633

After the corn harvest, Posuwa-i walked away from his pueblo, named San Ildefonso by the Ironskins. He was disgruntled and disgusted by the people that he'd grown up with. He never felt like he belonged. He resented the boy who was the son of the shaman because everything worked for Hi-waq-kwiyf. Everyone liked Hi-waq, and nobody liked Posuwa-i.

The young man brushed his hair back and thought. He was a relatively handsome man of the Tewa people, even though he had only seen nineteen winters. He wore his braids wrapped in bobcat fur and had his sacred bundle hanging from his belt. Over his leggings and fine white shirt, given him by a kind friar, he was wrapped in the woven wool blanket his mother made him for his day of manhood. But none of the mothers in San Ildefonso approved of him, calling him lazy and heretical. So none of the girls his age would even look at him.

The weather turned cold that afternoon, and he was glad for his blanket. He wandered in the wilderness, avoiding Ironskins and other Tewa Indios.

At dusk, as he knelt to drink from a spring, he jumped back in surprise when a man, Navajo in dress, jumped from a high bank to land on the other side of the stream. He had similar leather leggings, like Posuwa-i, but his ears were pierced, his hair was shorter, and he wore a necklace of blue and red beads to carry his sacred sack around his neck. And he was not as young as Posuwa-i.

The man spoke in the trade language. "I am Tse-bit-a, and this is my stream. Why should you drink from it?"

Posuwa-i stood up and pulled his knife from his belt. His pride stung at being addressed by this stranger. There weren't many Navajos near his village, and he considered them worthless. He had never killed anyone, but still couldn't let the insult go without some threat. "I am Posuwa-i. I drink from this stream because I want to and nobody can tell me not to."

Tse-bit-a laughed and put his knife away. "Then drink your fill. I don't want your blood polluting my water."

Posuwa-i didn't put his knife away, but stepped down into the water towards the other man. He held his knife out away from his body, and with his thumb spun it slowly in hand, showing his knife skills.

Tse-bit-a flopped down on the ground in the pine needles and grass. He leaned back on his elbows and laughed again. "I am not frightened of you, young one. I have seen real evil."

Posuwa-i stepped out of the water, put his knife away, and sank into a customary squat. He was a little hurt that he wasn't as intimidating as he thought. "What do you mean by evil? I thought all Navajo were evil."

Tse-bit-a laughed again. "You know nothing of evil. I can still see your mother's fingers on your face. You have never seen evil. But I can show you." He stood up, and started walking. When he'd climbed back up the bank, he turned and looked at Posuwa-i, he stopped. "Aren't you coming?"

Posuwa-i shrugged. "Why not? You are at least more entertaining than my family was." He climbed up and followed Tse-bit-a. They scrabbled through the rabbit brush and juniper trees for some time, and then Posuwa-I noticed that the trees were gradually getting taller. There were fewer juniper trees but more pine trees. At first, they were the scrubby piñon, but they gave way to the huge ponderosa pine. And the two men were steadily climbing higher and higher.

The Navajo leading him was older, maybe as much as thirty. But he kept going even when the younger Tewa was puffing and slowing down. They came to a spot that looked down in a canyon, and Posuwa-i stopped. He recognized this canyon as the one his father had pointed out when they were in a hunting party. He'd said, "Here, it was said, is Litsoof, the cave of darkness. Remember, my son, you should never enter." The thought of the forbidden cave made his heart beat faster. What could be better than Forbidden?

This canyon was narrower and angled so that the sun rarely reached all the way to the sand at the bottom. It was almost winter, a time of more darkness. Posuwa-i thought of those dark spaces down there.

Tse-bit-a kept moving, and they finally reached the sandy bottom. There were signs of some violent flash floods, but this was not the rainy season. Boulders and tree trunks were caught in brush, some of them very large. Posuwa-i was glad that he wasn't here in flood season. He asked, "Is there a settlement here? I didn't think this canyon was livable."

Tse-bit-a laughed again, and this time the laugh wasn't one of carefree joy but of dark delight. "No, the canyon isn't livable. But there are living spaces down there. Are you afraid of the dark?"

"No, of course not." Posuwa-i threw his shoulders back to demonstrate his courage and grit.

But the Navajo kept laughing. "Yes, you are. I can smell it on you. I bet your mother let you keep a lamp by your bed at night." Then the laughing cut off, and the man disappeared. That was frightening enough, but a monster appeared right where Tse-bit-a had been just a moment before. It had pale skin and black circles where the eyes should have been. The fangs were so large they stuck out of the face like spears, and there was no hair, just some ragged fur on the head, seen through wrapped bandages. This was a horrible monster lit momentarily by the last ray of the sun before it slipped behind the mountain. Then it was dark.

Posuwa-i's hand was reaching for his dagger when something struck him on the back of the head. There were stars for a moment, and then he slipped to the ground, senseless.

✳ ✳ ✳

That had been Posuwa-i's introduction to the cult of Tocatl Coztic. He'd come to his senses in a cage built of sticks from cholla cactus. Someone had removed his blanket, his shirt, and his leggings, and he only had a crude cloth wrapping his private areas. He already had several cactus thorns in his arms and back and some in his legs. He tried to move carefully and not bump the thorny sticks, but it was no use. He continued to feel them bite into his flesh in diverse spots.

He heard moans around him and realized that his wasn't the only cage in this chamber. It was very dark, darker than he had ever experienced, but he could hear breathing around him. And echoes. This was a very large cave.

He heard footsteps and held still, wondering if it was better to acknowledge the presence or to pretend to still be unconscious. But he couldn't resist opening his eyes. There was a light. It was more red than yellow, a smoky torch. He watched as the torch wove in and out of cages, stopping here and stopping there, but not in any discernible pattern.

Finally, he could see more details of the figure holding the torch. It was a man, shaved head with some sort of long feathers near the top. The man didn't seem to be wearing many clothes, but the reddish light fell on well-sculpted arms and chest. By now, he was four cages away, and Posuwa-i could see what looked like piles of clothes in the cages near him. He couldn't tell if they were alive.

The torch stopped above his cage, and he looked up into the eyes of the man. He had a hawk nose and a wicked smile that never touched his black eyes. The eyes, though, were captivating. Posuwa-i looked into them, and it was if he was falling from a great height. He felt his stomach jump and twist, and yet he was still falling in the blackness. As he passed out again, he heard wild laughter.

Palace of the Governors, Santa Fe
Meeting of the Provincial Council
April 1634

Governor General Francisco de la Mora Ceballos sat in the chapel that today doubled as council chambers, shaking a fist full of papers in the air. Attending him was the full New Mexico council consisting of himself, Xavier Bautista, the Father President, and the heads of the land-grant families. This was the first large council held in the tenure of this Governor General. Every single land-grant holder and village leader had been required to attend. Some were attending under protest, escorted to Santa Fe by a detachment of the Army. But all were there, in compliance with the Governor General's wishes. All were seriously concerned about the new information from the Jesuits.

The Governor stood and threw the selected parts of Father Philip's letter onto the council table. "A revolt is intolerable. It says here that the natives revolted, and every last Spaniard was ejected from New Mexico, with more than four hundred killed. We can't let this happen. The Indios can not be allowed to revolt. It is our solemn duty as servants of the Crown to maintain the Province of New Mexico for Spain. So before they revolt, we should show them how costly a revolt can be. I want the Indios reminded where the power lies, just as our first Governor, Oñate, did. We will show them the error of their ways by blood and fire. We will correct them by crushing the spirit out of them, and they will not revolt. Tell the Army, tell the priests, and tell the colonists, we must be united in this effort, this must not come to pass."

Then the Governor General sat down with his arms folded across his chest. Father President Bautista stood to emphasize his own opinion. "As the Governor says, we cannot allow our differences to permit the natives to revolt. You must be most firm and diligent in your efforts to inspire the fear of the Lord in them. In this I agree. As the Governor says, so must it be."

After the Father President sat down, everyone sat in silence for a moment. It was such an unusual moment for the Governor General and the Father President to agree that the council was shocked. Then the entire room erupted loud discussion.

Father Philip, sitting behind his superior, secretary to the Governor General, turned to his companion, the priest of the parish north of Santa Fe. "Father Jose, this will not end well. If I read the article correctly, it was this kind of repression and the curtailment of religious liberty that caused the Indios to revolt in the first place."

Father Jose nodded. "All I can see happening is making them revolt forty-five years early." He waved his hand at the dignitaries in front. "But, Father Philip, how can we stop them?"

Father Philip sighed. "The Governor General only seems to understand blood and steel. I respect the wishes of the Father President, but we should do what we can to persuade the Indios, not force them. If they respond as I fear, this will all end in bloodshed."

✳ ✳ ✳

The meeting continued for several hours. First, the heads of each land-grant family had to stand and pledge their family and their honor to the decree of the Governor General. Father Philip, who was taking notes for the Governor General, was saddened to hear the fear and hatred of Indios in so many voices. He had been in Santa Fe for two years, and genuinely liked the natives he knew. He found it hard to understand how much some of the Spaniards hated the local tribes.

Finally, the leader of each village, hacienda, and land-grant were given their responsibilities. Goals were set for the bureaucracy. When the meeting broke up, Father Philip frowned. He gathered his writing materials, thinking of all the copies he would have to make now. The orders were to confiscate food from the villages; perhaps hunger would keep the Indios from revolt.

And he realized that it was this bureaucracy that made conquest of this place possible. In Spain, organization and the ability to precisely define the task required had been one of the most powerful weapons Spain had ever deployed. The Indios had no defense of such organization. In his heart, he prayed for tolerance and empathy and yet knew it would not come to pass.

Village of San Felipe
April 1634

The mounted troop came to a halt at the gate of the village. It was past noon, and Teniente Ramirez wanted to get this over and get back to Santa Fe. But he was on orders from the Governor General.

So he spoke to his men from horseback. "Fill the wagons from the storerooms. I don't want to see one single grain of corn or one sack of meal left in the village. Don't worry about them, they are like rats, they'll have stuff hidden. We have been commanded to show them who's powerful. If they fear us they will not fight us."

The soldiers were like a swarm of locust as they went through the village. Anybody who objected to their search was rudely shoved to the ground. Two men were killed when they tried to protect the village storehouse. The soldiers had been ordered not to kill unless necessary. After all, the placid Indios were valuable workers, and their services were still much in demand by the colony.

Santa Ana Pueblo
April 1634

In the dusk, a horse and rider ambled along the river and took the path up to the gate of the village. It had been shut at sundown.

by Kevin H. and Karen C. Evans

The rider was Eduardo Griegos Bernal, heir to the Bernal land-grant. He had been born at home only seventeen summers past. He was a good son of his father, the Alcalde of Bernalillo. He was tall, almost five feet eight inches, and had black hair from his mother. That night he was wearing a black cloak to hide him in the darkness.

But when he'd heard from his father what the Governor General and the Father President planned to do to the Indios in this village, he'd stormed out of the house. The thought that his friends in Santa Ana would be pushed to the edge of starvation for no other reason than to keep them from revolting burned deep into his heart.

So here he was, just past sunset on a chilly spring night, contemplating his actions. Yes, Eduardo agreed with his father that the commands of the Governor General were madness and the way the Indios were treated was a crime. His education had been very thorough, more so than many of the young men his age. He studied with the family priest, Father Tómas, using the scriptures and the declaration and official paperwork that the family retained in pride, showing their land-grant and the document signed by the king. He had read for himself the declarations by both King and Pope demanding fair treatment to the Indios.

Although his father could not afford to be seen in defiance of the Governor General, Eduardo could not stand by idly. So he was going to take action that night. But it wasn't seemly to do so in a way that put his father and family in danger. He pulled out a black hood he'd fashioned at home and pulled it over his head, obscuring his features. He could see through the eye holes. He was not ready to disgrace his father or himself. It was best if nobody knew who he really was.

Eduardo had a plan. He knew he was a day ahead of the soldiers confiscating food. He was going to champion the Indios and not allow the Father President or anyone else to treat the natives as less than people.

When it was full dark, he checked to make sure nobody was watching, then banged on the gate of Santa Ana Pueblo, the closest Indio village to Bernalillo. When it opened, the Indio gatekeeper, who had obviously been sleeping, said, "Who is there? Do you know how late it is? Why must you wake us?"

The young man tried to disguise his voice, but he spoke in trade language. "You will call me Ka-ansh, the mountain lion. I come with a warning for your village elders, it is urgent!"

The old man was about to close the gate, and Eduardo's irritation bubbled up. His voice got higher and louder. "Please, Tsigu-may. I am Ka-ansh, the mountain lion. I am here with a message. Just call the elders."

The old man looked at him for a moment and nodded. "I will get them. Wait here."

Eduardo worried for a moment that he had been recognized, but didn't have long to wait. Within moments, a crowd gathered. Ka-ansh climbed down from his horse and bowed to the shaman and elders. "I am sure you have heard rumors of what has happened in the villages north of you, when the soldiers burst into their villages and confiscated the food. It is about to happen here as well, tomorrow morning. You must hide your food tonight. The garrison will arrive tomorrow morning. They will take all of your food, as they have done to the other villages. You must hide it tonight."

The shaman tried to peer into Eduardo's eyes. "Tomorrow? Are you certain? Perhaps . . ."

Ka-ansh interrupted. "No, it is certain. It was discussed in the council of Santa Fe last week. Make sure that you leave a few ears of the oldest corn and one or two sacks of meal in the storehouse so they think they have it all. But make sure the rest is well hidden, and not in the village. Not even the sacred kiva is safe. The orders of the soldiers are to make you uncomfortable. They want you to feel powerless."

The elders looked at each other. Tsigu-may said, "Ka-ansh, can we trust this information?"

Ka-ansh straightened his shoulders. "I swear it is true, on the life of the Alcalde of Bernalillo. He has always treated you fairly, even when his neighbors laughed at him for doing so. You must take precautions now; tomorrow will be too late."

Then Ka-ansh climbed into the saddle. "I must go. I have to warn two other villages. Do not delay." Then he spun his horse and rode off into the darkness.

Santa Fe Garrison
May 1634

Colonel Carlos Martinez looked with an inordinate amount of pride at the two guns mounted on their carriages in the garrison. His men called them pipas, or water pipes. They were six pounders, meaning they fired six-pound cannon balls. And they were the only large caliber guns in the Province of New Mexico.

He and his cannon crew, Santiago and Pablo, were enjoying the cool of the evening. Martinez sipped his wine and frowned at the palacio in the darkness. "I have been at this station for almost three years now, and there's one thing I really hate. It's as if the whole world is made of mud. Our houses are mud, our walls are mud. Sometimes I feel like my bed is made of mud."

Pablo leaned back, looking at the stars. "I don't mind the mud, it does make the rooms cool in the summer and warm in the winter."

Santiago drained his cup and set it down, wiping his large mustache. "I heard an interesting bit of gossip today. Teniente Ramirez told me that they have had very little luck collecting food from the Indio villages. He said that someone must have warned them."

Pablo blinked, a little drunk. "I heard that too. There are whispers that a big cat has come down from the mountains to protect the Indios."

Martinez laughed. "Oh, of course. A savior. Haven't you heard? They have a new kachina in the villages. They call him Ka-ansh. I think it means wildcat or something. They say that this Ka-ansh has been sent by the Corn Maidens to save the People from the Ironskins. But it's just ignorant superstition. That's us, you know. Ironskins. Don't believe everything you hear from the Indios. They are liars."

The wine skin was empty, so Colonel Martinez stood up and stretched. "The Indios can have all the kachinas they want, for all I care. Let the Father President be concerned with that. All we need to worry about is taking the best care of our Pipas. I want you out here before dawn, and make sure everything is ready. We are rolling out at first light. We may be stuck here in this mud-covered wilderness, but with cannons like these we can't fail."

Santiago and Pablo stood as Colonel Martinez left. Santiago said, "Well, I guess we should get some sleep. We have to be up early tomorrow."

Pablo said, "We're supposed to destroy something valuable tomorrow. What do you think Colonel Martinez will choose?"

Santiago yawned and shrugged. "I don't care, just so we can blow up something, and then get back in time for lunch."

Pablo said, "Do you think the Governor General will come to watch?"

Santiago frowned. "That's possible. You know the Governor General is also enormously fond of our cannons."

Santiago and Pablo knew it just meant a lot more work hauling the cannons and their ammunition back and forth through town. But that's what they got paid to do.

by Kevin H. and Karen C. Evans

* * *

By the time the sun peaked over the tall mountains to the east, Colonel Martinez had his Pipas ready and targeted on some rock walls in the north part of Santa Fe. The Indios worked on them all the time. They had been built across stream beds in the area to serve as dams for irrigation, to divert water away from the fields and into the holding ponds that the Indios used in the dry times.

Martinez pointed toward the first dam. "Well nobody lives in those. It will fulfill our orders from the Governor General and not kill any Indios, which is what the Father President wants. All in all, it will be a good day's work and keep everyone happy. Get started."

The crew set up for a drill designed to smash up years of the Indios' work. Even though it meant more sweating and hauling, Santiago and Pablo did enjoy the boom of their *Pipas*.

And Santiago was pleased, because they finished the job before lunch.

Jemez canyon
August 1634

Father Philip mopped his face with a handkerchief. The hot August sun in the blue sky seemed to beat the juniper trees and sage brush flat with the heat. There was the taste of dust in the air, but the wind was still. The monsoon clouds that usually showed up in July had been weak this year, and the corn and beans in the fields were small and dry. It would be a hard winter if they couldn't get water.

So far, Jemez village still had water. The Jemez river was fed by mountain springs and usually didn't dry up in the hot summer. Their village was higher than the valley below and got cool evening breezes. It was protected from the drought below.

The village was situated in a spot not too far from the hot springs, about where the red rock stopped and the tall pine trees started. The Ponderosa pines shaded the village nicely, and the climate was much more comfortable than that around the Rio Grande river dwellers.

Father Philip was here for something dangerous. He had been invited by Raymundo, his Indio assistant. He sat near the gate of the village and watched as furtively, in the darkness of a moonless night, delegates from Pueblo Indio villages as far north as Taos and as far south as Isleta gathered. Many had traveled on foot for days to get here.

This was a secret meeting that the Ironskins could not know about. Jemez had been chosen because while it was central to the villages, the deep canyons and rocky terrain made it difficult for large numbers of the Ironskins on horseback to reach it.

The Indio leaders gathered underground, deep within the round ceremonial kiva of the village. Not only were the religious leaders and wise men present, but the village governors appointed by the Spanish had come as well. There were even a few white men in the gathering, including Father Philip. He was not sure what would happen, but Raymundo seemed to feel it was important for him to be here. Raymundo stayed by his side to help translate the trade language, of common use in the area.

First, or course, were the gathering and cleansing rituals, and the Jemez shaman took care of that. Then, Chief Hana-chu of Jemez pueblo stood to speak. He looked at Father Philip, and said, "Friend Blue-eyes, perhaps you can help us understand. The Ironskins have taken away our food stores, they have burned our kivas and kachinas. Why do they hate us now? We have done nothing to cause the troubles."

Father Philip stood up, accompanied by Raymundo. He was nervous because he was uncertain of his language skills, but Raymundo was there to translate if necessary. He frowned, ordering the Indio language in his mind. "Wise chiefs, this is all a misunderstanding. I am saddened that your people have suffered. The Spanish are taking action because of a piece of paper sent from the Spain. The Governor General and the Father President have both become convinced that all of the local tribes in the Rio Grande valley are planning a revolt. It is thought that you plan to murder every Spaniard along the Camino Real al Dentro."

They received this news in silence, and Father Philip glanced at Raymundo. In a low voice, he spoke to Raymundo. "Do you think they understood me?"

Then Wa-tu, shaman for San Filipe pueblo, and oldest man present stood up. "Friend Blue-eyes, can't you convince them it's not true? We hardly even speak to some of these tribes. The Tiwa speakers of Isleta cannot be trusted: they are liars and thieves."

There was a rumble of anger, and several younger men stood with spears in their hand. Father Philip's stomach clenched with fear, and he held up his hands. "Please, we need to keep personal slurs to ourselves. I know there are a lot of bad feelings among the Pueblos, but we must put our differences aside here and talk. Otherwise, my people, the Ironskins, will continue to set you against each other and continue their atrocities."

Wa-tu bowed his head. "I bow to your wisdom, Friend Blue-eyes. My feelings for Isleta and all the Tiwa mumblers can wait for another day."

Father Philip sent a silent prayer heavenward, and continued. "I'm afraid that fear is the temperament of the Ironskins because there are so few of us and so many of you. As they are convinced you all wish to kill them in their sleep, they will strike first, in hopes of winning before a war is started. They wish to intimidate you into total submission."

The tribal elders discussed this among themselves. Father Philip whispered to Raymundo, "How are they taking it? Do they understand the serious nature of these talks?"

Raymundo nodded. "They have always had a distrust of outsiders. This just proves why they should continue to hold the Spanish as enemies."

The discussion became angry, and Father Philip could no longer follow it on his own. But Raymundo stood up, anger blazing in his eye. "If it were not for this outsider, Friend Blue-eyes, you would not know the threat. Not all outsiders are the enemy."

Father Philip placed a hand on his assistant's shoulder, but spoke loud enough for all in the kiva to hear. "There is no reason to raise our voices, Raymundo. For me, I know the law, sent from the King and the Wise One of our religion in the old world. They are strictly prohibited from exploiting the local peoples in this fashion. It is against the law to make you slaves or steal your property. I am here tonight because I believe that what the two majesties of New Mexico are doing is wrong. And because of their decisions, I can no longer support them. I'm warning you, and I will warn everyone I can, that the abuses will continue. I have become convinced that you may have no other option, save rebellion."

That silenced discussion. All eyes turned on Father Philip. Raymundo said, "Father, what are you saying?"

Father Philip rubbed his face with his hands, praying that he had made the right choice. "I have thought on this for a long time. It is a hard thing for me as I am truly a son of my church. But I cannot tolerate the abuses being heaped upon you, especially from some imaginary slight perpetrated by the records brought back from the future town that appeared in Germany." And then he sat down on the ground next to Raymundo. His head was spinning, and his hands were shaking, but in his heart he knew that this was the right decision.

The discussion went late into the night, with many penetrating questions. Water was brought to everyone, and small corn cakes. Father Philip was sleepy, and it was difficult to understand anything but the basic words. But somewhere around dawn, a miracle happened. The leadership of the Pueblos of the Rio Grande valley finally agreed on something.

Together they hammered out a plan that all agreed upon. The Indios were finally drawn together in rebellion.

Palace of the Governors, Santa Fe
August 1634

The Governor General and the Father President sat across the desk from each other in the Governor's quarters. It was a rare but necessary private meeting. Both knew that someone was listening from the Governor's staff and that the Father President had paid spies in the palacio, but the privacy was important.

Francisco de la Mora Ceballos, Governor General, was a large man, well muscled, with the look of a hawk in his eyes. His neatly trimmed beard didn't show any of the gray hair coming in at his temples. He leaned back and wiped sweat from his face. "Xavier, I don't understand it. Everything we do seems to make the possibility of revolt more likely. We absolutely have to obtain control, or that rebellion from Father Philip's mail will become truth in fact. A rebellion can't break out now. I only have one more year of this assignment. I refuse to be known as a failure."

Xavier Bautista, the Father President, folded his hands across his stomach. He was older than Francisco Ceballos, his beard was salt and pepper, and his hands and face were wrinkled. He had been here a long time. He was dressed in robes, not as ceremonial as he would wear for Mass, but still elaborate. And he never seemed to sweat. "Indeed, Francisco, I agree that at times, you and I have been at cross purposes. I think it's time for us to put aside our differences and do something significant. We must show everyone, Spaniards and Indios alike, that we do indeed have control over the situation. Perhaps we could invite all the governors of the various native pueblos to the capital and make it sound like some kind of impressive gift-giving ceremony."

Ceballos waved his silk kerchief at a fly. "Why? What good would that do?"

Bautista smiled slowly. "Once we have them all together, they will come to understand that we control their destiny. We can quell this rebellion by separating its head from the body."

Ceballos smiled as well. "Xavier, that has merit. Before I arrived, the previous Governor General gave each of the village governors a silver-headed cane to demonstrate their authority. I know none of them appear in public without their canes. Perhaps we can demand they appear to swear fidelity to Spain or surrender their cane. They have become a great status symbol among the different tribes. Once they are here we can exert our authority."

Bautista sat forward. "We need a little something more, Governor. As both you and I know, the real power in each village is not the official governor. They are just toadies selected by us. We need the secret religious leader of the tribe. That is the person that we most need to get our hands on. If we eliminate the tribal elders, we can probably control the nation. As far as I can determine by church law, they could all be classified as witches, and indeed we can either hang or burn them. That might give the message that we need to emphasize."

Ceballos steepled his fingers. "Very well. I will call my secretary and draft a letter to be delivered immediately. That will put our plan into play."

✻ ✻ ✻

The secretary to the Governor General, Father Juan, appeared at the door to Father Philip's scriptorium. "Father Philip, I need your help."

Father Philip stood up immediately. "Of course, Father Juan. What can I do?"

Father Juan gestured, and they walked down the hall to the larger workroom. "We must send letters to the Governor of every Indio village. The Governor General wants to invite all of them to attend a special council. He has also requested that they bring their silver-headed canes as a mark of their leadership, along with at least two advisers. The more advisers, the more status. Emphasize that if we work together we can resolve our situation. So I need you and several of the other churchmen to help in the wording and copying of these letters as soon as possible. The meeting is to be held on the first of the month."

Father Philip smiled sat down by the writing table. "This is good news, Father Juan. I have been praying for a peaceful solution. Perhaps this would resolve in peace after all." He was already forming phrases in his mind about peaceful coexistence, and honor between the Spanish and the native pueblos.

✳ ✳ ✳

Back in his room, Father Philip read through the letter he had just finished for accuracy. It was the twelfth one he'd finished writing. Only two to go. The only other person there was Raymundo, his assistant. "Here is the last of my share of letters. I have made sure that these messages are positive. But I don't know."

Raymundo gathered the stack of folded documents and placed them in a leather satchel. "What are you worried about, Father? Aren't the letters supposed to show the governors that the Spanish wish them no ill will?"

Father Philip stretched and stood up to pace. "I'm not sure why, but I have misgivings. I've never seen the competing Majesties cooperate like this. The Governor General and the Father President are proud men. Proud men do not give in easily. Somehow I sense all will not go well."

Raymundo stopped at the doorway. "What do you mean, Father?"

Father Philip pulled a fresh piece of foolscap out of the stack and started writing again. "I mean that I have suspicions about their motives. The Governor General and the Father President are up to something. Do you still have your contacts with the southern Apaches?"

Raymundo shrugged and blushed. "You mean the Jicarilla? Well, I know this girl ..."

Father Philip smiled. "Raymundo, your exploits are numerous, but not pertinent to this situation. I need you to get a message to their Tribal Council. Shaman Kuruk is a reasonable man. And besides that, if we offer him some horses, enough warriors will come if we need a rescue. Make sure he knows this is serious. The Governors' meeting is in two weeks, and who knows what may happen?"

Hacienda Ordoñez, near Santa Ana Pueblo
August 1634

The rising sun reddened the morion of Hidalgo Ordoñez as he sat tall upon his horse. He was an older man, late forties, with a gray beard and moustache. But none of his workers doubted that he had the strength to beat any one of them to death. He surveyed the group of Indios assembled before him.

He turned to his foreman, Jose. "Take twenty of these men. Twenty should be enough. I want the field next to the river, on the north end, harvested and plowed today. If they don't accomplish the work in the daylight, light fires, beat them, and make them work all night. These Indios are useful, but lazy. Don't let me find you turning a soft heart to them. I must spend the day with the sheep; it's time to move them to the high pasture."

Jose nodded and started to shout in a pidgin dialect of Spanish and Keres. Don Ordoñez shook his head and turned his horse away. It was disgraceful that these Indios who had grown up on this grant still couldn't speak proper Spanish.

✳ ✳ ✳

The sun was high, and it was hot all day, as the men struggled in the field. It had been another long hot summer, with few rainy monsoons to relieve the heat. The crop was sparse, and the clay was as hard as iron, baked and unyielding. As the sun settled in the west, there was still almost half of the field to be finished. The foreman rode up and down on his burro with his lash. Many worked harder to avoid his notice.

But the foreman didn't notice what some of the men saw. A horse was tied in the shade of a juniper near the dry creek bed, and the dry grass rustled between there and the field.

Suddenly the foreman was pulled from his burro by a man wearing a black scarf as a mask. Ka-ansh didn't kill the foreman, just knocked him unconscious and tied him to a tree. The Indios laughed among themselves as they faded into the darkness to hide from the next work detail. Many whispered the name Ka-ansh.

Santa Fe Plaza
September 1634

When Father Philip stepped out from the palacio, he noticed that the central plaza in front of the palacio was immaculate. The two brass cannons that the Governor was so fond of were prominently displayed, with their crew standing by. A large platform had been built, upon which the Governor General and the Father President sat. Behind the platform were gathered the alcaldes of every Spanish settlement, along with the heads of the land-grant families and the churchmen of the Franciscans.

Father Philip took his place with the others in the hot sun behind the platform. He felt the light fingers of a breeze and looked up for a cloud to give a little shade, but there were none. Father Juan, next to him, whispered, "I have never seen a gathering like this. You have been here longer than I, what is happening?"

He whispered back, "I would say that the Governor General and the Father President want an audience for their actions today. Why do you think we are so far separate from the Tribal Governors?" The Indio dignitaries were gathered in front of the platform. Each Governor prominently displayed his silver-headed cane.

The Governor General stood, and the crowd fell silent. Ceballos ran his eyes over the people in front of him and smiled. "Welcome, honored guests. You heeded our call for a meeting, and I'm very pleased to see all of you here. Everyone is here except for the Jemez people, who threatened our messenger, and refused to attend. They shall suffer my wrath."

Then, without hesitation, the Father President stood and signaled Don Miguel, who sent the guards to surround the Indios. Horsemen rode closely, and all the soldiers drew their swords. There was a sudden blast of horns and shouts by the soldiers to deliberately disorient and distract the captives as they were taken into custody.

When all the Indios had been led off to the cells behind the palacio, there were shocked gasps from the witnesses, but no one dared to intervene. Nobody was as well armed or well trained as the Garrison of Santa Fe.

Father Philip was near the platform as the Governor and the Father President exited. He pretended not to listen to their conversation.

Bautista smiled at the Governor. "Well, that came off better than I expected. I think the next step will be the most important. We should have some pretense of legality about this, or the administrators in Spain will condemn you and me."

The Governor General grinned, almost giddy, looking at the pile of silver-headed canes that had been confiscated. "That is not a problem. My staff delights in bureaucracy. There will be paper, documents, and records by the barrel-full. We will confuse them with statistics and paperwork. All we need is a wagon load of paper, and we are safe on that count."

Across the Province of New Mexico
September 1634

Father Philip sat meditating in his scriptorium when Raymundo appeared. "Father, I just came from Jicarilla. The news of the arrest and confinement of the tribal elders and the tribal governors is on every tongue, like a torrential storm. From what I've already heard this morning, every village along the river, and even the villages further away in the far western corner of the colony, are angry and shouting."

Father Philip shook his head, saddened and weighed down with the news. "I never thought I'd see Spaniards fall so low. The delegates from all the pueblos came peacefully and were betrayed. The thin pretense that brought the elders to Santa Fe was a travesty."

Raymundo frowned. "What do we do now?"

Father Philip stood. "Come with me to the chapel. We're going to pray."

✳ ✳ ✳

By the next day, messages from Raymundo's contacts poured in to Father Philip. The betrayal in Santa Fe was the spark that set the colony alight. Young men, eager for a chance to show their courage, exulted in the news. The rebellion that had begun in Jemez sparked and caught fire from Taos to Isleta.

Preparations were made. Messages were sent back and forth. For once, the Keres agreed to listen to the Tiwa; Jemez was the center of it. Many of the younger men were overjoyed with the opportunity to do something about their frustrations.

Of course, there were still some hold-outs. They argued against rebellion, pointing to the depredations of the demon Oñate almost forty years earlier. War was not the way of the people of the River Valley. But those voices were few and far between. Most felt that when violence is necessary, they would provide it.

Two days after the betrayal, Father Philip rode a burro out of the palacio stables on an assumed errand from the Governor General. In reality, he was going to meet with his friend, Don Federico, Alcalde of Bernalillo. They came together near the village of Cochiti at sunset.

Both men tied their mounts, walked to the rim of the hill, and admired the sunset. It was magnificent, bands of orange and pink, with thin gossamer clouds shining like gold filigree over darker blue clouds.

It was true that the beauty of the land and the sky in this frontier region were unmatched. The longer Father Philip lived here, the more he came to love it. He sat down on an adobe bench overlooking the reservoir lake. Don Federico joined him.

Father Philip said, "Federico, I'm pleased you could meet me. I'm certain you know the temper of these times. I know the Indios around Santa Fe are boiling with rage."

The older man was a little stiff after the long ride. It was almost twenty miles from the village of Bernalillo. "Yes, I witnessed what our two Majesties did. They have no shame or fear of reprisals from crown or pope."

They both sat silent for a moment, sad at the state of affairs. Then Don Federico said, "Father, the letters you got from Europe, is there anything in them to encourage us? Or are we to suffer the indignities of the Two Majesties for the rest of our lives?"

Father Phillip sighed. "I read the Bible, looking for answers. I have read every word of the missives, and I haven't found a solution. There was an article in them about negotiating peace, but there is much of it I don't understand, and the examples given are not familiar to me."

Bernal shook his head. "We are far from the Viceroy, and it would take months to get a message to Mexico City. What can we do?"

Father Philip looked to heaven for a moment, praying he was making the right choice. The sunset darkened, going from melon colors to blackberry. He watched as a small rain cloud seemed to be raining on the valley. But it was called virga, the dry rain that evaporated before it reached the ground.

It was as if God had given him a metaphor for how useless he felt. Just like that little rain cloud, ineffectual at sending rain to the ground. He knew that any effort now to keep the peace would have the same effect as the virga.

Then he reached his hand into his shirt and pulled out a rolled piece of parchment, tied with a leather string. "I found out that their two majesties plan to kill the captured Indios on a pretense of witchcraft. If you are willing, I have a plan that will save the lives of those Indios held in prison at the palacio in Santa Fe."

The Alcalde took the rolled messages, and made the packet disappear inside his jacket. His face showed no emotion, but he old man's eyes were troubled. "You know, if anyone found out we we're talking like this, we would see the inside of that prison as well."

Father Philip nodded. "Yes, but Don Federico, what else can we do? You know that the actions of our two majesties are against the laws of God and man. If we turn a blind eye, we are a guilty as they. I know you have friends not only in the Santa Ana pueblo, but many others. Your hacienda and village are more tolerant than many others. Can I count on your support?"

Federico Griegos de Bernal, Alcalde of Bernalillo, sighed. "Father, you must give me a chance to consider. I have a wife and children I would risk."

Father Philip nodded. "Send me word by the end of the week. It will be difficult, and we can no longer risk being seen together. God be with you." The men shook hands and left the lake village behind in the darkness.

Santa Fe, New Mexico
Evening, September 1634

On the third day of the Inquisition, rumors spread out from the prison wing of the Palacio of the Governors. Beatings were the order of the day. Prisoners had been manacled to the wall, denied sleep and food. The Inquisitors were certain that they could get the chiefs to confess to fomenting rebellion throughout the colony or the shamans to admit to witchcraft.

It was still very early in the morning. Father Philip had been pacing in his room, unable to concentrate on the letters he had to write. He was interrupted by his assistant, Raymundo. "Father, a boy came with a message that you should visit the parish in Agua Fria. They have asked you to come help with a baptism."

He looked with surprise at Raymundo, who slowly winked and handed him a slip of paper. He smiled. Raymundo must have been practicing a wink, it was not something Indios did. "Oh, yes. A baptism. I remember that Father Jose contacted me a couple of weeks ago. Thank you, Raymundo."

The burro he checked out today was a little fractious, so it took a little longer than expected. Finally, dusty from the trip, he strolled into the small plaza with the mission church of Agua Fria, near a natural spring. He sat on a bench and asked a girl to bring him some water.

The old man on the bench next to him faced the opposite direction, and they ignored each other. Father Philip examined the clothes of a peasant, but when the hat lifted, he looked into the eyes of the Alcalde of Bernalillo. Father Philip whispered discreetly, "I thought you were going to send word. You risked yourself again?"

Federico smiled slowly. "I decided a ride would be nice. And I'm in charge, so I gave myself permission."

Father Philip smiled as well. "So you have heard about the actions of the Inquisition?"

Don Federico squinted against the bright summer sun. "It's a state secret, so of course, everyone has heard."

Father Philip turned and stretched his legs out in front of him, placing his back to the Alcalde. He didn't want any spies of the Father President to see him talking to anyone. His voice was low. "I am pleased to see you here today, my friend. Does this mean that you have decided?"

Bernal snorted. "Not me so much as my wife. Garciella had much to say on this issue and convinced me that we must do something to protect our friends the Indios. The people of Santa Ana saved her life as a child and gave her shelter during an Apache raid. She has never forgotten."

Father Philip smiled and crossed himself. One good deed is remembered for a lifetime. "I'm glad to hear it, my friend. God works in mysterious ways. So, have the young men carried the messages?"

Alcalde Bernal stretched, yawned, and stood up. His voice was a mere murmur. "Yes, everything is ready. When do you want to begin?"

Father Philip stood. "Tonight. Meet me by the prison gate after dark. Bring only those that you feel you can trust. With luck, no one will get killed."

The Alcalde stifled a yawn. "You will not see me this evening. I must maintain my position. But my son, Eduardo, has already been helping our friends. Not many know, but he has become a champion of the local population. I've worried because he's vocal in his opposition to the abuses of church and state. The Indios call him Ka-ansh."

Father Philip's eyes widened. "I had heard certain rumors about a mountain lion that made me wonder. I am pleased that it turns out that the phantom kachina is your son. I look forward to making his acquaintance tonight."

✳ ✳ ✳

About nine o'clock, when it was totally dark, they gathered outside the city walls of Santa Fe. Father Philip looked over his group of freedom fighters and was pleased. Or at least not quite as afraid. Eduardo Bernal, not yet disguised as Ka-ansh, was accompanied by some armed farmers from Bernalillo and a couple of hot-headed Navajos who were co-conspirators with Ka-ansh. Father Philip had his servant, Raymundo, and Raymundo's cousin, Mateo, both armed with clubs and belt knives.

The farmers were handed torches, and Father Philip stood near the rear of the crowd with a floppy hat pulled over his eyes to hide his identity. They boldly marched up to the prison gates, and young Eduardo brandished a large scroll complete with ribbons and elaborate wax seals. He let Father Tómas, the priest from the Bernal Hacienda, do the talking, in case anyone in the palacio recognized his voice.

Father Tómas shouted, "We hold here written orders that you are to turn the Indio prisoners over to us immediately. The Father President is not pleased with the actions of the Inquisition today, and he is taking the prisoners to a secret location to continue the interrogation."

The jailers, mostly poor uneducated men, looked with reverential awe at the elaborate document. They could not read it, but they knew it was important because of the ribbons and seals. Their foreman, Antonio, stood at the large bolted doors and shouted back. "You are not the Father President. And I don't recognize any of your soldiers. Who are you?"

Father Tómas sneered. "It is not your place to question me. I am part of the Inquisition, sent by the Father President. Bring them immediately. Make no delay. Who are you to question written orders? The signatures are there. Do you not recognize the signature of the Father President? You must obey!"

While Antonio deliberated, Eduardo whispered to Father Tómas, "Father, I didn't know you were such a good liar."

The priest didn't look at Eduardo. "I've already assigned my penance. So I might as well go full force today. Tomorrow will be prayers and self-recrimination."

They could tell that the reason Antonio hesitated was because he'd begun to suspect that this was a rescue effort. The whole affair was a bad situation.

Antonio said, "Father, the scroll may or may not be official. I don't know because I can't read. But I do know that if I release these Indios and your paper isn't what you say, my men and I will be tortured instead. I will release them to you, but you must allow us to come with you, for if we remain we are surely dead."

Father Tómas smiled. He knew that many Spaniards feared and detested the Inquisition. "Bless you, Antonio. It is appropriate that you accompany us. Bring them out."

Antonio had tears in his eyes. "Father, many of them cannot walk on their own."

Father Tómas patted the distraught man on the arm. "Never fear, Antonio, God has provided a way." He waved down the street, and a wagon and several carts appeared in the darkness.

It was not many minutes before the prisoners, their guards, Ka-ansh in his mask, Father Tómas, and Father Philip, were ready. Father Philip had a word with Ka-ansh. "You and your farmers follow behind us, rearguard. Keep an eye out for a squad of cavalry; we don't want to tangle with them.

Ka-ansh's eyes grinned from behind the mask. "Don't worry, Father. Everything is well in hand."

Palace of the Governors, Santa Fe
The next morning

The Governor General and the Father President met in the Governor's office. Ceballos was furious, pacing and shouting. Xavier Bautista, the Father President, watched his opposite stomp up and down for a few minutes. It was true that somehow, the Indios were all gone from the prison, as were the guards. It was almost as if they had evaporated in the night. Most of the underlings in the palacio had also evaporated, not wanting to witness the anger of the Governor General. Don Miguel Quezada, commander of the Garrison of Santa Fe, stood near the doorway. Bautista could tell that he wanted to escape as well, but his duty held him in place.

Ceballos started shouting again. "All of our plans have been disrupted because the Indio prisoners are gone." He pounded on the table. "Quezada, this is your responsibility. You must determine how they escaped, and arrest them. Find the prisoners, and have them executed.

Have the guards executed. Have the conspirators who freed them executed. I will not tolerate this!"

The Father President stared out a window, stroking his neatly trimmed beard. "You know, Francisco, that's not such a bad idea. By escaping, the Indios have broken the law, and if we execute them, we are justified. Their original guilt or lack of it no longer has any bearing, because by defying us they have shown we were correct to distrust them."

The governor stopped and turned. A slow smile crossed his face. "Very good, Xavier." He pointed at the garrison commander. "Quezada, assign someone to the investigation. You are to call out the garrison. In half an hour, we will ride out of the palacio to begin the search. I want every available soldier."

He sat back down, still smiling. "It's as if they want us to retaliate. We will track them and burn them out. And if a Spaniard is helping, we will burn them out as well. And if the person that helped the Indios has a land-grant, I'll divide the land among the soldiers. That should make them more enthusiastic."

Siege at Bernalillo Chapel
Two days later, September 1634

Boom. Boom. Boom. Father Philip tried to ignore the battering ram at the doors. He put the last heavy bench into the barricade. He turned to check the escape of the wounded, the women, and the children. There were still some waiting to crawl out a small door in the nave.

With each booming strike, the great chapel doors flexed and shuddered on their hinges. Father Philip was crouched behind the barricades when Raymundo slipped up and whispered, "I think we are ready. How long do you think the door will hold?"

Father Philip smiled. "I don't know, but watch when it fails, fire that thing when you see a gap big enough for the cannonball to get out."

Raymundo grinned at him. "Yes, Friend Blue-eyes. I've been wanting to fire this Abus gun since we found it in old man Paco's house."

Father Philip looked alarmed. "Raymundo, do you mean you have never shot that thing before?"

Raymundo's grin widened. "Of course not, Father. There are only three big bullets after all. I didn't want to waste them."

Another boom echoed throughout the chapel, and two sections of the door splintered wide. The resulting gap was just what Raymundo and his cousin Mateo were waiting for. They balanced the Abus gun evenly between themselves. Raymundo squeezed the lever, and the slow match descended to the powder pan, on the side of the big Abus gun.

Now there was a boom from this side of the chapel door and a very large hole exploded out toward the attackers. Surprised shouts were heard from outside. Father Philip whispered another prayer of thanks that the old gun didn't explode in Raymundo's hands.

At that moment, Marcos, the twelve-year-old boy from the village who was in the bell tower said, "Father Philip, the smoke, the pillar of smoke you wanted to know about has been seen from outside the town. It was very straight, and it started and stopped like they were putting a blanket over the fire."

Father Philip visibly relaxed. He looked up at Marcos. "Thank you, son. Stay there and watch." Then he moved from the barricade toward the small crowd of people in the nave. "At last, we have received the signal from the Jicarilla. The help I was hoping for has arrived. Everybody get ready. As soon as the battering ram stops, we should all go out the small side door of the chapel."

He glanced over to the Alcalde of Bernalillo. "Federico, they have probably searched all the rest of your hacienda by now. It was brilliant of you to take our rescued prisoners out to the cocinas. We're going out the side door and splitting up. It will make us harder to follow. Everybody head for the cocinas, the outdoor kitchens, by the river. After dark, we will make more plans. Remember, as soon as the attack on our doors ceases, we leave."

Don Federico nodded. "The kitchens. We will see you there. God go with you Father."

The women and children who were crouching in the darkness moved toward the side door, and Garciella, wife of the Alcalde, touched Father Philip's arm. There was an unaccustomed tension, probably from fear. "Father, you didn't really call the Apache, did you?"

Father Philip smiled piously. "They did offer to help, and it didn't even cost very much."

Marcos called down from the bell tower. "Apaches! I see Apaches in all the narrow alleys. They're throwing bundles of burning branches into the plaza. There's white smoke everywhere!"

Father Philip turned to Father Tómas. "Tómas, my brother, you need to decide now. If you go with us you will be branded as a renegade as I am. And if you stay you'll be treated with suspicion."

Father Tómas just smiled. "Don't worry about me, Philip. I have an idea. You should lock me in the cupboard with the vestments. By the time they find me in there they will be convinced I was made a prisoner when you occupied the chapel, as the only defensible structure around the plaza. I should be fine. Besides, the Father President has been wanting a good incident with the soldiers; he may even give me a bonus for creating one."

Father Philip laughed and embraced Tómas. "God go with you, Father Tómas. You are almost wily enough to be a Jesuit."

Tómas laughed. "I could never write that many letters." Then he allowed himself to be hustled into the cabinet by Raymundo and locked in. The whoops and shouts increased in volume outside the chapel.

Marcos, who was still in the tower, shouted. "The plaza, it's completely covered in white smoke. Ew, I think they used stink weed. It smells really bad, even up here."

Father Philip called up the tower. "Marcos, where are our allies?"

Marcos had started down the ladder. "The Apaches? They are running in out of the plaza, striking a few soldiers with clubs, and running back through the alleyways. The block of soldiers is beginning to break up. Oh, and the Apache even have a few muskets."

Father Philip looked up. "Hurry down, Marcos. It is time for us to go." Father Philip and Marcos hurried out the door, and Raymundo, his Abus gun over his shoulder, was last out. Just as the chapel doors burst open, he closed the side door and was gone.

Plaza of the Hacienda Bernalillo
September 1634

Teniente Ramirez, commanding the assault of Bernalillo, scowled at the messenger. "What do you mean, they are attacking the horse line? We left guards. Those horses are the only thing that can keep us alive in a mass attack."

The soldier shrugged. "But it is true, Teniente. The Apache, they are attacking and trying to take our horses. You know how they always want to steal horses."

The Teniente shook his head. "I still don't understand why the Apache are attacking right now. We haven't threatened them or even spoken to them in months. Very well, signal retreat. Everyone to the horse line! If we can keep the horses, we can run these savages down. Without them, they may well trample us themselves. We can't allow that to happen."

With the discipline that was the hallmark of the Spanish forces in the New World, the soldiers withdrew to the horse line. The battle of Bernalillo was over.

Las Cocinas on the river bank
September 1634

The outdoor kitchens, next to the river, were built to offer cooking space for large gatherings and also to keep the cooking heat outside in the hot weather. They were about a half mile from the hacienda. There was a large ramada, or shaded patio, and cooking surfaces around a hardened dirt floor.

Ka-ansh and his cohorts were anxious to engage in battle, but Don Federico had admonished them to stay here and protect the rescued Indios. Eduardo no longer wore the mask, hiding his identity; all the Indios just accepted him as Ka-ansh.

He and his friends made friends with Antonio and the two guards who came with them, Paco and Esteban. They all had families north of Santa Fe and wanted to return soon. Ka-ansh asked them to stay until other arrangements could be made, and they agreed. Besides, they didn't want to be caught by soldiers searching for the escaped Indios.

When Father Philip arrived, he found the rest of the villagers reassembled there. They took a headcount, and the miracle was that nobody was killed. There were some minor injuries. It had been a long and stressful night and day.

Father Philip checked on the rescued tribal leaders and governors. He spoke in the Tewa he had learned. "Good elders, are you well?"

There were nods. The twelve hours rest they got here in the kitchens had helped. "Elders, today we must decide. Will you hide, hoping that the Ironskins will not find you, or will you go back to your villages and teach your young men to resist?" The time had come to set the match to this powder keg he had created. This was the first time he had seen these leaders and shamans in the light, and they were a pitiful sight. All had been beaten, and some had been further tortured. But there was defiance in all their eyes. It was time.

One of the men, Wa-tu from San Felipe struggled to his feet. "Friend Blue-eyes, we see now that you were correct at our last meeting. We can not trust the leaders of the Ironskins; they have lied to us too often."

Father Philip nodded. "It is true, Wa-tu. Now, the Governor General and the Father President cannot afford to leave you alive. If they recapture you, they will kill you on the spot. From the papers I received from Germany, much history has been repeated. Now the only way for you to survive is to band together and drive the Spaniards out."

There was silence as all considered what Father Philip said. Finally, Don Federico cleared his throat. "Father, do you really think it will come to that? Will we all have to abandon our homes and return to Spain?"

Father Philip looked at the gathered leaders for a moment. "I cannot see the future, but from the historical information I received from my brothers, that is what has previously happened."

Don Federico looked at his wife and the other Spaniards scattered around the cocinas and sighed. "I know of several Spanish families that don't want to return to Spain, or even Mexico City. We have made a life here, and it is a good life. Perhaps we can write this history to our own liking. Perhaps we can come to an understanding, just as you and I have, tonight. We do not need to be different peoples. We can be all one people with the Spaniards aiding the Pueblos, and the Apache alongside. Perhaps we can create our own version of peace here in the Frontiers of New Mexico."

Eduardo, dressed as the Ka-ansh, stood next to his father and Father Philip to speak. "Yes, just like we did tonight. Governors, you must go back to your villages and tell them what has happened. You must convince them. If we don't all band together, the Governor General and the Father President will hunt us all down separately and destroy everything. But together we outnumber the soldiers, even if they call in all the troops from every garrison in the district. Yes, I was born an Ironskin, but I was born in the Rio Grande valley, as were each of you. We must fight for our life here, fight for what we love."

That brought cheers from the Indios and the Spaniards alike. Father Philip smiled. "For my part, I was not born a Spaniard, But I am a loyal son of the Church. I will begin by writing letters to everyone in Europe I can think of. I know that neither the government in Spain nor the leadership of the Church will countenance what is happening to the Indios. Perhaps, if it is known what kind of treatment you have received, there will be sympathy and support in Spain. I must send a record of this atrocity to the Viceroy in Mexico City before the bureaucrats in Santa Fe have the chance to sanitize the record."

Pos n'ou, Governor of Nambe pueblo, stood up painfully. "Friend Blue-eyes, while you battle the mysteries of the Ironskins, what are we to do? Some of us are not strong enough to travel."

Father Philip's eyes were sad. "If you cannot travel, send word to your pueblos. And for those that are still fit, go and talk to your people. It is time to lay aside our hurts and differences and join in rebellion. It is time for you to drive the Ironskins out. This is more than the old hatreds between clans and villages. You must decide, but do not delay. Given the chance, the Governor General of Santa Fe will crush you one by one."

The Indio Governors and their shamans gathered in the courtyard by village language groups. The discussions were intense for over an hour.

Natoto-kwata, from Ohkay Owingeh, stepped away from his Tewa group and called to Father Phillip. "Friend Blue-eyes, is there information in your letters that can guide us? What does your secret knowledge say? Is it time for war?"

The group went silent, all wanting to hear Father Phillip. He stood and crossed himself, praying that he would know exactly what to say to this group. "It is true that there are records indicating that there was a previous Pueblo Revolt in 1680. But my wisdom cannot tell you if it is time for war. We know that according the record, the revolt was successful but did not last, as the Ironskins returned twelve years later and reconquered the Pueblo people. That may be the case here, and it may not. It is in God's hands."

The groups went back to discussion, and Father Phillip sat down. He was ready to give them all the time he needed, although he hoped it would be a consensus.

Finally, Tseji, governor from Pojoaque, stepped forward. "We agree that they beat us like dogs, they threatened to hang us, and now messengers from our villages say that there is a warrant of execution declared for all of us, even for you, Friend Blue-eyes. We are all fugitives, as well as anyone who helps us. We have no choice. We will all return to our villages and prepare. In five days we will strike."

Then the shaman from Sandia pueblo, Wa-hwayku-a, who spoke in Tiwa, stood. "And just to be sure that you know when we will strike, we will each take a piece of rope with five knots; each morning we will untie a knot, and when there are no more knots, we surround Santa Fe and strike. Those villages too far from Santa Fe shall drive the Ironskins out from your area. If we do this all at the same time they will not be able to concentrate the soldiers against any of us."

Father Philip looked on solemnly. "I weep to see the declaration of open warfare, for many innocents will suffer. But it must be done. To help, I will pledge all I have, up to my own life. I will be with you at the gates of Santa Fe in five days. May God bless you all."

by Kevin H. and Karen C. Evans

CHAPTER 2

The Garrison of Santa Fe
Friday
September 1634

Don Miguel Quezada, the grizzled military commander, glared at his assembled captains and lieutenants. "I am concerned. I expected more action against the Indios before this. It is far too quiet. Five days ago, after the Inquisition tortured them, the tribal elders somehow escaped from prison. You tracked them to Bernalillo, and you engaged in battle, but then left empty-handed. And since then, nothing has happened for the past three days. Something should have happened by now. Teniente Ramirez, what do your scouts report?"

He was interrupted by another messenger. The man hurried into the garrison, out of breath, and held out a folded paper he took from his shirt. "Sir, a message! It came from your spy in the village of Tesuque. He says they are going to attack in two more days."

Don Miguel grabbed the dispatch. "Who's attacking? Tesuque?"

Fear was foremost on the messenger's face. "No, Don Miguel. The Indios. All of them. They have agreements to band together and drive us out."

Teniente de Bances stood up. "Don Miguel, if we ride out now we can ambush them on the road."

Quezada signaled for silence. "I understand that you all think we have better weapons and better protection than any Indio in the Valley, and that is true. None of them have our armor or weapons. And this is all true. But there are at best only two hundred of us, and there may be as many as five thousand of them. If we leave here to confront them, who will protect the women and children here in Santa Fe? We should prepare for them here. When they are weakened, then we will attack. Then we can ride out and break them. If we prepare for a siege, the hatred between the tribes should break up their alliance before we do anything. We just need to be patient. Start by barricading the plaza. And make sure the cannons are ready. Dismissed."

Santa Domingo pueblo
Saturday night

All the leadership from villages near Santa Fe met to plan the attack. Ka-ansh burst through the group of warriors who stood around the circle of the council of village elders. "There is a traitor. The Ironskins know everything about the attack."

Wa-tu, shaman of San Felipe, stood. "Ka-ansh, *you* are sure? That we are betrayed?" The rest of the council buzzed with whispers and suspicious glances.

Ka-ansh nodded. "It is certain. I was in Tesuque and saw the traitor himself hand the message to a runner. I slipped out and followed the runner to Santa Fe. The Governor of Tesuque has already turned the traitor over to the Navajos. The traitor revealed that he had told them that we are attacking the day after tomorrow."

Wa-tu scowled. "Very well, send out runners. We attack in the morning, a day early. If we do not, we may never push them out."

The First Day
Sunday, Outside the mission at Cochiti

The light had just begun to show above the crest of the mountains to the east. It was time. Wa-tu, leading the band from San Felipe pueblo stood and raised his spear over his head. All heads turned to him as he shouted a war cry. "It is time. Attack!"

The war cry echoed from a thousand throats. Men flung themselves toward the adobe walls of the monastery.

The priests were awake; after all it was Sunday. Father Garcia was in the chapel lighting candles when a throng of Indios charged into the chapel and threatened him with clubs and spears. "My sons, what is this?"

The Indios shouted in their native tongue and attacked without mercy. The massacre spread throughout the monastery and out into the streets. Soon flames begin to flicker above and around the eaves of the chapel. Every building of the compound was put to the torch and livestock was driven off to the local village.

The First Day
Tiguex Hacienda

Ana Hernandez looked through a window of the hacienda. She saw smoke from the village nearby but didn't know its source. Before she could find out, her vision was filled with an Indio on a horse. "What is this? Pablo, why do you have all of these men here?"

The tall Indio looked down at her. "My name is no longer Pablo. I am Kwa-kay, a proud warrior of the Tiwa people."

Ana's face showed fear for the first time. Kwa-kay continued, "You and your family have treated us with respect so we will not kill you. But you must leave, and you must leave now. If you do not leave you will surely die. I will not be able to protect you."

Ana hurried into the house and gathered the children. She didn't take time for more belongings than the family Bible and her mother's lace shawl. Then they were outside. Her husband, Jose, had hitched the horses to the carriage, and she loaded the children in before climbing in herself.

As Jose turned the carriage toward Santa Fe, Ana gazed sadly back at the village. Most of the roofs were in flames.

The First Day
First mesa, western edge of the province

Sergeant Sanchez and his men ran up the path to the chapel, with unnumbered Indios screaming behind them. Most soldiers had pants and shoes, some had armor, and many carried a pistol. When the chapel door was slammed shut and barred securely, they found they were missing three men, and nobody had thought to pick up a musket or halberd.

Father Pablo hurried up, still wiping sleep from his eyes. "What is this, Sergeant Sanchez? What is all the noise?"

Sanchez directed his men to use the benches to barricade the door before turning to Father Pablo. "I don't know what happened, Father. But from here you can see everything south and east of us is on fire. Before we were aware, the Indios attacked. They have already killed three of my men.

The priest crossed himself as they heard the crash of tree trunks pounding on the door. Then one of the soldiers screamed. Nobody noticed until too late the bundles of burning twigs and branches that were falling from holes in the roof.

The First Day
Santa Fe

First by trickles, and then in mobs, the refugee Spanish inhabitants of the Province of New Mexico filled the small town of Santa Fe to the brim. Nobody wanted to stay in the buildings on the edge of town, so they were all milling around in front of the palacio.

Governor General Ceballos burst into the throng of humanity that filled the central plaza. "What is happening? Why are you all here? I demand clarification as to why you have left your haciendas."

The mob murmured, and someone in the crowd shouted, "It is the local Indios. They have attacked. They are burning everything."

Another man shouted, "They are killing anybody too slow to leave. And they are driving all of the Spaniards out of the haciendas."

A voice in the back of the mob shouted as well, "You are the Governor General. You are responsible for our protection."

Now many people were shouting. The Governor General started backing toward the doors of the palacio. "Go back to your shelter. You can't stay in the plaza all night. Go back to the church, or the monastery." By that time, the governor was in the doorway of the palacio. He stepped in and the guards slammed the door. The mob was looking ugly.

The governor shouted as well, stomping through the hallways to his quarters. "What have we heard? I thought they weren't going to attack for two more days!"

The aides and guards scattered like cockroaches as he moved. As he sat down in his chair, Don Miguel Quezada stepped in and saluted. "Governor, we have reports from every part of the province, and ..."

Ceballos waved his hand, and Don Miguel fell silent. "Your reports are late. Haven't you seen the plaza?"

Don Miguel stopped. "No, Sire. I just rode in from Tesuque."

The governor snorted. "The plaza is full of refugees from the haciendas. They have been driven out this morning by attacking Indios. I thought your spy said we'd have two days."

Don Miguel stood very straight and gripped his sword. "Sir, when I left there before dawn, Tesuque was in chaos. Perhaps you didn't hear, but the Father President, accompanied only by one guard, rode to Tesuque yesterday to examine the church's assets."

Ceballos sat back in his chair. "No, I hadn't heard that he left the palacio, but I don't keep track of him. Did he return with you?"

Don Miguel stared at the floor. "I saw his body, Governor. He is dead, along with at least twenty other men. I don't know what happened to the women."

The Governor General jumped to his feet. "What? How could this have happened? What of the garrison in Tesuque? Didn't they raise a hand to protect the Father President?"

"Governor, the garrison was attacked first. I've had reports of upwards of a thousand warriors surrounding Tesuque. They slaughtered the soldiers before they knew there was a threat. Then they went to the church, dragged out everyone inside and killed them, then burnt the church to the ground. I've been unable to get more information that I can trust."

"What of our spy? Why didn't we hear from him before this morning? Last night?" Now the Governor General was pacing.

"Governor, I fear that our spy has been compromised. I couldn't find him in Tesuque. I suspect foul play."

"Of course there is foul play, Don Miguel. We are surrounded by rebellious Indios. I want you to assemble the men. Immediately. They are to strengthen the barricades. I want all of the streets into the plaza blocked except for the Southeast corner. Have the six-pound guns emplaced there. And have Teniente Ramirez send one of the scouts to Isleta. If this is a rebellion, I will need reinforcements from there. I'm relying on you, Don

Miguel, on your honor as a Spaniard. You must do all you can to protect the inhabitants of Santa Fe and all the surviving refugees."

Setting the barricades was not easy. The whole time that the barricades were being built, more and more of the refugee Spaniards were flooding into the plaza. Don Miguel took matters firmly into his own hands. He grabbed Sergeant Castenada. "Jorge, I want you to get the women and children under cover. Inside the palacio is best. It's the strongest building here. I don't care what the seneschal says. Women and children inside. They can't stay out here underfoot. The men and older boys will boost the garrison and help us defend against the Indios."

Sergeant Castenada saluted. "Yes, sir. I'll get my men on it."

When the women and children had been bustled inside, everyone took a deep breath and got to work. Don Miguel strode over to the Teniente supervising the northwest barricade. "I have a job for you as well, de Bances. You need to evaluate which refugees have some military training and form them into troops. Put sergeants or lieutenants in command and give them assignments. I am not feeding anyone who can't be useful. We have a siege, and if we are to survive, we have to be well organized."

Young Teniente de Bances saluted. "Of course, Don Miguel." Then, as the commander moved on to bigger problems, de Bances grabbed one of the Governor General's aides. "We need to find those men who have military training. Send those with firearm training to the stables and those who have some sword or pole-arm experience to the parade ground. Report back to me before sundown."

The local Spaniards had many problems, but bureaucracy was not one of them. They learned delegation and prioritizing from a young age. The

Spanish propensity for minutia and exacting detail would finally show its value.

Immediately, aides to both the Governor General and the Father President began to filter among the crowd, sending people to the various places they needed to be. Boys as young as fourteen were pressed into service, and the old men, depending upon their health and strength, were sent either to be soldiers or to go inside with the women and children.

By sunset, the refugees were organized. The governor emerged from the palacio, fully armed and armored. He signaled for his horse to be brought forward. When he swung into the saddle, the crowd became silent. "Men, tonight we work together to protect everything we hold dear. You must stand up and show these Indios what a Spaniard is made of. We will win victory for the King!"

The cheers raised the spirit of every man in the ranks. Now, more quietly, the governor continued. "Don Miguel, how many men do we have to defend the city?"

The garrison commander saluted. "Governor, trained or mostly trained, we have about eighty men. Local landowners, their sons, and volunteers comprise perhaps another seventy more. Of that we can field about sixty pikemen, forty musketeers, and fifty cavalrymen. That accounts for all of the armor we had available. And it does not include the crews with the brass cannons or the locals with their own hunting pieces."

The governor pointed at his favorite unit of the garrison. "What of the brass cannons?"

Don Miguel nodded. "They and the local militia will guard the barricades. That way, we can use our soldiers to scatter the Indios. Our weapons are better, our men are trained and blooded in battle. They cannot stand before us."

As they spoke the men were rapidly forming into a group at the southeast corner of the plaza. The governor gestured outward, outside the barricade. "And the Indios? How many are out there? How many Indios are here in rebellion?"

Don Miguel turned to Colonel Martinez. "Colonel, you have sent scouts out. Have any of them reported back?"

Colonel Martinez saluted. "Right now there about eight hundred Indios surrounding us, carrying some kind of weapon. Mostly bows and arrows and hunting spears. One of my scouts rode as far as La Bajada and could see several groups of Indios traveling in this direction, so more are gathering."

The Governor General interrupted the report. "Do you mean that this is more than one or two pueblos attacking? How have they organized? Who is responsible?"

Colonel Martinez continued. "Governor, there is more. Apparently, somebody has been training them. My scouts have observed the Indios formed up into disciplined groups. As they can't enter Santa Fe, right now they are burning the farms and other buildings outside of town. Some of the fields are burning, and they have taken the best of the outer buildings as a headquarters."

Don Miguel murmured to the Governor General, "If your predecessors had not been so lax about the city plan we would have a proper grid of streets to defend and attack from. But with the exception of the plaza and a few rows of houses around it, the streets are chaotic. The houses do not provide much in the way of defensible territory."

The Governor General bent down, and put his hand on Don Miguel's shoulder. "No use complaining about our circumstances; there is nothing we can do for it now."

As the governor sat back in his saddle, Don Miguel straightened, and saluted. "My men will do everything we can do to protect this palacio, Governor."

Cavern of Tocatl Coztic, Jemez mountains
September 1634

It had been three years since Teopixqui arrived in this canyon, and as he recruited men and women with darkness in their hearts, the cave had finally been transformed. Now it was no longer a crack in the ground that one had to crawl in on hands and knees. Now there was an opening five feet high and a screening wall that hid the entrance. Rabbit brush and young juniper had been planted to help hide the entrance.

The Nahuatl priest came out in full darkness and moved to the top of the rise. From here, if he looked north, he could see the tops of trees in Santa Fe. And if he looked south, he could see the Rio Grande valley, with several small villages of Ironskins and Indios. There was smoke rising into the night sky from both directions. Something was happening.

He stepped to the leather curtain that covered the door and spoke to a slave. "Send for Tse-bit-a." Then he went back to his observatory spot. That much smoke usually meant fire and suffering, and it was rather enjoyable to see it all around him.

It took several minutes for Tse-bit-a to find him. The man immediately fell to his knees, then bent and touched his head to the dirt. "What is your wish, Serene One?"

Teopixqui ignored him for a moment. Then he said, "Rise, Tse-bit-a. I have a task for you."

The Navajo stood, and Teopixqui pointed toward Santa Fe and then to the south. "There is conflict. Go find out who is burning the villages. I need to know if the Ironskins are searching for us, or if they are spending their wrath on the local Indios.

Tse-bit-a bowed. "It shall be done, Serene One." And then he ghosted into the darkness.

✱ ✱ ✱

The tall Navajo warrior skulked in the woods above Santa Fe. It was interesting to see, because never had he seen so many Indios together in one place. He couldn't tell much in the darkness, but he estimated that there were at least five hundred warriors outside Santa Fe, carrying torches and singing war chants.

He turned and headed down toward Agua Fria to get more information. This was not an unfamiliar trail. He had come this way several times in his recruiting trips. The ground became less steep, and he was able to move down to see the village.

The surprise was that it was not the Indio village burning, but the Ironskin one. This was not what he expected, so it was time to get more information. He moved to a screen of bushes, and waited until he spotted an Indio moving somewhat carelessly. The man was armed with a spear, and moved through the bush like a cow drunken on loco weed.

Tse-bit-a waited until the man was close to his hiding spot, then he stood up, grabbed the man around the throat, and dragged him back into the brush. He held the man's neck tightly until he stopped struggling, then hoisted the limp body up on his shoulder and moved back uphill.

At a sheltered spot that was probably a resting place for deer in the springtime, he dropped the man to the ground and tied the captive's hands and feet and then sat back to wait.

About ten minutes later, the unconscious man stirred. It amused Tse-bit-a to watch the fear flare in the captive's eyes as he realized that he was tied up. Finally, the man's gaze swung to where Tse-bit-a was lounging under a juniper tree. "Where am I? Why have you tied me up?"

The Navajo came to stand over the man and laugh. "Well, you were moving in the night like a drunken cow, and it irritated me. So I tied you up. I have some questions." Tse-bit-a took a knife from the sheath on his waist, and held it so the captive could see the moonlight on the knife edge. "First of all, who are you, and where are you from?"

The man trembled, but answered. "I am Kwampo from San Felipe pueblo. I am here as a warrior. We are going to drive the Ironskins out of the Rio Grande valley or kill them all."

That surprised Tse-bit-a, and he squatted down by the man, thoughts of torture receding. "San Felipe is going to drive the Ironskins out? And how are you going to do that? There may be as many as a thousand Ironskins here."

Kwampo's arms were tied behind him, so he couldn't roll on his back or sit up. But he rolled so he could look Tse-bit-a in the eye. "We are not just the San Felipe. We are the Indios of the Rio Grande valley. Warriors are arriving every day from as far as First Mesa and Ohkay Owingeh. We are united in our purpose. You are a Navajo, you should join us. Driving out the Ironskins would benefit you as well."

Tse-bit-a looked at his knife and at his captive, then moved in, with the knife forward. The captive jerked back. But a look of surprise crossed his features as the Navajo cut his restraints. Tse-bit-a stepped back and gestured. "You are right, the Ironskins should be driven out. Go and join your brothers."

Kwampo sat up, and rubbed his wrists, then looked one more time at Tse-bit-a before scurrying away like a frightened rabbit. It left Tse-bit-a with a lot to think about as he made his way back to the cave of Tocatl Coztic.

CHAPTER 3

The Second Day
Outside Santa Fe, early morning
September 1634
Monday

Father Philip stood outside the barn that was now a council chamber. The morning air was cool and dry, and to the east, the mountains glowed with the coming sunrise. The rest of the sky was clean, clear of cloud or dust. He watched as the sun peeped over the mountains, sending rays of light into the valley, waking the plants and animals. The dawn was so innocent, unaware of the conflict going on in the valley.

He sighed and stepped into the door. There, the leadership of the pueblos gathered to discuss the plans for the day. Yesterday, plans had gone much better than any had predicted. The Spaniards were driven from every village within twenty miles of Santa Fe. Word was arriving all the time about attacks in the outer villages and haciendas, and there was a steady stream of refugees hurrying into Santa Fe.

This barn was on the outskirts of Santa Fe, south and west of the palacio and in the oldest part of town. The sun was just lightening the building as the small windows above were spilling with sunlight.

by Kevin H. and Karen C. Evans

Father Philip looked over the leadership of the uprising, sitting in a circle in the center of the barn floor. When they were gathered like this, he could see resemblances, as if he were attending a large family reunion. The people of the Pueblos in the Rio Grande valley were different than their neighbors, the Apache, the Navajo, or in the north, the Utes and Paiutes. All of these groups came through the area for trading, and girls were brought from those groups for wives. But these people were more alike than different. They wore loose leggings and fine shirts, and each had a wool blanket with the traditional weaving of their village or tribe.

He had been given permission to address them, So with Raymundo by his side, he stood and addressed them in Spanish with translation. "In spite of their anger toward the Spanish invaders, you must offer them the chance to surrender. Tell them you'll let them leave, then fall behind them and push them out of the territory. It is not a good thing to execute all of them. The Great Father will not bless us if that is done." Then he sat down.

Okuwa-oky, from Santo Domingo, waited for the priest to finish. He stood for his turn to speak. "Friend Blue-eyes, they have done many horrible things to us. The anger runs very deep. For over forty years, longer than many of the young men have been alive, they have trampled upon us and treated us like beasts of burden, stolen our young men, destroyed our sacred objects. The Great Father is not pleased with the Ironskins. Nevertheless, for the sake of those who treated me kindly, I say we give them a chance."

Wa-tu stood for his turn. When he spoke, he pointed at Father Philip. "Friend Blue-eyes, You must go to the Spanish. You are well respected by the black-robes. You must make a demand. Tell them that if they leave peacefully, they will not die. Tell them that if they stay we will kill every one of them."

At that speech, there were many nods, and grunts of agreement. But before Father Philip could stand to speak, another chief, Natoto-kwata, stood quickly and spoke. "But, Friend Blue-eyes, it is best if you make them talk long and loud. The longer they talk, the more men we will assemble here."

Many laughed at Natoto-kwata. When Okuwa-oky could see that the council was in agreement, he stood to speak. "My slave name was Carlos, but I am again called Okuwa-oky, given me by my tribe. I say that if we can convince them to leave, many lives will be saved of the Tewa, the Tiguex, the Keres, and the Pecos. The Taos and the Piciru. These are lives we will spend if we must, but if they leave peacefully, we can live to old age."

This brought shouts from the whole council. Father Philip could still see some anger, but for the first time, the council was in agreement. One by one, the chiefs of the villages sat and held up their war sticks. Each stick showed agreement.

Father Philip stood counting. "Eight, nine, ten," Finally it was unanimous. If the Spanish would leave peacefully, the Indios would not attack.

Okuwa-oky stood with his stick on his arm. "We are in agreement. I will send another with Friend Blue-eyes to keep him safe. Make for me two crosses about the size of your hand make one white and make the other red. Then find some white cloth, and place it on the end of the lance. They will know that you come in peace, and that you want to talk."

So that morning, Father Philip set out with a delegation of chiefs and warriors. They were all on horseback, except for Friend Blue-eyes, who straddled a burro. He was trembling but tried to keep a brave face. The truth was, he was not at all sure that either side would honor the white flag. And the Spaniards were just as likely to shoot him on the spot as they were to listen to him.

by Kevin H. and Karen C. Evans

The Second Day
Santa Fe Garrison, Just after noon

Sergeant Juan Sanchez ran up to Don Miguel, out of breath. "Excellency! Excellency, the Indios have a flag of truce. They wish to talk. They are approaching the opening to the plaza now."

The commander stepped to the stirrup of the Governor General's horse. "Sir, we have a delegation approaching under the flag of truce. I wish the Father President was here. He always seemed to be able to talk the Indios into doing anything he wanted."

The Governor General looked over his meager troop. "Don Miguel, we should go out to meet them. Get your horse. I will go with you and an additional ten soldiers. Be sure to choose the ones with the best-looking armor. We want to impress them. Maybe we can talk them out of this rebellion."

The group of men assembled on foot behind Don Miguel and the Governor General, both on horseback. The Spanish procession proceeded until they were just outside the opening in the plaza.

The two delegations faced each other at the crossroads. Don Miguel noticed that one of the Indios was wearing familiar bloodstained clothing. He leaned over to the Governor General and whispered, "These Indios are in no way innocent. That one is wearing the Father President's robes."

Ceballos' lips clamped into a firm line. He raised his voice so it could be heard by the Indio delegation. "I recognize you, Carlos. Why are your people savaging outlying haciendas? Have we not always treated you well? You were a respected member of the counsel."

Okuwa-oky was one of two on horseback, along with Wa-tu and Father Philip. "Governor General, I was never truly a prosperous member of the council. I was only called Carlos because the priest said my name was an abomination. Many years ago, when your people came to the Rio Grande, we gave you homes to live in and food for the winter. But now that you are many, you take our food and burn our homes. This is how you treated us." The chief pulled the bloody robes from his shoulders and arms, and showed welts and scabs from healing wounds. "I was captured and tortured in your palacio for no reason. If you had not broken your promise, we would have had no rebellion in our hearts before the tortures. You are an evil man, as was the Father President." He threw the torn robes on the ground.

Then Okuwa-oky motioned to Father Philip, who was holding up two crosses, one white and one red. "This man speaks for us. He will explain our demands. You must choose."

Then he turned his horse, and the other Indios followed him down the street away from the plaza. Father Philip was left alone in the street.

The Governor General sat back into his saddle and watched the Indios ride off. Soon, the priest holding a red and a white cross was all that was left of the enemy delegation. "So are you a prisoner, returned as a show of good faith, Father Philip?"

The priest sat very still, trying not to look at the soldiers behind Don Miguel and the Governor General. Most of them had muskets aimed directly at him. "No, sire. They sent me to persuade you. Depending on how these talks go, I am to go back to them with the cross of your choice. Are we to continue this discussion out here in the sun, or may we not retire to the palacio and let me explain my mission?"

The Governor General snorted, and turned his horse. He spoke loudly to Don Miguel so that Father Philip could hear him as well. "Take this traitor to the chapel." Then he rode back into the plaza, leaving the soldiers and Don Miguel.

The garrison commander sighed. "Father Philip, I know you well. You are not a wicked or corrupted priest. How could you turn against your people? How could you be part of the murder of the Father President?"

Father Philip sighed as well. He looked as if the weight of the world sat on his shoulders. "Don Miguel, it's not that simple. I was not there when the monastery at Tesuque was burned. I didn't have the power to stop the forces that the Father President primed himself. You know as well as I that the choices made here were not in keeping with the law of the King and of the Church."

Father Philip watched Don Miguel's face as he silently turned his horse toward the plaza. Don Miguel was not pleased with the Governor General, but his duty remained to command the garrison in Santa Fe.

That left Teniente de Bances, in command of the foot soldiers. "Come, Father Philip. We will escort you to the Governor General. And I pray that there is a way for all of us to come away from this travesty alive."

Father Philip rode up to Teniente de Bances. "I have prayed for that outcome from the beginning." He stood as the crosses were confiscated and manacles were snapped on his wrists, and then followed the soldiers into the palacio. So much for negotiations.

Second Day
Sunset, Santa Fe

Father Philip sat in a chair in the center of the chapel floor. He had been there for quite some time, alone. His manacled hands sat in his lap. He was familiar with so many of the sounds around him. He could hear murmurs from the lay brothers behind the screens in the chapel. And farther away was the rattle and scrape of the indoor kitchens.

Finally, he heard measured footsteps, and he knew that the time had come. They were the boots of the Governor General, coming around the corner from his office. Father Philip whispered another prayer, and fingered the rosary hanging from his belt. He silently told himself, *Your time has come, Philip. God, send me the voice that will make them choose peace. Or at least delay until the Indios have time to build their forces.*

Several feet in front of Father Philip's chair was a table and two chairs. The Governor General entered the chapel, still in his armor. He made a show of sitting in one of the chairs, facing him. It was obvious that the empty chair would have been for the Father President. This was more of a tribunal than a delegation discussion.

Father Philip sat silent, waiting for the Governor General to open the discussion. The silence stretched for some moments, but Father Philip remained calm. He was resigned to the possibility that the Governor General would order him executed.

Finally, the Governor General looked directly at Father Philip. "Here he is, the man that caused an Indio rebellion. It was you who received the letters that put this idea in their heads. It was you who released the rebellious leaders from the Inquisition. I am sure that if the Father President were here, you would already be stretched and roasting over coals. So are you ready to confess your traitorous behavior, or shall we bring in the Inquisitors?"

Father Philip stood, as he felt the position of spokesman demanded some decorum. "Governor General, it is true that I received a letter from the Jesuits about future history of this place, but I did not foment rebellion. I did not dictate to you your actions that brought the Indios to war. You stand accused of negligence towards these people, allowing them to be enslaved and tortured for your own gain. I do not feel that I acted as a traitor to you or to this colony of New Spain. I was at the Hacienda of Bernalillo when your men were sent to attack us and burn the holding. This was the spark that set this rebellion in motion."

Ceballos' eyes glittered but he said nothing.

Father Philip continued. "The Governor of Santo Domingo, who was known as Carlos, was one of those I rescued from the prison. As a spokesman of the Indios, I was sent to give you their demands. The white cross is for peace, and the red cross is for war and death. If you take the white cross, you must gather your people up and leave. If you choose this, the Indios have sworn a solemn oath that they will let you leave in peace."

The Governor General was on his feet immediately, his face red with anger. "And how do we know we can trust the solemn oath of savages? They have no souls. They have nothing sacred to swear by. They are incapable of giving their solemn oath."

Father Philip was silent for a moment until the Governor General sat down. "Begging your pardon, sire, but it has been my experience that the Spanish are more likely to break an oath than the Indios. They have kept bargains that you yourself have broken. May I continue?" The Governor General leaned back and folded his arms across his chest, so Father Philip took a deep breath and went on. "If you choose the white cross, you will live. If you do not, then the Red Cross shows their intention to stain the land red with your blood and not one Spaniard will leave here alive."

The Governor General snorted, then stomped from the room without another word. The rest of the men in and around the chapel were unsure what they were supposed to do next, so they tiptoed out, and Father Philip was left alone in the chapel with just one candle burning. He thought for a long time about what a calming and intelligent force the Father President had been. Now that he was no longer alive, what was to keep Governor General Ceballos in check?

Father Philip still sat in the chapel. He was tired. He couldn't tell what time it was, but it was probably well past midnight. He had been awake for almost two days. Reality was starting to seem very unreal. He sat there for a long time, until the candle, which was burning low, sputtered and went dim. It flared again, but it would not be long before he was sitting in the dark.

There was a disturbance out in the vestibule, near the entrance of the chapel. Then the palacio doors were thrown open. Father Philip heard Don Miguel's voice as he ran towards the Governor General's quarters. "Wake the Governor!"

Father Philip sat in the darkness of the chapel, and was unnoticed. He saw Ceballos meet Don Miguel just outside the chapel. "What is the meaning of this? It's the middle of . . ."

Don Miguel interrupted. "Governor General, we are under attack. The Indios have entered the Plaza and have taken the cannon."

Ceballos ran toward his quarters. "Bring my horse. We must not lose the cannon."

by Kevin H. and Karen C. Evans

CHAPTER 4

The Third Day
Santa Fe cannon revetment,
Two hours before dawn,, September 1634
Tuesday

S antiago Fuentes yawned. It was true the Indios were in rebellion, and there was a chance he could be killed at any moment, but not much had changed. He had come to New Mexico al Dentro to be a cannoneer, and so this guard duty was something he did every day. He punched Pablo's arm and said, "Look there, I can see light just over the mountains. Our shift is almost over. You want to go find some beer before we sleep?"

Pablo Garcia rubbed his arm. "Yes, that's a good idea. I need something extra to help me sleep in the daylight. But if the fighting gets fierce again they will wake us up and make us fight all day before we stay awake all night on watch again. Explain to me again why you wanted the night watch."

Santiago said, "At least there's a chance we might get some sleep in the morning. At night, there's no place to sleep inside the palacio. There is wall to wall people, everybody hiding from the Indios. This morning we will have the barracks to ourselves."

It was not even ten minutes later when Santiago nudged Pablo awake. "Did you hear that?"

At that very moment, the shouts of the Indios could be heard rolling across the end of the Plaza. Santiago peeked around the corner and saw Indios. "Quick, Pablo. Hand me the slow match. We must fire this cannon, we are under attack."

Pablo woke up with a jerk, and they made sure the load was secure and fired the cannon. "Santiago, what do we do now? With only two of us, they will reach us before we can reload."

Santiago was already gathering things off the ground. "Pablo, push the cart with the powder towards the center of the Plaza. I will get the ram rods. We can't hold them off, but we can't leave them the ability to fire on our own people."

Frightened by the screaming Indios, Pablo gripped the handles of the cart and started pushing with all his might. Santiago secured the fuse from one and then the other of the cannons. They would be very difficult to fire now. He grabbed the ram rods and followed after Pablo.

The Third Day
Outside the Santa Fe Plaza, Before Sunrise

Wa-tu looked at his society brothers, maybe for the last time. "Look at the peaks, the sun has begun his travels. It is time. At the word of the senior chiefs, we will go."

For the young Indio men, the stress and pressure was building enormously. Then came the sound of wood beating on wood. It was the signal, time to run forward into battle. Wa-tu screamed his war cry, encouraging his brothers. "Forward, we will bathe in Ironskin blood."

The movement was unorganized, there were no lines of men, but clot or clump, group by group, a human wave washed towards the open corner of the Plaza. The Indios filled the winding streets, shouting, screaming, waving their weapons in the air. Eight hundred men scrambled towards the enemy artillery. The attack started only about seventy feet away from the entrance to the Plaza. It had taken all the skill that the Indios had, to creep forward without alerting the Spaniards within the fortification.

With an earth-shattering boom, cannon shot flashed out from the fortified position. It was like the hiss of a thousand snakes, all around. Watu saw gaps open all around him as his brothers fell to the shrapnel. But the men behind kept moving, carrying him forward.

When they reached the guns, they were surprised to see no one there. Rapidly they tried to put the guns into the operation, first turning them and pointing toward the palacio. When they tried to load the cannon, they found no powder and no loading tools, just a pile of cannonballs and a few buckets of water.

That didn't stop them from pulling the cannons from the installation and rolling them toward the street outside the plaza.

The Third Day
Palacio barracks

Colonel Martinez was already awake. His orderly had just delivered hot water to his room in the garrison. He was almost ready to apply the razor to his face when he heard the sharp double report of the cannons from the Plaza. He put his head out the door. "Find out what's going on, and report back to me immediately."

Then he spoke to the other guard in the hallway. "You, make sure everybody's awake, equipped, and prepared. I think we have trouble."

Mateo El Gordo rushed out the door and looked towards the cannon revetment in the flickering light of the torches. He could see a mob of Indios swarming the revetments where the cannons had been emplaced.

Turning slightly, he saw the two artillery watch standers pushing a cart towards him as fast as they could move. He ran over and got his shoulder on the side of the cart, moving them faster. "Santiago what happened? What about the guns?"

Santiago replied, "It was just as the light reached the top of the mountains, the Indios screamed and charged. This cart has all the ready gunpowder for the cannons. We had to leave the guns, but the Indios only have some cannon balls and buckets of water. They may have stolen our beautiful cannon, but they will never fire them. Send a troop out there, though. The Indios might find the powder store between the revetment and the center of the Plaza."

Colonel Martinez had followed the guard out the door. He grabbed Mateo by the shoulder. "I am right here; I heard their report. Go tell Teniente de Bances to gather the musketeers in front of the garrison."

Then he turned to Santiago. "That was good thinking, son. Now I want you to run across the way to the palacio. Find Don Miguel, tell him we are under attack, and then gather that troop of farmers from the haciendas. Tell anyone with a musket or pistol to fire from the windows. If we are quick, we may be able to break them before they can settle into the gun position."

Then the Colonel riveted Pablo with his hawk-like stare. "You, go to the stable in the garrison; tell them that if the cavalry is not formed and attacking within ten minutes, I'll make them cut off their beards and eat them."

The three men in front of the colonel scattered like cockroaches in the light. The colonel turned and ran towards the garrison.

The Third Day
At the revetment in the plaza Santa Fe

Hundreds of Indios swarmed around the hated brass cannon. Wa-Tu turned to the members of his society. "We should prepare. The Ironskins will not let us stay here unmolested. They will attack soon, and we must be prepared. If we can keep this place long enough we can fill the Plaza with our brothers and drive them from our land."

The Third Day
Palacio Chapel, during the Indio attack

Father Philip woke with a jerk and realized he had been dozing, still sitting in his chair in the middle of the chapel. He had been dreaming that the evil Governor General was about to hang him when he woke.

He watched through the open chapel doors as people scurried around him, but found that he was completely ignored. Finally, the soldiers were all outside, and Father Tómas was at his side. He had a key, and was unlocking the manacles.

"Father Philip, we must hurry, now, before anyone notices. I have two burros outside. We must ride."

So, exhausted as he was, Father Philip escaped the palacio with his good friend from the Bernal Hacienda. They passed women and children huddled in the dark hallways, and it tore at his heart to see so much fear. But there was nothing he could do. He left.

The Third Day
Santa Fe plaza, near the barracks

Colonel Martinez shouted, "Get the pikes assembled, do it now!" Then he addressed the musketeers. "I want two volleys fired together, and reload as quickly as you can. Then draw your swords and advance. Do not shoot my pikemen. Anybody who fires after the pikemen start to engage will have their guts ripped out, nailed to a post, then we will chase you around the post until you are tied up like a fly in a spider's web. You will not shoot your brothers in arms."

The men, some as young as thirteen, scurried to their positions, and Colonel Martinez waited for them to be in place. "Do this quickly and we will reclaim the cannon revetment. Strike them hard and strike them fast! Remember everything starts when the trumpet sounds."

Then the Colonel strode over to his warhorse. As he swung into the saddle he shouted at his personal valet. "Make sure the musketeers know that there will be only two volleys, and then they must stop. Have Don Miguel and the Governor General been informed?"

Santiago nodded. "Yes, Excellency. They have been informed, and at least this end of the palacio is close enough that everyone heard your bloodcurdling threat to the musketeers. I do not think we will have any trouble."

"Good. Get the rest of the cannoneers, and take your powder and tools with you. We are going to need those guns. There must be four thousand Indios outside the walls. They are not getting into the plaza, not if I can help it."

With a grand motion Colonel Martinez drew his sword, flashing it the dawn. "Sound the trumpet, it is time."

The harsh trumpet blared across the plaza. In an instant, every musket vomited flames. The half visible knot of men around the cannons convulsed. Moments passed, then the musketeers lashed out another blast of fire. From the palacio, however came scattered steady fire. The militia seemed to be reloading their muskets at their own pace.

As the fire from the palacio trickled away the pikemen shouted, lowered their weapons, and charged. Not to be outdone, the musketeers shouted as well. With their muskets slung, they drew their swords and rushed into the fray.

While the gunfire had made the group of Indios scatter, the charge of the pikes and that of the swords and bucklers made them splash. The natives broke and ran.

The pikemen pushed between the cannon revetment and the entrance of the plaza, while the musketeers scrambled into the revetment. Then the ground began to shake. The cavalry had arrived.

Standing in his stirrups Colonel Martinez cried, "Now my sons! Hit them hard." There were only fifty horsemen, but they had some of the finest mounts in New Spain. Nowhere in this territory did horses exist to match the cavalry of New Mexico. More than that, they were as finely armored as any group of knights in history. Men of steel mounted on the backs of ferocious animals, they smashed in to the group of natives like a boulder dropped on a nest of eggs. They were like a sudden gust of wind ripping a cloud to shreds. The cavalry drove the rest of the Indios out of the plaza and into the streets.

Colonel Martinez waved his sword. "Sound the recall, follow me!" The trumpet blared and the Commander led his men back into the Plaza.

When the cavalry arrived at the palacio, Don Miguel and the Governor General had just mounted their horses. Don Miguel shouted, "Colonel Martinez, report."

The Colonel was still on horseback. "Excellency, the pikes formed into a square of almost eight ranks by eight files. The muskets are divided into two squares of twenty each on the sides of the pike. We have driven off the Indios that tried to steal our cannons. Now, we are ready for your command."

Don Miguel nodded. "Well done, Colonel. Teniente de Bances?"

The young Teniente saluted. "Your Excellency, we have fifty horsemen with lances, well mounted and eager to attack at your will."

Don Miguel turned to the Governor General. "Your Excellency, we are prepared, we are yours to command."

Ceballos drew his sword. "I am proud to lead you all. We will disperse this rabble. Don Miguel will see to the security of the plaza. Colonel Martinez will command the musket and pike. They will march out and fire two volleys at the largest concentration of Indios. Then the pike will close and shatter it. I will have command of the horse, and our job is to break up any concentrations that form against the pike square. Once we have shattered the biggest group of rebels, we all march on their encampment and burn it to the ground."

That speech began the attack. It was near morning, but still very dark. Huge torches burned in the Plaza. The musket and pike marched rapidly to the crossroads of the only street that was unblocked to the Plaza. Both wings of musketeers fired shattering volleys into the mass of Indios before them.

With a shout, the pikemen lowered their weapons and strode rapidly forward. At the moment of contact, another volley from the muskets shattered forth.

The Indios ran forward, swinging their clubs and screaming. Arrows rained down, but the stone points were ineffective against the morion helmets and steel cuirasses. There were a few pieces of Spanish armor worn by the natives, evidently taken in during the earlier raids.

When the two groups met, the long pikes of the Spaniards obliterated the center of the Indio formation. The musketeers had drawn their swords and provided support to the pike square on its edges. The small band of Spaniards became the center of the huge mass of Indios, as more and more Indios streamed towards the conflict.

Then came the call of a trumpet, and the ground began to rumble. Fifty trained cavaliers lowered their lances and charged into the side of the rebellious Indios. The shock shattered the cluster of Indios. The pike square and its accompanying muskets marched steadfastly towards the farm buildings where the Indios had their headquarters.

Howling Indios, shouting Spaniards, flames, and fire ruled the twilight. Finally, in the gray daylight, the Governor General commanded his troops to the Plaza. "We must protect the women and children. The buildings are burning, and the Indios have fled. We'll see what the day brings."

When the Spanish soldiers regained the Plaza, they saw that both of the brass cannons had been returned to the well-constructed revetments made from adobe bricks. The Governor General gave one of his rare smiles. "It's good to have the cannons back where they belong. Colonel Martinez, double the guard. We don't want this happening again."

Don Miguel rode up and saluted. "Sire, the dead are piling up near the palacio, and I want to send out a crew to push the bodies farther away. I also noted that some of those Indios had helmets, or breastplate, and a couple had muskets. I would like to recover those as well."

The Governor General considered for a moment, and nodded. "Good thought, Don Miguel. Recover what you can so the Indios can't sneak in and re-arm. But make sure you have sentries set. Put them up on top of the walls, so they can see if Indios are moving up on you. Don't take any unnecessary chances."

by Kevin H. and Karen C. Evans

CHAPTER 5

The Fourth Day
Just after midnight, second Indio council
chamber, September 1634
Wednesday

T he council of Chiefs had gathered in their new headquarters. Natoto-kwata, chief of Ohkay Owingeh, looked around. They were in a barracks for workers, which had very little in amenities. "I liked the last place better. This one is smaller. But at least this keeps the morning cold out. How many men do we have assembled?"

Okuwa-oky, chief of Santo Domingo, said, "We started the day with about eight hundred. Last night, many died or were wounded too much to fight. But today, many more have arrived. So we now have over two thousand. And many more are promised by the village elders. We should see as many as five thousand tomorrow. After that, I don't care how they fire on us with their guns, we will swallow them like the flooding river and drive them before us. There will be so many warriors but they cannot possibly stand against us."

Kwa-kay from Tiguex stood up suddenly. He was not a chief, and so usually would not be recognized to speak. But Okuwa-oky stood up as well. Kwa-kay gestured, and Wa-Tu was carried in on a stretcher. He was gravely wounded. Kwa-kay said, "This man is a survivor from the madness yesterday. I think you should hear his report." Then Kwa-kay and Okuwa-oky sat down.

Tze-nat-ay from Teseque stood before Wa-tu could speak. "Weren't you in the raid to take the cannons? What happened? You had ten times their number, and yet the Spaniards swept you out of that place like an old woman sweeping dust from her doorstep."

Although Wa-Tu had blood still seeping from a chest wound. He struggled to sit up with the help of his two society brothers. There were only three of them who had survived and escaped the plaza before the cavalry charge. "Honored chiefs, I come to tell you of our glorious battle. Members of our Society sacrificed themselves so that I could escape and report to you. Many of us knew the power of their musket. I have a musket ball in my leg and will soon die. But we have never seen the destruction they create with their long axes. When they ran at us with the axes on poles, we had nothing to stop them."

The chiefs looked on, and Tze-nat-ay continued. "Was that all? Men with long axes? That doesn't sound dangerous."

Wa-Tu was trembling, but refused to lie back down. "First, we faced the musket fire, then the long axes. After the long axes, their horsemen rode at us, and we were forced to leave. My brothers stood and attacked the horses so that I could escape, but they are dead. The men and the horses are all Iron-skins. The clubs did nothing to them."

Natoto-kwata stood. "Wa-tu, you have shown your bravery. I wish you peace before you die. I am pleased, even though we didn't succeed in taking the cannons. Wa-tu, last night, we were almost successful. We must try again and keep them from sleeping. Prepare to attack now, before dawn. Then they will be sleepy and we will be prepared. We must be victorious."

Before anyone could ask more, Wa-Tu swooned, and collapsed. He was taken out of the council. Okuwa-oky stood again. Others were silent, affected by Wa-tu's report. But Okuwa-oky's eyes burned in hatred. "We must resist these Ironskins. Do not forget how they stole our food, our houses, and even our young men, who were sent carrying salt and never returned. Assemble everyone; it is time to cover them with men as the river covers our fields in the floods."

Outside, a large group of men from the surrounding area began to assemble. Others, who had not been involved in the early morning attack, began to join the group. Slowly but forcefully, the drums beat, and the men lifted their voices in song.

As the song strengthened, the group of men solidified and they began to flow toward the opening into the plaza. The closer they came to the entrance the louder they go. Finally, the song dropped off into a wave of overlapping shouts, the Indios raising their weapons as they rushed toward the entrance like an unstoppable river.

The Fourth Day
Before dawn, cannon revetment

Colonel Martinez stood behind his freshly loaded weapons, his men in a circle around him. "Remember, fire the cannon one at a time. Reload as rapidly as possible. Do not forget to sponge out the barrels between shots, or when you're pushing powder down the barrel it will all boil out and burn your face off. We need continuous fire."

Then Martinez turned to the group of men next to the horse trough behind the position. "Many of you are inexperienced in combat. But I have a vital job for you. You are my bucket men. Your job is to cool the barrels of the cannons, because if they get too hot they will burst and not only will we not have any cannon, but we probably won't have any crewmen left either, and that most assuredly includes yourselves. Do not let my cannons get too hot."

Santiago listened as he prepared his gun. He had heard this all before. If nothing else, Colonel Martinez believed in preparing to fight. Under his breath Santiago whispered to Pablo. "I guess we won't get any sleep after all. However, we will be able to express our displeasure to the Indios denying us our rest."

Pablo shrugged. "I would rather have the sleep, Santiago."

The sun had not fully cleared the mountain when the rush of Indios reached the opening of the Plaza. With more of a bark than a roar, the first cannon let fly with its cargo of death. Moments later the second cannon added its bark to the noise. Then the musketeers, formed on both sides of the revetment, let fly with everything they had.

The Indios, receiving this expression from their Spanish overlords, recoiled with each bark. Gaps formed in the Indio mass, and with each volley from the musketeers, men fell. No matter what the Indios in front wanted, the men behind kept pushing forward.

The cavalry was preparing to charge when, at last, the Indio assault faltered and began to wash away. It seemed the Spanish artillery position was a rock that didn't particularly care about the flood of the river.

Colonel Martinez watched from his horse. His eyes gleamed as the Indio charge faded. He shouted, "Hit them hard and they will break! Now, charge!"

The trumpets sounded, and the cavalry began to move forward. From the other side of the gun position, the knot of pike-men lowered their weapons and advanced into the fray.

The cavalry charge was just too much for the Indios. They scattered away from the plaza, disappearing around corners and into the smoke. They were done for the day.

So the Spaniards had a respite throughout the hot day. Don Miguel organized another expedition to retrieve dropped armor and weapons and to push the bodies out of the plaza.

When it was dark, Santiago had the night watch again. Pablo was with him, and they both struggled to keep their eyes open. This siege was putting a lot of strain on them. They had not slept well through the day, and now, the night seemed to fill with watching the Indios, who were about to attack again. Pablo startled at every sound. He could see many small fires, where one by one, the buildings in Santa Fe were set ablaze.

Around midnight, Santiago turned to Pablo. "Well at least, if we cannot sleep they are not sleeping either."

Pablo just grunted. "I'm afraid there are a lot more of them than there are of us. I feel like we are at the bottom of the pitcher, and somebody keeps pouring more and more water in it. I fear that soon we will be drowning in Indios."

by Kevin H. and Karen C. Evans

CHAPTER 6

The Fifth Day
Cannon revetment, September 1634
Thursday

J ust before dawn, Colonel Martinez, on horseback, lead a whole troop of musketeers to the corner of the plaza near the only opening. The gunnery position was stuffed with soldiers. A breathless messenger came running up from the palacio. "The Governor General, he commands that all water barrels be filled immediately. The scouts have found the Indios blocking the canal that brings water to the village. The Governor, he fears that there will not be enough water to cool the cannon barrel."

Grunting and cursing, Pablo dug out the buckets while Santiago shouted at the cannon crew. "Wake up, you lovers of goats. Get the buckets. The Indios will not destroy these beautiful cannons if I have anything to say about it."

Soon a steady trickle of men ran back and forth from the central fountain of the plaza to fill water barrels and a horse trough at the gun emplacement. Santiago and Pablo supervised. "You know, Pablo, it's just as well we woke them when we did. This way we will be first in line for breakfast."

Don Miguel rode out of the garrison with a troop of cavalry, commanded by Teniente de Bances. Don Miguel walked his horse up to Colonel Martinez at the fountain before they finished and spoke quietly. "Well done, Colonel. It appears you have everything ready. At least today we won't have any surprises."

Martinez grinned. "Let's hope not, sir." He signaled the trumpeters with his raised sword. When the plaza was ringing with the music, he nudged his horse forward, followed by a small force of Spaniard muskets.

Colonel Martinez stopped near the cannons, and nodded to de Bances. "Teniente, make sure you keep a close eye out. You have the command of these horsemen. The scouts brought word that the Indios are gathering to the south. Steer directly into the thickest part of them. We need to break their lines and show them the value of good Spanish steel."

The Teniente saluted and grinned. "Yes, Colonel. Today is the day we break this rebellion." Then de Bances led his men out of the fortified plaza. Behind them was the collection of scouts, led by Teniente Ramirez. Some were mounted, others on foot. The colonel moved his horse close to Ramirez. "You are my second set of eyes, Ricardo. Do not hesitate to advise me when we are about to be attacked from the sides or the rear. And when the Governor General takes command, you are still to report to me."

Governor General Ceballos stood near the cannon and stared down the empty street that lead to the rest of town. So far in this conflict, the fighting had been productive. On a number of occasions, the Indios, buoyed by optimism or their numbers, had stood fast and allowed the Spaniards to fully engage them. That was when bodies piled in heaps on the ground. Mostly the attacks had not been sustained. Those that looked like they were going to overwhelm the infantry had been broken up by the cavalry.

Today presented new problems. The canal was blocked, and the palacio needed water. Ceballos took his horse's reins from the stable boy, and pulled himself up into the saddle for another day of fighting. He scowled at Teniente Ramirez, reporting from his scouts who stood next to his horse. "You've found the blockage?"

Ramirez nodded vigorously. "Yes, Your Excellency. They have driven poles into the canal bottom and stacked brush behind it. Over the brush, they have put skins. Very effective dam."

The Governor General slapped his gloves on his thigh. "Then, Teniente, tell me why you didn't destroy the dam?"

Ramirez started to sweat. "Your Excellency, the scouts are not in armor, and there were only four of us. Our estimate indicates that there are more than a thousand Indios, both on the hillsides and in front of the dam. They are armed with bows and arrows. Several threw spears at us, and I saw an old Abus gun that they were trying to set up on a tripod. They will do whatever it takes to keep the dam intact. It does not look like they mean to leave."

Ceballos rubbed his forehead under his helmet. He found that he truly missed his arguments with the Father President. They had been irritating, but they had always served to focus his decisions. He had to do something to keep the confidence of his troops. Where were the reinforcements and supplies he'd requested from Isleta?

"Splendid, Teniente. That means they are all in one spot. We will attack the dam with everything we have and drive them off for good. If they do stay to defend their work we will crush these rebellious Indios once and for all. I don't want to see one of them get away."

Ceballos drew his sword and turned to faced the troops assembled in the plaza. As he spoke, he waved the sword over his head. "Men of Spain, we ride to victory. Start the attack, destroy them, and we will drink in peace tonight."

Teniente Ramirez nodded and waved his men forward. Governor General Ceballos spurred his horse to the front of the force. He waved his sword in the air, and shouted, "For Santiago! For Santa Fe! En nombre del Rey. Ataquemos!"

Every man in the expeditionary force answered, "Ataquemos !" and charged out of the plaza.

The Fifth Day
Outside Santa Fe, at the canal
Before dawn

Wapinnuge was a seventeen year old boy who was slow of thought. He could not remember his Tewa name, so the men in Santa Domingo who cherished and protected him used his Ironskin name, Pepe. He had been sent on this task because it was something he could do to help. So he was perched in a tree as lookout while his brothers worked through the night.

Amu-chukwa, who grew up in Santa Fe as Mathieu González, directed the men who had labored by his side throughout the night. The creek was down to a trickle, and no more water was flowing to the Ironskins. "You have done well. They will get no more water from this part of the river. We will let the hot sun do our work for us. The Spanish village will soon become an oven. We will let the Ironskins stay, baking in their own grease."

Pepe said, "Are we finished here? The sun will be hot for us as well."

Amu-chukwa shook his head. "We must stay and protect this dam. The Ironskins will try to destroy it, but we cannot allow it. They must go without water and leave here, or all the effort we put in last night will have been for nothing."

Pepe listened to Amu-chukwa because he admired this strong man. But he glanced toward the city and yelled, waving his arms, "The men, the Ironskins! They left their Plaza with horses and guns. They are marching this way!"

Amu-chukwa looked toward the plaza, then raised his spear. "Pepe and I will stay here and watch. The rest of you, go to the streets before they arrive. Protect the dam. Remember, stay hidden from their long-axes and guns. Shower them with stones and arrows, whatever you can. They must be stopped, but don't sacrifice your lives. We have more fight to come. If we have to, we will block the water again. If they get past you, return here. We must not fail."

The Indios melted away. Amu-chukwa and Pepe kept watch from the hillside. They could see Indios from villages near and far. There were more Indios than Pepe could count. The Indios washed across the fields outside the village.

The Ironskin soldiers, musket, pike, and cavalry, rolled like a huge boulder smashing down a hillside. Nothing could stand before them. Men fled from their faces. But when they passed by, the tribes filled in behind them like the waters of a flood. The Ironskins were like a bubble bouncing in a sea of men.

As the Ironskins fought their way closer to the dam, the Indios from Santa Domingo returned to protect their dam. Amu-chukwa waited until he saw the horsemen at the end of the street, then shouted to his men at the dam. "Nothing has stopped them. They are coming now, prepare yourselves. Remember the plan. People with bows, throwing spears, and throwing sticks, go to the top of walls and on the hillside. If you run out

103

of things to throw or shoot, big lumps of stone may be very effective; see if we can break their backs. The rest of you with clubs, stand in front of the dam. We must see if they will charge. When they do, retreat over the dam and up the hillside." The Ironskins seemed too invulnerable. For the first time, Pepe began to feel fear.

The Fifth Day
Streets of Santa Fe

Rodrigo Ortega was not one of the soldiers. He was a sixteen-year-old weaving apprentice, near to earning his journeyman designation. His uncle held a land grant north of Santa Fe, near the sacred spring of Tyi Mayo.

But today, he was not weaving. His uncle had assigned him the care of his aunt, cousins, and the small children of the village when the others evacuated. His uncle stayed behind to protect the hacienda, and they had not heard of him for almost a week.

When Rodrigo reached Santa Fe, riding a horse next to his aunt's carriage, he had been gathered into the ad hoc cavalry. There had been a couple of days training with Teniente de Bances. They had familiarized themselves with the lance and done some small work with the sword.

Now, in uncomfortable and ill-fitting armor, he watched from his horse as the muskets advanced towards the Indios in front of the dam. The fear he had felt as they left the fortified plaza had dissipated, replaced with a worry that he would make a mistake. But his first battle encounter was going better than he thought it would.

The Spaniards halted about fifteen paces from the Indio rebels formed up in front of the dam. On command, the musketeers raised their weapons and everything was swallowed up in a huge cloud of white smoke. Then the trumpet sounded, and Rodrigo, with the rest of the cavalry around him, lowered his lance and began to advance towards the enemy. As they came into the cloud of smoke, Rodrigo's eyes and throat burned for a moment, but he didn't have time to do more than notice.

Before they connected, there was another shattering crash, which came from the musketeers. The wind began to twist the smoke into spirals above the ground. Teniente de Bances pulled his sword and shouted. "Steady, all advance in a walk. Move to a trot on signal. Lances until you break them, swords after that."

Rodrigo flinched. They had practiced this maneuver and chased Indios for a couple of days now, but this was the first time they were facing men who held their ground. The Indios were trapped against their dam. Rodrigo felt his stomach tighten, and he gripped his lance. He had been excited to be included with real soldiers, but now it didn't seem all that glorious. The line of cavalry began a slow walk.

✳ ✳ ✳

Amu-chukwa watched the Ironskins move forward. The Spaniards with their spears and their muskets were approaching like a log in a flooded river. They moved over anything in their path and then withdrew unscathed.

He shouted, "Everyone down!" just before every musket in the Spanish formation spat fire and smoke. He'd thrown himself to the ground with the sound of musket balls whistling past his ears.

Some of his companions started to get up, but Amu-chukwa shouted again. "Stay down! They always shoot one more time, and then they will walk towards us." He covered his head as fire roared forth from the muskets again.

At that point Amu-chukwa stood and shouted, "Do not attack until you can see them through the smoke. Then fire as quickly as possible."

The small valley that held the canal at its bottom seem to attract the wind. Quickly, the smoke began to flow away from the defenders. First the tops of the spears, then the helmeted heads of the attackers began to appear out of the receding smoke. Amu-chukwa shouted with glee. "Shoot! Shoot them now. Use the iron arrowheads. We have them at our mercy."

The arrows arched out, sounding more like a flight of birds than the thunder of the muskets. But when the shafts reached their targets they skipped off the steel armor of the Spaniards. Amu-chukwa shouted out again. "Faces! Shoot them in their faces or their hands. Hit them where they have no iron skin."

The next volley of arrows arched out. This time a few figures staggered and went to their knees. At that moment the horses, carrying riders like towers of steel, appeared out of the smoke.

Amu-chukwa jumped up and pointed to the large man in the center. "It is the Governor General! Shoot him in the face! Cut the head from the snake, and the bite will not follow."

Now with a single purpose, every archer, every spear man, every man with a throwing club, on each hillside made it their goal to strike the Governor General. A cascade of projectiles fell upon him.

✳ ✳ ✳

Rodrigo scowled. The arrows were thick enough to shade him from the hot September sun for a moment. But he could see as they fell that they were too light and were skipping off of the armor of the footman. Steel helmets and hard cured rawhide over thick padded jackets shed the arrows with ease. He could hear the voice of Teniente Ramirez, commanding the ground troops and scouts. "Steady, men. Steady all. Advance smartly."

The sudden trumpet call focused Rodrigo's attention. The cavalry advanced on the western side of the small valley. Surely they would catch them before they could scramble away. Ahead of him, the Governor General couched his lance and touched his heels to signal his horse to advance. Behind their leader, the fully armored cavalry moved up to a trot behind him.

As Rodrigo watched, the arrows were like a cloud of flies buzzing all around Governor General Ceballos, skipping off his armor.

Rodrigo could see that the Indios were all trying to kill the Governor General. He shouted and kicked his horse into a run, but it was too late. Before he could warn or intercept the governor, an arrow fell from the sky and found its home inside the governor's helmet. Ceballos fell off his horse, the shaft of the arrow clutched in his hand. Every Spaniard who saw it hesitated for a breath.

* * *

Amu-chukwa saw the governor fall, and shouted, "Now, now is the time! Everyone return to Pepe, at the observation tree."

Like a cloud being ripped by the wind the Indios scattered running uphill or over the dam, but in every case away from the Spaniards.

The Fifth Day
Santa Fe plaza, afternoon

Colonel Martinez strode up to the canvas sunshade and peered inside. When he saw a friar with a bowl and a rag, he asked, "How is it? Is the Governor General dead?"

Before the friar could answer, Ceballos struggled up on his elbow, then rolled around until his feet hit the floor. "Not dead yet, Martinez. They tell me I've lost my good looks. However, a scar, fairly won, is not to be despised. Apparently the arrow hit on the wrong side of the cheek plate on my helmet. It didn't really penetrate but skittered down the side of my face. The surgeon even gave me the arrowhead." Ceballos held up the metal head.

The Colonel took it and shook his head. "Sire, you are very lucky that this didn't kill you. When we saw you fall, we thought for sure that it had."

The Governor General lay back down, exhausted. But his voice was still strong; it was low and chilling. "Iron arrow tips. Tell me again whose idea was it to teach the locals how to smith?"

Martinez smiled. "It was one of your predecessors, sire. And it seems they learned the lesson well."

Ceballos held out a hand, and Martinez returned the arrowhead. Ceballos sighed and slipped it into a sleeve pocket. "Many more arrows like this, and we could be in serious trouble. When we succeed in driving out the rebels, I plan to catch me that blacksmith. I want his hands, and maybe add a few coals just to light him up some."

Colonel Martinez sat on the stool near the cot. "Sire, after you fell, the Indios fled, surely thinking you were dead. We worked all afternoon and will have the plug out of the canal within the hour. I recommend we keep some troops there until an hour before dusk and then march back to the town. You know they'll plug it up again tonight after we leave."

Ceballos nodded. "Yes, I agree. But at least for now, water will get into town and they can refill our storage vessels. When the water is flowing again, fill every container we have."

The Colonel stood and saluted. "Yes, Governor General. I will return to the canal and supervise clearing and then protecting it."

Wearily, Ceballos acknowledged the salute and eased back down on the cot. "Make sure you are not in full darkness, there are too many of them still out there. We can't lose our best men. Send in Quezada on your way out."

The colonel saluted again and left the tent. Moments later, Don Miguel Quezada ducked into the tent and saluted. "You sent for me, Excellency?"

Ceballos sat up again, "Don Miguel, when the water returns, make sure that every barrel and bucket we own is filled with water. Above all, we must protect our cannons. I've been listening to them fire all day. And now they are slowing down. It probably means they are hot and cannot be fired as rapidly. Tomorrow, I think is the time for the deciding strike."

by Kevin H. and Karen C. Evans

CHAPTER 7

The Sixth Day
Santa Fe plaza September 1634
Friday,

I t was perhaps two hours before dawn. These were the cool hours, just before the sun peeked over the eastern mountains. The clear sky lightened, and only the brightest stars still shone. Nobody had taken the time to appoint a new Father President, and many of the duties he had performed were left aside. Right then, Father Diego, who had been Father President Bautista's secretary, took up his vestments and went to the troops to perform last rites. The priest and his acolytes processed up and down through the soldiers and then the refugees, performing their benedictions in clouds of incense, with their crosses held high.

The Governor General and Don Miguel stood together just outside the door into the garrison. Governor General Ceballos said, "The scouts report that the water is stopped again. And I have had complaints from the cooking staff that there is very little food left. The armorer says that we're almost out of powder and shot. This can't go on much longer. Today we must make the difference. Today the rebellious Indios have to be crushed or we will lose."

A thoughtful look crossed Don Miguel's face. "I have an idea. Why don't we leave half the muskets behind? We can arm the remaining musketeers with sword and buckler and put them around the pikes. It will strengthen the pike square and keep the Indios from swarming them under. It will also let me use the best marksman on the muskets, or at least the ones who can reload fastest. We want every volley to shatter the enemy."

The Governor General was feeling the bandage over his cheek. It felt hot, and throbbed in unison with the headache behind his eyes. But Ceballos was never one to show distress. He clapped Don Miguel on the shoulder. "That sounds good. Steel against wood is still a great advantage. Also, today I want the troops to stay inside the village streets, because as long as we're in the streets they can't bring their numbers against us. We'll be able to pursue them through the streets as long as we wish. I want to shatter their formations, I want to shatter their enthusiasm, I want them to lose all taste for this fight. I want to drive them off of this mountain."

Don Miguel grinned. "That sounds excellent, Sire. We will play to our strengths and against their disadvantages."

✳ ✳ ✳

It was still dark when Father Diego murmured his last prayer. He gathered his staff and went back inside the chapel. Governor Ceballos could tell when Don Miguel issued orders because he could see a stir among the men as the new orders were passed.

While his horse was saddled and brought to the loading step, Ceballos strode into the cannon emplacement. "My sons, today we are going to drive them through the streets. Be prepared. Every time we can push a group of Indios past the opening to the Plaza, I want you to fire. Hit them hard, like a hammer falling from the heavens. If we do that enough we can break their nerve and they will run."

Santiago rubbed his hand in anticipation. "Excellency, that is a superb idea; we will do it in your honor."

Ceballos nodded, but did not smile. "Keep my pipas cool, keep them firing." And he strode off and mounted his horse.

✻ ✻ ✻

The sound of trumpets announced the readiness of the formation. Rodrigo was near the middle of the line but had a great place to see and hear. His heart beat faster thinking of the fighting and the thrill he had experienced already. He was in line with his new friend, Cézar Garcia, who was also a refugee with a horse. Although Cézar was twenty, they stuck close to each other.

The sun was almost visible behind the peak when Governor General Ceballos led the cavalry contingent. At the barricade that led out into the streets, he stood in the stirrups and waved his gauntleted fist over his head. "Never in the annals of New Spain has there been such a great opportunity for valor as this day. Together we shall sally forth, and together we shall shatter the enemy. Today we'll create such fear in their hearts that a thousand years from now they will still be speaking of the valor of Spain. For the Viceroy! For New Spain! For New Mexico!"

Everyone shouted in answer to the challenge, and Rodrigo and Cézar shouted with them. Their hearts were racing as the Governor General spurred his horse. Then the cavalry led the way out of the plaza. From that moment onward, it was the measured tread of feet and the jingle of harness that sounded through the streets of Santa Fe.

by Kevin H. and Karen C. Evans

As the formation turned the first corner on their march through the streets they found a huge group of Indios crouched in the darkness. Rodrigo whispered to Cézar. "It looks like they had the same ideas as we did, a dawn attack. Too bad that we are prepared and they are not."

Cézar laughed and tightened his grip on his lance. "We will trample them for Spain!" And since Cézar was older, Rodrigo followed his lead.

As the formation of Spaniards advanced, it was if a sudden fanaticism gripped them. They were here to destroy, and they were good at their jobs. With an unstoppable, frenetic energy, they smashed through the first wave of attackers.

As the Indios began to break, the muskets were fired. The twenty men so armed were shooting in groups of five at the same moment, as rapidly as possible. The effect was devastating. Suddenly all opposition broke and fled.

Ceballos stood in his stirrups, shouting at the top of his lungs. "Forward, men! We have them now!"

The Sixth Day
Afternoon, Tribal camp outside Santa Fe

The council of chieftains settled in another barn. This one had no roof, but it kept them out of sight, and cut the wind. There were noticeable gaps in the leadership, with maybe ten or twelve leaders here. Many faces in the circle showed grief and weariness. And in the distance they could hear the clash of the fighting.

Amu-chukwa stood to speak. "The ditches have been blocked again. This time we filled it with stones and earth for over one hundred paces. They will not clear it easily again. Further we have burned every field, every blade of grass, and every roof in the village, except for those immediately adjacent to the Plaza."

Qua-stiju from Acoma stood to speak as well. He had been silent for many of the councils because he spoke Keres, and it was at times difficult to make himself understood. But he had something to say now. "My brother Amu-chukwa, you may have done too well. Very little water is here for our warriors. There is no food left in Acoma. The Ironskins burned our grain stores. Our children will cry this winter."

Amu-chukwa stood and looked at the other chieftains. "We have done what had to be done to drive out these devils. Our brethren are hungry, but the Ironskins are hungrier still."

Okuwa-oky stood to speak. "Our warriors cannot stand before them. Their guns are devastating. Inside the village, the streets are a maze of confusion, and we cannot bring our numbers against them. They have nothing to eat, and they have nothing to drink. I say it is time for us to withdraw and let the Ironskins starve."

After that, Chieftain after Chieftain spoke. The day wore on to its finish, and Indios died in the streets of Santa Fe. Finally, at dusk, the senior Chieftains stood in agreement. "When it is dark, we will leave. Let the Spaniards drink mud and eat the dust of the ground, for there is nothing else here for them. Let us go home and celebrate our victory and mourn our losses."

The Sixth Day
Cannon revetment at dusk

Santiago slapped Pablo on the back. "Now, that was a glorious day. We must have broken their formations four or five times as they passed us until they finally stopped coming. I guess even the Indios can learn something if you teach it to them with enough fire."

Pablo pointed to the opening of the plaza. "I hear someone coming, Santiago. We have no more gunpowder. What shall we do, throw the cannonballs?"

Santiago laughed. "Don't be a fool my friend. It's the cavalry and footmen returning. Look, there's Rodrigo and Cézar."

When Rodrigo heard his name, he nudged Cézar, then turned and waved at the cannon crew. "Well, we're back. They just melted away, about twenty minutes ago. It was like the attack dried up, and they all vanished. So we have returned victorious. Is there anything left to eat?"

✻ ✻ ✻

The rest of the cavalry entered the plaza, surrounding the Governor General. Ceballos sagged, but remained in his saddle by strength of will. The bandage on his face was dirty and seeped blood from underneath. Obviously, the battle of the day had taxed the Governor's strength.

As they reached the dismount step, Don Miguel hurried over to help Ceballos out of his saddle and down to the ground. Father Juan, with clean bandages and two servants, waited in the doorway of the palacio.

Ceballos held on Don Miguel's arm as they walked into the darkness of the doorway. "My thanks, my friend. Bring the commanders into the chapel, I want to talk to them."

Rodrigo and Cézar looked at each other. They were young, and unwounded, and had not realized that the Governor General would have any weakness. They were silent as they rode their horses to the stable.

Ceballos sat in the dark chapel, alone for a moment. He breathed deep, and took off his morion helmet. It had been a long day. There were not many casualties because their armor repelled most of the attacks the

Indios could use. But today it took more effort than ever to be strong for his men.

He heard sounds in the corridor and sat up again. His face set to the standard scowl as his commanders gathered. The surgeon bustled in and tsked at the condition of his wound. Ceballos ignored him and looked at Don Miguel Quezada, Colonel Martinez, Tenientes de Bances and Ramirez. He did not stand but waved the surgeon away as he spoke. "I have not seen a more glorious day. You have all done well, and I will mention your names in my report to the Viceroy. For tonight, see to your men and horses. I want reports of stores and casualties. We must do it again tomorrow and for every day thereafter until they disappear. We must not fail, for our honor and all those that depend on us."

Colonel Martinez took off his helm, and shouted, "To Victory!" and the others cheered and saluted their governor. Then all went to their quarters. Ceballos was finally able to collapse on his bed. He was asleep before food was brought. They left it on a table by his bed, and blew out the candle.

by Kevin H. and Karen C. Evans

CHAPTER 8

The Seventh Day
Predawn, Santa Fe plaza September 1634
Saturday,

The morning of the seventh day was ominously quiet. The fire of conquest that had burned so brightly within the Spaniards the day before was now subdued Everyone was tired and hungry, and the children seemed unwilling to play. Even the trumpets did not seem bright and cheerful but more just noise heard on the edge of their consciousness. Again it was the darkness before dawn, and Ceballos stood in the doorway of the palacio, watching Father Diego perform last rites for the gathered troops. They had no casualties from the previous day, but this little comfort was essential to the morale of the men.

When they finished, he gestured for the stable boy to bring his charger Fausto. The horse was thrilled, and some of that optimism lifted Ceballos' own heart. He mounted and addressed the troops. "Men, this is a new day. Let us go forth and punish them once more."

Cézar and Rodrigo sat on their horses and looked at each other uncomfortably. It was only a shadow of the speech of the day before. Rodrigo felt a little fear now where he had not had a shadow of it the day before.

by Kevin H. and Karen C. Evans

Before Ceballos could issue any more orders, he was interrupted by Símon, one of the scouts who stood watch on the rooftop of the palacio. "Governor General! Don Miguel! They are gone. We haven't seen any Indios anywhere around Santa Fe. We waited for daylight to be sure. That farm house they were using for the chiefs is burning. The Indios are gone."

Don Miguel, already on horseback, looked suspicious. "Excellency, it could be a trap. I advise strength and caution. March the foot together and break the cavalry into detachments, so that we may cover more ground quickly, but let them stay within sight of each other and return at the first hint of resistance."

Ceballos listened and nodded. "That is prudent, Don Miguel. Let the orders be given and let us march forth."

The jingle of harness and the tramp of feet were the only sounds in the village. Outside the barricaded plaza was a waste land. Not a roof remained on any house in the town, and there were no bodies of dead or dying Indios. Only the palacio and the garrison had roofs. Even the chapel roof, near the edge of the plaza, had been burned, with the thick adobe walls standing like a blackened skeleton. The canal had been filled with stones and debris for a great distance, and it would take more than a week to clear it.

After a cursory ride through town, Governor General Ceballos returned to the palacio. Many came in and out with reports. Finally, about noon, Teniente Ramirez, in command of the scouts, was announced. When the Teniente stepped into the governor's office and saluted, Ceballos looked him over. The Teniente was smoke stained and fatigued. The governor knew that Ramirez had not slept but spent the night coordinating reconnoiter. "Teniente, report."

The Teniente saluted again. "Sire, we have ridden patrols for ten miles on all sides of Santa Fe. We have not encountered any Indios or any life at all. Every field, every source of food, has been burned to the ground, and there isn't a blade of grass to be seen. Even the birds seem to have left the area. While there were probably Indios watching us, they were all watching from hiding. It is silent out there."

Ceballos sat in thought for a moment, then stood. "Teniente, go get your ration of food, then rest. I have some decisions to make." The Teniente saluted and left.

The Governor General then announced a council meeting in one hour. There was a lot of bustle in the palacio as the servants ejected all the refugees from the larger common rooms. The senior leadership was ushered in, and the doors were closed.

Although everyone was enjoying the quiet, outside the apprehension was intense. Refugee families gathered children and counted heads, the cooks scraped the bottom of food barrels, and the soldiers stood near the barricades and watched the silent village. The only movement outside the plaza were trailing streamers of smoke darkening the sky.

Finally, the doors opened, and Governor General Ceballos, with Father Juan at his side in bright vestments, stepped out to address the crowd. They climbed the small platform as all the inhabitants and refugees gathered near.

Ceballos drew himself up to his full height. It surprised some to see grey in his black hair and beard. This week had taken a lot from the governor. "I have an announcement, my fellow citizens of Spain. Our efforts have been blessed by heaven. All of the opposition has been crushed. We have won."

The crowd broke out in cheers. Many were laughing, and many were crying. It was a great moment.

When they subsided, he continued. "I have some bad news, though. The canal is blocked, and it will take a week to bring water to the palacio. And there is little food. Winter is close, and if we are to survive we must evacuate to the South Valley and join with our brothers at Isleta. I had expected reinforcements, but our messenger may not have even arrived there yet. So we will go to Isleta, and find out why they sent no help. Men, see to your families. Prepare yourselves then, for tomorrow we march."

Alonso, a father from the village near Cochiti, had been working in the prison after Francisco deserted. He called out, "Governor General, what of the Indios we have captured? There are almost eighty of them. They sit in our prison. Are we to feed them our limited supply all the way to Isleta?"

Ceballos pulled himself into the saddle and didn't bother to look at Alonso. "They are of no consequence. Hang them."

Santa Fe plaza
Evening

Teniente Raum de Bances sat on the bench near the north wall of the plaza. None of the barricades had been removed except for the parts made up of wagons or wheels. These were needed for tomorrow's exodus. He had a couple of tasks that needed attention now that the fighting was quiet. Right now, he was rewinding leather for the grip of his sword.

Someone walked up behind him, and since Teniente de Bances could hear the sword rattling in a sheath, he knew it wasn't an Indio. But when he heard the voice, he knew it was Don Miguel, commander of the Santa Fe Garrison. De Bances jumped to his feet and saluted.

Don Miguel waved an acknowledgment of the salute and sat down. The Teniente did so as well. Don Miguel's voice was tired but sounded cheerful. "Don Raum Angel Santiago de Bances, you have either succeeded beyond your wildest dreams, or you have been part of the sorriest mess in history."

Raum re-sheathed his sword. "Don Miguel, you know how I feel about my inherited title. At least not until I've earned it."

Then two men from the stables came up with two horses. Don Miguel stood up and pulled himself on his war horse, and he had another fine mount beside him. "The Governor General has officially acknowledged your courage and ordered that we address you as a knight. Also, his Excellency has sent you his warhorse, Fausto, because you've been given an important command. And do not give me any trouble about calling you Don. If nothing else, you have certainly earned the title."

Raum walked over and started a careful examination of the Governor General's white charger. The animal was in fine health, and the elegant trappings were all in perfect condition. The horse watched Raum as he checked the horse's teeth, hooves, saddle cinch. Raum patted the horse's neck, and Fausto blew in the Teniente's face and shook his mane. Raum smiled as he pulled himself into the saddle. It was nice when the horse approved. "So what's to be my command?"

Don Miguel gestured to the small squad of musketeers gathered in the plaza. Their muskets were stacked to the side, and the men were playing dice games or sleeping, waiting for the next orders. "You are to command the rear guard and allow the column to reach safety. And tonight, you need to go out to make sure we will have an open road tomorrow. So since you're leaving soon, this may be the last time we see each other."

Raum grinned and offered his hand to Don Miguel. "I was told I would have my soul tried, hammered, and beaten by this place, and now it looks like it may kill me. Nevertheless, I would not trade this time for anything on the world."

Don Miguel smiled as well. "Adios, my friend. This is a task for a young brave man, and you are the only one here that fits that description. If it be God's will, we will meet again." Then the old commander of the garrison turned back toward the palacio.

De Bances leaned down and patted the horse's neck again. A mount this magnificent could only be descended the from horses of antiquity, maybe even the war horse of Rodrigo Diaz de Vivar, hero of Valencia, the immortal El Cid. The Governor General owned the best horse in the province, and now Raum had the Governor General's horse.

He walked the horse over to the soldiers, and gave orders to the unit of musketeers. It took about an hour, and then everything was ready. He rode to the gate, gave the order, and they followed him out of Santa Fe. They didn't look back.

First Day of Exodus
Camino Real al Dentro, South of Santa Fe
September 1634

It was a long column. Twelve hundred colonists and their hundred and fifty defenders, moving slowly down the river road. The day had been full of alarms and apprehensions, but the only Indios they saw were drawn up on hilltops, far from the river. The Indios were just watching from a distance.

Santiago and Pablo, along with the rest of the gun crew, were marching down the side of the column. It was a sad day for the cannoneers, because late last night, when the cannons had been examined, the left cannon was found to have a crack along the side. Even if they had a qualified cannon smith, nothing could be done for it. The right cannon, which was Santiago's favorite, had actually begun to melt in the heat of battle. This made Santiago sad. He had worked with those guns for six years. He called them Maria and Jose, with his favorite being Maria.

The previous night, when he'd reported to the governor, Ceballos shook his head. "Those aren't even worth hauling back to Mexico City. We must destroy them so the Indios can't use them against us."

And so the barrels were charged with their dwindling supply of powder. Then the ends were packed tightly and stopped up. Santiago himself lit the fuse and sadly ran to cover. They exploded in place. Now they were smoking heaps of scrap metal.

Santiago was a gunner no more, and neither was Pablo, but they were alive. And marching south. The column had passed many haciendas, all of which had been put to torch. There wasn't a stick of wood or a sack of meal left in the entire upper valley.

As they passed the smoking ruins of the chapel at Santo Domingo, Pablo punched Santiago in the arm. "How long do you think it's going to take? That is, for us to get to somewhere safe?"

Santiago shrugged. "You know the answers, Pablo. It's usually is a four-day trip from Santa Fe to the South Valley, but we are moving slowly because of the women and children on foot. We have only three hand carts for supplies and almost no horses or other transportation. The cavalry has to guard us against attack. Perhaps a week, perhaps more. I don't know what we will find at Isleta. I thought sure that they would be able to come up and support us and they did not."

Pablo said, "We are on siege rations now. What could be worse than that?"

Santiago thought for a moment, then shrugged. "I think we are out of beer."

Pablo sighed. "That's worse."

by Kevin H. and Karen C. Evans

CHAPTER 9

Second Day of Exodus
La Bajada

Teniente de Bances and his squad stayed behind the slow-moving caravan. He sent men to either side of the road, looking for sign of an ambush. But so far it had been mostly dull, simply keeping to the pace of the caravan and paying attention.

As the sun settled toward the west, he warned his men to remain vigilant. There was some suspicious movement on the edge of the mesa to the east. Something stirred up Raum's subconscious. Perhaps a rustle in the brush or stones sliding over each other, but something had pushed the young man into alert.

Raum kneed his magnificent horse, Fausto, toward the movement. When some of the musketeers made to follow him, he stopped. "Sergeant, you keep the squad here as rearguard. If I find something over that hill, I'll signal you with my pistol. Remember, our first duty is the welfare of the caravan."

He could tell that Sergeant Ruiz didn't like the idea of his officer riding off alone, but he acknowledged the command. Raum galloped off toward the mesa.

He finally found a way up to the edge of the mesa. The sides were steep, but he found a small creek that drained off the top. His horse could climb the dry stream bed with ease. At the top, he could see miles of countryside. He could see the head of the caravan of Spaniards retreating to the south valley. He got off his horse, and eased over the edge of the mesa to see what he'd thought he'd seen before.

The sight made Raum's breath catch in his throat. The valley on the other side of the mesa was black with Indios. There could be a couple of thousand down there. Many were women, cooking at fires, but he didn't see any children. This was a war camp, preparing to attack the Spaniards again. They meant to destroy the retreating column.

He jumped up and caught the reins of his horse. As he pulled himself in to the saddle, he caught up the trumpet where it hung on the side. Quickly Raum lifted the trumpet to his lips and began to blow for all he was worth.

Then he jammed his spurs and began to ride for his life. He made it down off the mesa, but stopped as he neared the road. Already his rear guard was out of sight down past La Bajada. He gripped his reins, about to race the horse for all it was worth and outrun the Indios he could already hear behind him.

Then duty brought the young man to a halt. His command was musketeers, on foot. They would require time to protect the caravan. And time was what Raum had to buy the caravan.

So, with determination, the young man turned to face his foe. Already, he could hear war cries, and he could see hundreds of dark-haired Indios boiling out of the hills on both sides. He pulled out his sword and nudged the horse. The great-hearted warhorse charged. Both Raum and the horse issued a screaming challenge as they neared their foes. Raum's focus narrowed down to the point where his sword would first contact a target.

The Indios swarmed around him like angry ants. Raum was pushed back against the edge of the mesa, fighting hand to hand. More and more of the wounded began piling up around him until he was pinned against the steep hillside.

The young man slid off his mount and slapped the horse on the rump. The horse surged forward screaming and trampling. The Indios backed away from the fearsome animal. That gave Raum room to use his sword. First he fired his pistol into the face of the man at his right, then shoved it inside his chest armor. His shield was battered, blood was running off his elbow, and the attacks kept coming. The young man stood resolutely blow upon blow of his tired sword. And what kept him fighting against impossible odds was the knowledge that the column had been warned.

* * *

Sergeant Ruiz limped into the camp after darkness had swallowed the land. Don Miguel strode forward, glowering. "Where is Teniente de Bances?"

Ruiz saluted. "Sir, he saw some suspicious movement on the Algodones mesa, and left us to protect the caravan while he checked it out. My man Juan, at the end of our formation, saw him after he contacted the enemy. The Teniente blew the trumpet to warn us, then turned and rode right into the teeth of the attack. He was an extraordinary young man. I would have run for my life, and on that white horse, I'd have probably have made it. If he'd have done that, it would have brought the howling horde down on our heads. As it was, we only had a small skirmish, and are here to report."

Don Miguel said, "How many casualties?"

Ruiz grinned. "Only one, sir. One of the men tripped on a rock in the dark and scraped up his chin."

As Sergeant Ruiz left to find some food, one of the sentries, Andres, shouted a warning from his post. "Colonel Martinez, one of the scouts spotted the Governor General's horse."

Don Miguel walked to Andres' position. "Is the horse coming into camp? And what of Don Raum?"

Andres said, "They're bringing the scout in now, sir."

The young man, barely sixteen, saluted. "Don Miguel, we were not close to the horse, he was on the top of a mesa about five miles from here. We saw him in the moonlight. He was still wearing his trappings, but we saw no sign of the Teniente. One of the boys, I mean, scouts tried to climb the mesa to catch him, but the horse would not be caught. It went back down the side of the other side of the mesa and disappeared."

Don Miguel covered his eyes with his hands for a moment, then looked out at the darkness. "I don't think we will see Don Raum de Bances again. What a waste. He was one of the best Spain has ever sent us."

✳ ✳ ✳

The march continued for a week, and finally the walls of Isleta were spotted. It was an historical village, the first spot that the Spaniards had wintered, forty years earlier. Now it had tall adobe walls topped with sharp stones and thorns. It was as secure as the plaza of Santa Fe had been.

But as the tired column filtered into the village, it was eerily silent. No people came out to the plaza to greet them. Governor Ceballos called a halt. "We will camp in the walls tonight. Father Juan, come with me."

They strode toward the mission church with the customary two towers. Father Juan pushed the old heavy door open; it was dark inside.

Not a candle was burning. Ceballos stood as Father Juan lit a candle, and then they walked towards the altar.

There was a frightened gasp, and they stopped by one of the benches. A small boy, maybe nine or ten, stood up, rubbing his eye and looking terrified.

Ceballos, his voice booming with command, said, "Who are you, and where are the villagers? I am the Governor General with refugees from Santa Fe."

The boy's voice was fearful. "I am Bartolome Gonzalez. They left me here with a message for you, governor."

Ceballos saw the boy tremble and modulated his voice to soft and kind. It was an effort; that voice wasn't used often. "It's all right, boy. You can give me the message. Is it written down?"

Young Bartolome shook his head and clasped his hands behind his back. "No, Sire. Your Teniente Governor made me repeat it so I could tell you. He has marched south towards Socorro and will await you there. The population that was here is intact with ample supplies, for nobody attacked us. However, all of the outlying settlements have been burned to the ground and many have been murdered."

The boy stopped, and Ceballos could see tears forming. He tried to keep his voice gentle. "How long ago did they leave here?"

Bartolome looked confused, then counted on his fingers. "They have been gone eight days, Sire. The rest of the message is that, should it be your pleasure, the Teniente Governor requests that you go to Socorro to reunite the inhabitants of the province."

Ceballos sighed and looked at Father Juan. The father put his hand on the boy's shoulder. "You are a very brave boy, and you have performed your task perfectly. Is there any food left for us?"

The boy smiled for the first time. "Yes, Father. I will show you."

by Kevin H. and Karen C. Evans

CHAPTER 10

Hacienda Bernal
October 1634

Father Phillip sat at the table, a glass of wine by his left hand, a quill in the other. He was writing a letter addressed to a friend of his in Jenna, in the Germanies. It was the fourth such letter he had written since he'd watched the column of Spaniards ride south.

He had written as eloquently as possible, setting forth all of the happenings within the province of New Mexico over the past two years. The refugees had been gone from Santa Fe for three days.

He sighed as he wrote about his part in the struggle of the Indios to gain their Independence. It had come at such a great price. Over five hundred men slain in battle. The local Indios had been content to let the Spanish leave and kept watch on them only to insure they were gone.

Then a party of scouts went into the empty Santa Fe plaza and found the seventy-eight men who had been captured in battle, all still hanging from the trees in the plaza. The scouts cut them all down and prepared the bodies for burial.

This was too much to be born. It was a death of ignominy, and the shamans would have to work to save the warrior's souls. That was the reason for the vicious attack on the departing column.

133

Here at the village of Bernalillo, Spanish stragglers were arriving every day. These were people who didn't evacuate to Santa Fe at the beginning of the war. They felt safer on their own land and wouldn't give it up easily. Many had seen the local Indios as good neighbors and had never treated them as heathens. It was surprising to see how many were gathering. Already, there were around two hundred adults, and Father Philip didn't know how many children. There were even a couple of families with mixed race children. They kept more to themselves, but Father Philip felt they should be included in this mixed bag of citizens.

Independence was now a fact in this part of the world. Other than himself and the arriving refugees, there were now no Europeans living north of Socorro.

He kept writing. "It is evident therefore that while our brave, local natives never won a battle, indeed they won the war. For although the Spaniards had an enormous advantage in the material of their arms, weaponry, and their tactics, we had the numbers and we drove them forth. I end this missive therefore with a warning and with a plea.

"You and the Committees of Correspondence must be aware that, no matter how great your advantages of weaponry are, there will always be more of the down-timers than there are of you. No matter how many you kill, they can overwhelm you in sheer numbers, and then you will lose."

He finished the letter with an appeal. "In the time since the Spaniards have evacuated, the tribes were already back to a state of conflict and acrimony. I humbly plead for help to establish a unified people that would be able to resist the return of the Spaniards."

He folded the precious vellum, tied it up with twine, sealed it with wax, and stamped it with his signet ring.

He turned with all the letters in hand and almost stepped on young Eduardo Bernal, who had quietly been standing near the table. Eduardo looked at the letters in Father Philip's hand. "Are you planning on sending that letter south? How are you going to get it back to Europe? Nobody there even knows what has happened here. Will they keep writing to you?"

Father Philip smiled. "I was just thinking on how I could send this letter. I don't want anyone in El Paso or Mexico City to open it and read it. I was hoping that it would not be noticed in a pile of other letters. Do you think there are others waiting to send letters?"

Eduardo shrugged. "I don't know, Father, but I will ask around. There may be someone trustworthy to take them."

✻ ✻ ✻

As Father Philip walked over to the chapel, a boy came running up to him. "Father Philip!"

The priest turned a kindly eye on the boy but didn't know his name. "What is it? And who are you?"

The boy, about eight years old stopped and grinned with pride. "I'm Dot'izhihíito, of the Apache tribe. Don Federico sent me to find you. He wants you to join him at the cantina."

Father Philip grinned as well. "Thank you, Dot'iz-hi. How long have you been in the village of Bernalillo?"

Dot'izhihíito frowned slightly at the odd pronunciation of his name. But he answered, "For a year, Father. When my mother was ill, she came here for the shaman at the cantina. My mother died, but I am here still, and I have learned Spanish."

Father Philip patted the boy on the head. "And you learned very well. Thank you for the message." The boy ran off to play, and Father Philip turned toward the cantina.

Father Philip moved through crowds of women and children, who were all in the plaza of Bernalillo. He was thankful that he was not the

135

leader of the refugees. That honor had been unanimously given to Don Federico Griegos Bernal, Alcalde of the landholding of Bernalillo. Father Philip served as his adviser. As far as they knew, it was the only village that permitted Europeans and Indios to live together peacefully. It was Father Philip's hope that the village would grow strong and establish the ideals of freedom and liberty. He opened the door to the cantina and was surprised to see it empty except for the Alcalde sitting at one of the tables.

Don Federico greeted him warmly as Father Philip sat down. "Father, thank you for coming. I thought it would be a little more private here, don't you think? Inez has promised to keep everyone else out, and we know she can keep secrets."

Inez, who ran the cantina, didn't even blush. "Don Federico, you have no idea. Can I get you something more than wine?"

Bernal smiled and shook his head. "Not now, Inez. Father Philip and I have some planning to do in order to insure we are on the same page."

Father Philip raised his eyebrow as Inez left. "Planning? What are you thinking, Federico?"

"I'm thinking that winter is all too close, and many of these people have come here with nothing. I need to call a council meeting, just to find out how bad things are. Have you been planning anything?"

Father Philip pulled his letter out of a pocket. "I just finished some lengthy letters to a some of my Jesuit friends. I'm hoping for clarification on the new town that appeared in Germany. Even more, I would like to get a promise of help, in case the Spanish come back soon."

Bernal nodded and pursed his lips. "Do you really think they will be back soon?"

Father Philip set his glass on the table. "Don't you?"

Bernal said, "No, and I'll tell you why. It will take time for the Governor General to reach Mexico City, and even when he does, he will still have to find money to gather materials. They will have to buy new cannons, wagons, food, and then convince men to return north with him. And what kind of political storm will be brewing both in Mexico City and Madrid? Will Ceballos gain any of the support he needs to return quickly? Even in your letters it says it takes them twelve years to return. And perhaps now even longer. I don't know, but I think it will be an uphill battle for him. It's not like we've ever found gold here, or even silver. What's here to make them take the risk again?"

Inez stuck her head in from the kitchen. "Alcalde, your son, Eduardo, is here to speak to Father Philip. Should I let him in?"

Don Federico said, "Yes, Inez, send him up."

Eduardo came close to the table and bowed slightly to his father, then turned to the priest. "Father, I have found three or four that want to send letters."

Father Philip smiled. "Good. Perhaps your father will allow you and a couple of your friends to ride to El Paso and get them sent from there."

Don Federico thought for a moment, then looked at Eduardo. "I think that's an excellent idea. Do you think you can find a way to El Paso?"

Eduardo grinned, and stood up straighter. "If I cannot, I will find someone to accompany me that can. We will deliver your letters and bring back any that have come that far for you, Father Philip."

The priest handed the letters to Eduardo. "I hope you can get to El Paso, place it secretly into the post, and return. Be cautious in your journey, going and coming home, Ka-ansh. This is an heroic task for you."

Eduardo turned and hurried out. His father, Don Federico, frowned after he was gone. "Father, do you really think your letters will make any difference?"

Father Philip said, "All we can do now is to pray, for Eduardo, for the letters, and for us. Perhaps my friends in Europe can help, and perhaps they cannot. We won't know for about a year. But for now, we're here and we're independent.

by Kevin H. and Karen C. Evans

Bernalillo village
October 1634

Several days later, Don Federico Griegos Bernal, Alcalde of the village, heaved a great sigh as he sat down to breakfast. His wife, Doña Garciella Maria Souza Bernal, put a bowl of gruel in front of him. "Are you well, husband? You sound as if you are carrying the whole village on your back."

Federico rested his head in his hands. "If only it were just the village. I am worried for the whole colony. Yesterday, a family came into town all the way from First Mesa, near the Hopi village. They were terrified and hungry. Of course hungry. Why is it that when they fled their homes, none of these people took any food with them? Why do they think I have it?"

When Garciella said nothing, he looked up just in time to see her side-eye towards the pantry. It was only for a moment, but he knew that his wife knew something she was not telling him. He stood up, and took her hand.

It was clear that this action surprised her. She jumped a little, then smiled. "What is it, Federico? Is there something I can get you?"

Instead, he took both her hands, and looked down into her dark eyes. They were as beautiful as ever, those liquid black eyes. He had always seen his future, his children, his desires in those eyes. "It's something about the food, isn't it, Garciella. Tell me. Do we have less than I thought? Are we going to starve this winter?"

Her eyes widened, then wrinkled into a smile. "No, my love. We will not starve. And neither will your colony. I have taken care of that."

Federico sat down again, not sure what he had heard. He had been worrying for a week about the food. The fields around Santa Fe were black and empty, and the cattle and sheep had been driven off or slaughtered in the field. And the Governor General had been persecuting the Indios by burning their food before the conflict blew up. As far as he knew, they would all be short this winter. And it was too late to do much about it. There was already snow in the high peaks, and the leaves on the sacred Sandia mountain were gold with coming winter. "What do you mean, wife?"

Garciella looked back and forth, as if the walls were listening. Then she pulled a chair close to him and sat as well. She leaned toward him and whispered, "I took care of the food while you were dealing with the revolt. I knew it would be difficult if we didn't have enough, and more. So whenever I heard that a village or hacienda had been abandoned, I sent the boys out to gather everything they could find. We have good boys. They brought home a bounty."

He stared at her, still not quite able to understand. "You sent our sons out? During a war? I had been comforted thinking that my family was here, safe, far enough from Santa Fe to be out of thought of the rebels."

Garciella grinned and leaned back. "Who said our sons? I said, our boys. That includes the boys of the village, both Spanish and Indio. And you should thank me. At first, I sent them with the cart and burro, just to keep them closer to home. The older ones really wanted to go and fight with you instead. But I convinced them that it was their responsibility to keep the younger ones safe, and to gather what they could. Once they saw my vision, they were eager to go. And they came home with so much!"

Federico was still slow. To be fair, he hadn't slept well; ever since the Governor General and the refugees fled, he had been sleeping with an eye open and his hand on his pistol, worrying about marauders. And nightmares didn't help. So he was exhausted and unable to grasp everything his wife was telling him. "The boys of the village? Eduardo was with me, helping in the war. That only left you Jorge, Jose, Anna, and little Paulo. You didn't send Paulo and Anna out, did you?"

Garciella pulled herself up straight in her seat, and her eyes shot fiery darts in his direction. "Do you think I am a fool? Do you think I don't love my children? Of course I didn't send Anna and the baby out. That came later."

That pulled Federico to his feet. "Later? What do you mean? Why am I just hearing of this now?"

Garciella said nothing, but pulled her lace handkerchief from her corset and waved it at a fly that circled her head. She looked at him and waited. And when Federico didn't sit down and talk, she said, "Can we talk now, if you are finished with your shouting?"

Federico turned to the buffet on the side of the room, and found the wine decanter and glasses. He was still angry. But he knew that Garciella, who had been trained in the Viceroy's court in Mexico City, would be good to her word that she would not discuss anything until he was calm. It was too early for wine, so he tightened his left hand into a fist and tried to force his frustration in between the fingers.

Finally he was able to take a deep breath and sit down at the table. He was not next to Garciella, but at the head of the table. He sat down. The servants had evaporated, so he looked at his wife. "I am listening. Start at the beginning, and tell me everything."

The facts and events that his wife laid out were astounding and thorough. Without his knowledge, she had been plotting and planning since the first incident of burning and confiscating food happened in early summer. When she heard the garrison was sending a unit to a village, she would send Eduardo the night before to warn the villagers. Then he would bring home a wagon load of dried corn, beef, salt, and spices. One time, he came with a herd of twelve hogs. She had instructed the foreman in the village to build additional barns and silos for the food.

Federico frowned. "But where did you get such an idea? Why did you start before there was a rebellion?"

"You know that I grew up in Mexico City and that my father was rich. My nurse was a woman from the Lowlands in Europe, a Hollander. She had been instructed to see to my catechism and prepare me for my confirmation. But she was secretly a Huguenot, a Protestant. She knew more of the Bible than I was ever taught She would tell me stories at night. And one story was of a man named Joseph. He had been sold into slavery like she had, and she loved the story very much."

Federico frowned. "I haven't heard of a Joseph, except for Saint Jose, holy guardian of . . ."

Garciella nodded. "It seemed very heretical to me, from the Jewish portion of the holy works. But this Joseph, as a slave, gained the confidence of the king because he interpreted a dream. And because of that dream, the king built storehouses, which saved the land when the famine came. I didn't remember this story until I had a dream as well."

Federico pulled his left hand into a fist again, trying to keep from bursting from his chair and shouting again. He took a deep breath and nodded, so Garciella continued.

"I dreamt of a man with a torch, and he was burning all the grain. And I could hear my nurse's voice telling me to build a storehouse. So I did."

Federico sat back. "How much do you have now?"

Garciella got up and sat in a chair close to him again. "I have filled three barns. And there is much to do. There are fields down near Isleta that need to be harvested and the grain stored in the storehouse. Also, there are hogs and sheep that need to be slaughtered and either smoked or salted in barrels for the coming winter. And it is not something I can ask of my sons, or the boys in the village. This is a job that needs men."

Don Federico plead with her. "I still don't understand how you could risk children for this business. Weren't you worried about anything? Attack by the Apache, or by the Spaniard soldiers, or by the Navajo?"

Garciella pulled her rosary from her skirt. "I was not worried because it was a task given to me by God, and I prayed the whole time the boys were gone. Nobody ever saw them, let alone attack. They were kept safe by the angels."

While Federico was still pondering this news, they were interrupted by Jorge, their second son. The boy was tall, with fine Hidalgo features and dark hair, like his mother. And for the first time, Federico noticed that he was no longer a boy, taller than his mother already.

Jorge stepped into the dining room, about to speak to his mother, when he saw his father as well. He stopped and bowed a little. "Father, there you are. They are asking for you at the church. There are new refugees, and the priest wanted to ask you something."

Federico stood, but Garciella put her hand on his. "That can wait for a moment. Jorge, I have been telling your father about your food gathering. Now he knows everything."

Jorge raised his eyebrows a little, and then relaxed. "Mother, you are wise. It has been difficult keeping a secret from Father since he got back from Santa Fe. Shall I tell Father Philip as well?"

Garciella looked at Federico, but said nothing. He rubbed his chin for a moment. "Jorge, I can see that you are ready for responsibilities. Since Eduardo is away on a mission for the mail, you will be my aide. I think it's time for a council. Send out runners to the nearby farms and pueblos, we will schedule it for the first week in November. Now that I know we can feed visitors, it is time for everyone to discuss things."

❋ ❋ ❋

Father Philip was in the scriptorium to the side of the chapel, reading a letter. Even if this rebellion had not happened, he would not have gotten any mail until some time next spring. And now, he was not sure that any of his correspondent brethren would assume he was still alive. So he was taking a quiet moment to reread the letters he had gotten since he arrived.

He was only six pages into the letter when there was a diffident knock on the door, and Don Federico put his head in. "Father Philip, do you have a moment?"

Father Philip put away his letter and stood. "Of course, Don Federico. Now is a perfect time."

Don Federico looked around the small cubicle, seemingly stuffed to the gills with papers. It astounded him, because this had only been Father Philip's scriptorium for two months. He pushed a pile of parchments from a chair and made himself comfortable. "Were you reading the letter with information about the future?"

Father Philip said, "As a matter of fact, I was. Did you have a question?"

Don Federico rubbed his face and straightened his moustache. This was a move he made frequently. "I suppose I was hoping you would give me another bit of information about what will come next."

Father Philip leaned back and laced his fingers together. "I am not a soothsayer or fortune teller, Federico. What sort of thing do you think the article can tell us?"

Don Federico leaned back as well. "I don't know. I guess I was hoping for some sort of divine revelation. But back to business. I have called a council for the beginning of November, and I would appreciate if you and I could put together an agenda."

Father Philip said, "Oh, I see. You are wanting to find a way to bring these people together after all the war and contention. I think that's a good idea."

Don Federico said, "To tell you the truth, I should have called for a meeting before now, but I was worried about feeding a large number of people on meager supplies. My good wife has just informed me that I have been worried for nothing."

Father Philip leaned forward, elbows on his desk. "Really? What has Doña Garciaella been up to lately?"

Don Federico smiled and relaxed. He remembered some of the other meetings he had attended with Father Philip. No matter what, Philip had been calm and wryly humorous. "Apparently, since the first sign that things were going to be difficult, she has been gathering food into her storehouses. The moment that the Governor General ordered his men to burn the food of rebellious Indios, she would send the boys from this village to take the food before it could be destroyed. And when the fighting started, she raided all the empty haciendas and villages. She has three barns full, and is still working to gather in all the food available."

Father Philip was startled at the single-mindedness this would take. And that put Doña Garciaella much higher in his estimation. He forced face into a blander expression. "That was very enterprising of her. What would she have done if the rebellion had been quelled?"

Don Federico shrugged. "Who knows. She says she had a dream, saw a vision, and sent the boys out while she stayed at home and prayed. She never worried because the angels were protecting them." The man paused, thoughtfully, and Father Philip kept quiet, to let Don Federico work through his thoughts. "Father, you know I am a good Catholic, and I come to mass and confessional. But it always surprises me when I learn my wife is a much better Catholic than me."

Father Philip smiled. "She is a better Catholic than me as well, Don Federico. Women are more sensitive to spiritual things. She has a strong faith that she doesn't question. We are both lucky to know her and learn from her piety."

Don Federico frowned. "At any rate, I no longer worry about feeding people. We have enough and more, and we will be able to care for whomever shows up next week. My next problem is administrative. What have we done? What do we have here? And are we going to be punished when the Spaniards come back to conquer us again? I don't know what our next step should be."

Father Philip leaned back in his chair. "It is true: when we agreed to support this rebellion, neither of us gave much thought to this moment. I truly was planning on being dead. But now, here we are. I do have some thoughts, but I think I want to know what you are thinking as well. We have to present a united front next month, because there will be a lot of opposing opinions. Did you send out runners to the Pueblos, and the Navajo, and Apache? They should have a say in this as well."

Don Federico blinked and then stood and strode to the door. He opened it, and shouted, "Raymundo, I need you. Could you step in, please?"

The Indio boy stuck his head in. "Me?"

Don Federico sat down. "Yes. Could you arrange messengers to the Apache and Navajo, as well as the Pueblo villages? They are to be invited next month as well." He turned to Father Philip. "Anything else?"

Father Philip smiled. "I don't think it is time yet, but you seem to have assumed the role of Governor General, which makes me Father President."

That made Don Federico laugh, and he left the scriptorium. That was just what Father Philip wanted. He sat back down at his desk and picked up the letter he'd been reading. He knew they were only at the beginning of this venture. If they could all keep their sense of humor, this transition would be much easier.

by Kevin H. and Karen C. Evans

CHAPTER 11

San Felipe village
October 1634

Raum de Bances realized that something in this darkness smelled worse than he did. He didn't open his eyes, but sniffed. He could smell dust and that stale sweaty odor of unwashed bodies. Some of that, he assumed, was himself, but there were more unfamiliar smells. Then he knew that the smell that brought him awake was something he was lying on.

He was a little startled to feel a hand on his forehead, but he still maintained the pretense of sleep. Raum was unsure where he was or how he got here. He hadn't expected to survive. The last he remembered, he had been on foot, with his back to the canyon wall, fighting off angry Indios. He had fired his pistol and stuffed it inside his armor, then continued with his sword. Then his memory was blank.

"So, you come back to us. I know you are awake, your breathing told me."

Raum opened his eyes and blinked. It was dark except for a flickering oil lamp in one corner. And even that was nothing more than a clay dish and a wick. And yet the light seemed to stab into his eyes and echo with the headache he noticed was there. He could make out a shadowy figure by his pallet on the floor.

He tried to speak but only heard scratchy moans come from his lips. The shadowy figure put an arm behind his head to raise him up and set a cup by his lips. He sipped, and it was good to have wetness on his lips, so he sipped again. It was bitter, but still so welcome in his dry mouth. "Where am I?"

The voice spoke very good Spanish, which was advantageous. Raum had not been here long enough to learn any of the difficult Indio languages, although he had picked up a little sign language. His eyes didn't focus very well either. The shape moved back, and Raum saw grey hair, small delicate hands, and a frown. He thought it might be a woman.

"You are the Ironskin that fought on the mesa. You are the ghost on the white horse. We saw you fighting, and we saw you fall. You should be dead. But the shaman found you, and ordered us to take you home with us. You are in the village of San Felipe."

Raum lay back, and tried to remember where San Felipe was. But he felt scattered and couldn't think clearly. "How long?" he scratched out in his dry throat.

"You have been feverish for a week. I did not think you would awaken, but the shaman is a great healer. I was sent because I could speak to you. I have no reverence or respect for Ironskins. Do not think me a friend."

Raum still felt confused. Her voice had an edge to it, and a part of him wondered if she would stab him even now. He even felt that the voice was somewhat familiar, but in his foggy state, he couldn't tell why. So he said nothing more. The person held a cup for him to drink from, and it was not water, but something slightly bitter. But the bitterness seemed to push the fog away.

He looked at her again. She was young, maybe twenty-five. Her hair was dressed in the odd manner of Pueblo women, with much of the long black hair bound in back in what was called a squash blossom. He could see her face, with typical cheek bones and dark eyes. "What name?" His voice was still raspy and unused.

She looked away and picked up a rag that she used to cool his forehead. "I am called Pov'op'u. I am the shaman's second wife."

He became more aware of hurts and itches. He could feel the sharp stab of pain from a wound under his left arm; his head was heavy on his neck. For the first time he could ever remember, he felt weak and old. He decided to try asking questions again. "How can I get to Santa Fe?"

Pov'op'u snorted. "I don't think you want to go to Santa Fe. The warriors have Santa Fe and are howling to the moon. They are ready to kill any Ironskins they find."

Raum thought for a moment. "Are there any other Spaniards nearby? Or am I the last?"

His nurse was silent for many moments. Raum began to think he would go back to sleep without an answer. Finally, she got up to go and stopped at the door. "There are some of your kind at the holding of Don Federico. Perhaps in a day or two, we can take you there. They can worry what to feed you this winter." After that, she left the room.

Jicarilla village, north of Santa Fe
Early November

The great mountains to the north had white snow above the yellow of the aspen trees. Kogen-lii, chief of the council in the village of the Jicarilla Apache, knew it was time to move south. Soon, the north wind would whistle over the badlands and freeze the river. All signs indicated that this would be a mild winter, but it was no good taking chances. It only took one surprise blizzard, and the village would totter on the edge of survival.

Kogen-lii had seen many winters, and now his hair was gray. He sat outside his wikiup and surveyed the activity. The men of the village were hunting, bringing in turkeys and quail, and less often, deer. The older boys, not yet going hunting with the men, were fishing. And the women were all working hard to preserve the food for winter. Their harvest of corn and beans was gathered and stowed in baskets in a nearby cave, where the cooler air would help keep their food dry and free from most pests.

When Kogen-lii was a child, they didn't stay in one place through the summer because they didn't plant crops, just gathered what they could find in season. They learned agriculture from the Pueblo people of the Rio Grande river valley. And since then, they had been more prosperous and healthy. They had also been easier for enemies to find and raid. This new way of staying in a place always made him nervous, especially this time of year when it was a race to preserve enough food before the heart of winter.

The recent battle of the Pueblos against the Spaniards had not been of interest to Kogen-lii. Some of the young warriors had gone to see if they could kill an Ironskin, but the village stayed in place. And when news came that the Spaniards were gone, and that the Pueblo people were occupying the palacio, he thought the matter was over. Now they could get back to normal without worrying that a black-robe would come and burn their sacred objects.

Kogen-lii sat near his door, enjoying the sunshine and planning. It was time to go south, and find new hunting grounds, a place that rarely saw snow. He had seen fifty winters, and his back and shoulders ached in advance of a storm. He looked forward to cool mornings and warm fires and one of his wives cuddled close. Less activity in the winter gave them a chance to rest and recover before the busy planting season next spring.

Those thoughts were interrupted when he saw his senior wife striding across the ground. She was frowning, and he knew that meant that her aggravation was about to be placed on his shoulders to solve. "I can see the storm on your face, Eda. What has happened now?"

Eda-adiso-oana continued to glare. She had grey in her hair, and she had seen almost as many winters as her husband. "That useless boy Mazhiia was supposed to be helping his mother with the fish drying. His job was to keep the birds and flies off the strips in the sun."

Kogen frowned. "Isn't he old enough to go hunting, or at least fishing, instead of being left at home to work with his mother? I seem to remember him about seventeen or eighteen."

Eda snorted. "He has twenty winters and is too lazy. None of the men will allow him to go on the hunt with them, and the last time he was sent to fish he was found sleeping, with no fish to show for his day. I sent him back to his mother, Ligai. She spoiled him as a child because he was a little slow of thought. And now, she has to live with her choices. He's become the laziest man in Jicarilla."

Kogen picked up his staff and used it to stand up. "Do you want me to talk to him?"

Eda shook her head. "That's not the problem. He was given the task of watching the fish racks. Now, he's nowhere to be seen. One of the racks was knocked over, and the dogs carried off some of the fish. That's less for us this winter. I haven't been able to find him and neither have any of the boys. He has disappeared."

Kogen said, "So the last time anyone saw him was this morning?"

"No, yesterday. I got busy with that buck the men brought in yesterday, and Ligai didn't check until just now. As far as I know, nobody has seen him since yesterday morning."

Kogen walked to the circle of old men, sitting to repair their bows and make more arrows. They enjoyed sitting together so they could gossip without the women. Men said many funny things that offended women. "Tset-soye, tell me about Mazhiia. Wasn't he sent hunting with one of your groups?"

Tset leaned back on his elbow. "Yes, he was to go with us, and we left before dawn several days ago. He was not awake, and when we tried to wake him, we were chased off by his crazy mother, Ligai. It just wasn't worth facing her to get Mazhiia out of bed. We left."

One of the other men, Itsa, laughed. "My little daughter likes playing with Mazhiia. He hides, and she tries to find him. He plays with many of the children. Perhaps he is playing now."

Kogen nodded. He had observed Mazhiia playing that way. He waved to the men and heard some of the comments about old men in charge thrown at his back. It was all in jest. None of those men wanted to have to listen to the complaining of everyone; that's what the chief did.

He went over to where some of the children were tending the smoking fire under some of the venison. When he walked up, the children all stood up and looked at their feet, partly in respect and partly out of fear. They worried that he would punish them for playing while they were to tend the fire. Kogen smiled and raised a hand. "Don't fear. I have a question. Who can answer me? I want to know who saw Mazhiia leave the fish racks. Any of you?"

A small girl peeked out from behind her older brother, then moved back behind him. But Kogen saw her. "Kai-ii? Did you see something?"

She peeked out at him and then came around her brother but held his hand for support. "Yes, sir. I saw Mazhiia. Yesterday. I was collecting sticks for the fire, and I saw him going that way." She pointed to the south. "He didn't hear me call him to come play, he was walking fast. He had a sack on his back. I think he left."

Kogen managed to go down to one knee. "Do you play with Mazhiia sometimes?"

Kai-ii nodded, as did most of the children. Her brother, Naakii, said, "We played with him sometimes. But we didn't like playing with him when he was mean. Sometimes he would cheat, and sometimes he would hit us with sticks and laugh if we cried. My mother told me not to play with him any more. He has been mean lately."

Kogen went back to Eda. "One of the children saw Mazhiia leaving yesterday, with a sack on his back. Maybe we are rid of him. I think the only one that will miss him is Ligai. Even the children said that Mazhiia was worse lately, hitting them with sticks. We are lucky to be rid of him."

Eda's face was sour. "Well, one less lazy mouth to feed this winter."

When she nodded and walked away, Kogen knew the matter was finished. He went back and sat by his wikiup.

by Kevin H. and Karen C. Evans

CHAPTER 12

Village of Bernalillo
November 1634

Father Philip was in his small scriptorium in the church, settling his vestments. He and Don Federico thought it best to appear at the meeting looking official. It was not often that Father Philip wore vestments, as most of his time was taken up with the schools and educating the children in the local area. But this was a new responsibility. He felt that if he could help the people into a peaceful transition and teach them all to exist together, they would become so strong no outside force could conquer them.

As it was, his vestments were rather plain. It was difficult to obtain brocaded cloth here in the wilderness, and his own talents never ran to embroidery. So he had the chasuble and scapular, both in red. They were a stark contrast to his normal attire, the black cassock. Raymundo helped him dress, and Father Philip was decidedly nervous. "I'm not sure how my students will react. It's not like I've worn these much. They're a little creased. Perhaps I should wait until they can be fixed."

Raymundo said little. It was not his place to instruct the Jesuit missionary. Luckily, Don Federico tapped on the scriptorium door, then stuck his head in the room. "Father Philip, what's the delay? We have everyone in the chapel because it is the largest indoor space we have. If only it weren't already on the edge of winter, we could meet outside and make everyone comfortable."

Father Philip held his arms out to the side, showing the fullness and sweep of the chasuble. "I feel a little silly in this. I've never been the one to direct meetings and such. Maybe I should just let you do in. You don't really need me, do you?"

Don Federico stopped and blinked. "Wasn't it you, only a couple of weeks ago, pointing out that if I am Governor General, you are Father President? We need to show them that we are united in purpose and intent, and that we're not engaging in personal conflict. Heaven knows that there is already enough conflict. I heard just this morning that a Navajo band raided the Apaches up north. We need to do what we can to unify and Christianize this territory. And I need you by my side. It's time to go."

Father Philip let his hands fall to his sides, and he let out a deep sigh. "Oh, very well. I guess there's no escape. Lead on, Don Federico."

The new Governor General was decked out as well, with his fine black doublet with gold braid and a half-circle cloak that fell to mid-calf, appropriate for horseback riding. He was also wearing a rather tall black hat that made him appear taller than his regular five foot seven.

The two left the scriptorium and made their way to the front of the church. Sitting in the pews was a mixed bag of men, some from Pueblo villages, some from the Navajo and Apache tribes, and some from Spanish settlements that had failed to evacuate. Father Philip could see that they were not comfortable with each other. First of all, they sat in groups, Apache with Apache, Pueblo with Pueblo, and Spaniard with Spaniard. Each group had wide space between them and anyone else. And they seemed to be simmering, on the edge of breaking out into a full-blown battle.

In front of the altar, Don Federico drew his sword, and the room went silent. He said, "Thank you all for coming. I know this is an uncertain time, and I am hoping that by meeting together we can settle some of that uncertainty for everybody. I would like to introduce Father Philip, without whom, as some of you know, many would not now be alive and free. I want you to listen carefully to him."

Then Don Federico stepped back and sat down on the first row in front of Father Philip. It was a little startling, as he had not anticipated getting blindsided like this. He silently prayed that he would say something marginally appropriate. When he opened his eyes, all other eyes were on him, waiting. He took a deep breath to try to slow his heartbeat. He looked to the side, where Raymundo stood, and gestured for the boy to join him. When Raymundo arrived, Father Philip whispered, "I'm speaking in Spanish. You translate into trade language." Raymundo nodded, and moved to the side so he could gesture with his arms.

Father Philip took another deep breath. "Men and brethren. I am blessed to be here with you today. I know the misery that many of you are suffering right now, with the loss of loved ones in our recent war. At this time, I want to invite all of you to pray with me." Many heads bowed. Some did not. Father Philip began in Latin and prayed for peace. Then he switched to Spanish and said the same prayer. And then he switched to his limited knowledge of Tewa he had learned in the last two years.

As he spoke he felt peaceful, as if a blanket were laid on his shoulders, and he could see that many men in the room were having the same experience. Don Federico seemed more relaxed, as did Tsigu-may from Santa Ana and Okuwa-oky from Santa Domingo.

Those who didn't seem to participate in the peaceful sentiment were Hana-chu from Jemez and Ma-iit-soh, chief of the local Navajos. Seeing this, Father Philip knew where his work would begin. It would be easy to spend time with people that were already in sympathy, but the real work would be with the dissenters of their locality. He let his arms fall, and he nodded to the group, then sat down next to Don Federico.

But Don Federico wasn't sitting any longer. He stood up, and gestured for Tsigu-may to stand up as well. He stepped over, and said something quietly to Tsigu-may. The old man nodded, and when Don Federico stated speaking again, Tsigu-may did the same in sign language. Father Philip smiled. At least Don Federico was concerned that everyone there understood the proceedings.

Don Federico said, "Please, I want everyone here to participate and tell us of your circumstances, so that if there is anything another can do, we can do it. We need to get through this winter and into planting season next spring, and I think that the only way this will happen is if we all work together, share our resources, and stop the raids and attacks."

That caused a grumble in the back of the room, but Don Federico ignored it. The sign language used locally had been developed as a trade language because the Athabaskan tongues of Apache and Navajo were unintelligible to the Pueblo speakers and vice versa. The Pueblos themselves had a wide variety of languages that the others didn't understand well. Sign language was the best answer. It was easily learned by men who wanted to trade or were looking for information from neighbors. And it didn't upset their spirituality, which somehow learning Spanish seemed to do.

Don Federico said, "I know that winter is close at hand. It is past harvest time, and many are evaluating their food stores and seeing shortage. I found out just the other day that my wife, Doña Garciella, has been engaged in gathering. She has sent the boys of the village to the haciendas and villages where the Spaniards evacuated and gathered everything that was edible, to share with others when the snow flies."

That statement brought a grunt of surprise from several of the attendees. Impulsively, Mondragón was on his feet. It was Alfonso

Mondragón, a landowner from near Rio Colorado. "What? She plans to share it? With some of these dirty Indios? Is that what you are saying? How can we survive if we are forced to share with these murderers?"

That brought Hana-chu from Jemez to his feet as well. "If you hate us so, why didn't you leave with the rest of the cowardly Ironskins when they fled south? Why did you stay behind for us to slaughter?"

Before anyone else could say something that Father Philip would lament, he next stepped to the angry Spaniard and put his hand on Mondragón's shoulder. "Alfonso, please. Just listen to Don Federico. You can express opinions afterwards."

Mondragón snorted but took his seat. He sat with his arms folded defiantly across his chest. And when Mondragón sat, so did Hana-chu. Father Philip turned and nodded to Don Federico. "Go ahead, sir. I think they will listen now."

So for the next half hour, Don Federico laid out his proposals. There were grunts and sighs, but nobody else interrupted. His plan was simple. He suggested that those Spaniards that lived more than a day's travel from Bernalillo should find a place to stay closer during the winter months and not return to their land holdings until time to prepare for spring planting. As for the more nomadic peoples, such as the Navajo and the Apache, they were already planning to move to a warmer climate for the winter. The Pueblo villages never left their valleys. Don Federico felt that this way they could all come to the aid of someone attacked by wandering bands of Spanish deserters or any of the more warlike Plains Indios.

When he finished, the men all sat in the chapel in relative silence. They were thinking. For some, it was a new thing to realize that things they had known all their lives, like the occupation of the Spanish, was over, and they were part of a new situation.

Finally, Fidel Trujillo stood up. His home was north of the Cochiti village, very near Santa Fe, and his land was some of that which was burned by the Indios during the war. He and his family had arrived in Bernalillo before the Governor General had led his forces to Isleta. Fidel had been born in Santa Fe and had no desire to see Mexico City. His wife had been born farther north, but felt the same way. They were young, with three small children. "Don Federico, not only have I and my family already moved closer to Bernalillo, we have occupied a home nearby that was deserted when the family evacuated. We are settled, and the children are attending Father Philip's school. My wife is happy, because they had not been to school before, and my oldest son, Iago, is already ten years old. More than time for education. I am willing to work with Don Federico on anything he thinks is necessary. I support everything you've said." He finished and sat down.

Tsigu-may stood next. "Our village is ready to work with Don Federico. We have lived hear near him for many years. We trust him and know that he has a straight tongue. We believe what he has said."

That opened discussion, and talks went until after dark. Finally, Doña Garciella came into the chapel and waited for the man, Okuwa-oky, to finish speaking. Then she stepped up near the altar and said, "Don Federico, you can't keep these men any longer. Their wives and I have prepared dinner, and it is cruel to keep them from eating it. All are welcome to eat with us."

Don Federico stood up next to his wife and smiled. "You heard the real Governor, and I think this is a good time to finish for the day."

There was laughter, and the first meeting of the Council of the Rio Grande was finished.

CHAPTER 13

San Felipe
November 1634

Raum found himself awake for most of the day. He was dressed in his pantaloons, some rags for bandages, and a white wool blanket. His armor, pistol, sword, and helmet were gone, and nobody he asked seemed to know what had happened to them.

So he sat against a sun-drenched south adobe wall on the ground floor of the village that was at least three, and in some places four, stories high. The small homes each had a doorway, and the upper ones were reached by ladder. Today, the sun was scattered with clouds, which had a different look. Someone told him that they were snow clouds, and winter was almost here.

He sat there until just before dusk, when the wind turned cold. He saw the first snowflakes settle into the dry grass. He grew up in coastal Spain, then onboard a ship to Mexico City, and then in the march north last spring. He had seen snow on tops of mountains, but this was the first time he had seen it actually fall. He had never realized the magic of it, as if thousands of tiny fairies danced in the cold and silent air.

Pov'op'u found him there, shivering, and ignoring the cold. "I will not have you sick again. You must go back to your room." She helped him stand up, because he was still weak. She left him at the edge of his pallet, and he managed to sit down in a fashion that wasn't quite a collapse. His apartment where he had been kept was empty except for the pallet. Through the open door-flap, he could see the younger children dancing and playing with the fluffy flakes as they floated through the sky. Some tried to catch them in their hand, only to see them melt. One little girl stood with her mouth open and her tongue outstretched until a snowflake fell in her mouth. Then she laughed and ran to find her mother. It almost made Raum long to be a child again.

But he was not a child. And he was not an Indio. His fever was gone, and the arm that he decided must have been broken was itching inside the wraps. He had not been allowed to scratch underneath the pieces of wood that held his upper left arm in place.

A shadow fell over his door, the door flap opened, and Te'n-ot jaka came in. Raum knew him as the shaman of this village. It was he who mixed herbs and tended his wounds. Also, the old man had been methodically teaching Raum sign language. It was surprisingly easy for the young man, because many of the hand signals seemed somewhat intuitive. He seemed to be able to understand, even having never seen a certain word sign before.

Te'n-ot jaka seated himself, said, in Tewa, "Good morning, Kawaayu-hau." And then he began signing. Kawaayu-hau was the name they called Raum. He wasn't sure, but he thought it referred to his horse and his fighting on horseback. He had seen none of the local Indios do that, so they would probably think it unusual.

The old man showed him the sign for home, and pointed at the roof. Raum tried the sign and smiled as he came close. The old man nodded. But a smile was rare. Next he made a new sign and pointed outside. Raum showed his confusion, so the old man stood up and held open the door flap, then pointed to the sky, and made the sign again.

Raum frowned and made the sign for sky.

The old man took a seat again, made the sign for sky, and then the new sign. He did this several times, with Raum repeating the sign. It was difficult because it involved both hands, and one of his arms was still wrapped in a splint, so he couldn't move it fully. At least it no longer hurt to try.

And then Raum got the idea. "Snow?" He stood up, and stepped outside. He looked up at the dark cloud overhead and saw feathery flakes falling. When some landed on his sleeve, he went back to Te'n-ot jaka and showed the old man the snowflake. The old man nodded, and there was a ghost of a smile that appeared then disappeared. Te'n-ot jaka gestured that Raum sit again, and the lesson and discussion continued.

By the end of the lesson, not only did Raum understand more of the language, he knew what Te'n-ot jaka was trying to tell him. Although he was not healed completely, the old man thought it time for Raum to go back to the Spaniards.

Raum was surprised that there were still Spaniards anywhere nearby. He had thought when he saw the caravan of evacuees that all the Europeans were gone, and he was alone with thousands of Indios. But apparently that was not the case. Te'n-ot jaka drew a crude map in the dust. Raum could see that he was a little north of where he left the caravan to defend their retreat. He studied the map, then said, "Is that the village of Bernalillo? I have been there one time. Don Federico didn't evacuate?"

Te'n-ot jaka frowned, then shook his head and made the sign for Ironskin.

After the old man left, Raum stood up and paced the lodge for a moment. He had agreed to go in the morning when it was light. He sat back down near the dust map and considered how he would go. He was on foot this time. It could take him several days to reach Bernalillo. But it would be nice to be back among his own people again.

163

Near Pojoaque
November 1634

O-Fuwapi was on horseback, riding to Santa Fe with a message from the village of Tiguex. The snow had fallen two days prior, and although it didn't last, the mud did. This horse was one that someone in the village found wandering after the Ironskins fled, so it had been brought into the village. They had not had the luxury of a horse, and he felt powerful riding so high off the ground.

O-Fuwapi had been sent to bring back the chief, who had been visiting those who had moved into the palacio for the winter. They had all heard the complaints of the Indios living in the Palacio of the Governors. The rooms were enormous and expensive to heat, so work had begun to put inner walls into some of the rooms to create smaller rooms that a family could live in. Then it didn't take so much wood to heat it. O-Fuwapi thought about this for a while and just couldn't imagine why the Ironskins would build such a house in the first place. How could they afford to waste wood on big empty rooms?

His thoughts were interrupted when his horse neighed. It was startling, as he had never heard a horse voice anything while he was riding. It was all still so new to him. But he pulled up the reins and looked around. He didn't see anything, but his ears heard what the horse had heard, something walking through the brush just uphill from them. It made the hair on the back of his neck stand up, and a cold chill, colder than the sunny day around, tingle down his spine and out his arms.

O-Fuwapi got off the horse and stepped to the edge of the juniper that screened them from the hill behind them. He peered through the branches and saw something move. It was bigger than a coyote, taller than a black bear. As he looked, he realized that he was looking at a man. It wasn't someone from his village, and it wasn't anyone from the villages nearby. But it was an Indio. He thought about calling out, and his hand even began to move over his head, but he stopped himself. Ever since the war, he was more cautious of people he didn't know. He watched as the person moved west, apparently not aware he was being watched downslope.

It was a man, dark-haired and dark skinned just like O-Fuwapi. But he was dressed differently than the local Pueblo people dressed. This one was all in deerskin leather, making him difficult to see in the brush. If O-Fuwapi had not known this area so well, he would not have seen much of this man at all.

Something about the way the man walked made O-Fuwapi think it was suspicious. The man seemed furtive, which would explain why he wasn't on the trail but breaking through brush above it. Really, it had been mere chance and the direction of the wind that had allowed O-Fuwapi to see him first.

And he noticed that the man had a sack of some sort on his back. It was rather large, and when O-Fuwapi moved a branch away from his face, he distinctly saw something in the bag move.

That made O-Fuwapi's heart skip a beat, then thud harder in his chest. His old grandmother had told him stories of bad men that stole into a village and kidnapped naughty children who should be safe in their beds. He had been certain this was just a story to train naughty children, but right now, watching the bag jerk on the man's back, he was no longer certain.

O-Fuwapi stayed in the juniper tree peering at the stranger until the skulker moved from sight. Momentarily, he thought of following the man, but as his skin crawled at the thought, he let it go, and climbed back on the horse, and they moved again toward Santa Fe.

by Kevin H. and Karen C. Evans

Teopixqui moved steadily through the woods. He had captured a small boy who strayed too far from his friends in the Apache village near Pojoaque. This boy looked healthy and strong for a five-year-old. The priest wanted a boy to train as a servant, and if he started with one this young, he wouldn't have to worry about retraining habits to his liking. Besides, if the boy had been much older, he would not have fit so conveniently in the sack.

Teopixqui's cave operation had come far since they started. Quimtchin was still with him, though not in any shape to explore the local area or spy out the people who would not be missed. So about once a month, or every six weeks, Teopixqui would leave on an exploration in another direction. He never walked farther than a week in one direction, so that he could circle back and find his way to his unmarked cave. But by now, he had a good idea of what was in the territory.

The recent war had been very good for Teopixqui. Between the fleeing civilians and the wounded men, he'd had a choice of victims to bring to his cave and hold in dark pits until they would be of use in the pagan rites he practiced. He did his best to keep out of sight of the Spaniards and their missionaries. The churchmen, especially the Franciscans, were very strongly against his practices of sacrifice and ritual eating on the holy days of his God. He had been called a witch many times, and each timeit made him smile and display all his sharpened teeth.

He had also picked up some like-minded men, not just from the Indios, but also from the Spaniards. Anyone that had a thirst for blood and suffering would fit in. On his explorations, he always watched the people working around the village and chose those who were dissatisfied, who were unattached, who refused to accept menial labor, anyone he felt was discontented. Then he would take an opportunity to come under cover of darkness and whisper to these men. And usually, it didn't take much convincing to make them want to leave the confines of their tribal structure and go to his cave. He always encouraged them to steal what they could of meat or strong drink. That way, the party never ended.

Teopixqui had been aware of the young man in the juniper tree, watching. He continued on as if he had not seen, but he kept note. This man was alone and riding a horse. He may be one of those that Teopixqui would recruit in his next foray.

by Kevin H. and Karen C. Evans

CHAPTER 14

Bernalillo village
November 1634

G arciella stood by the table in the kitchen, supervising. There were several women in the kitchen, so she was grateful that they had built a nice large area for cooking for the whole hacienda.

The planning and negotiations had been going on for almost a week, but today was the Matanza, or fiesta of the harvest. The men were outside slaughtering pigs and sheep for the winter. It would have taken a lot of hay and grain to feed the animals through the winter. Only a few were kept as breeding stock.

The killing outside kept the women inside busy, preparing salted pork and cooking a meal with the offal and meat from that day. And since this wasn't a religious fiesta, there was more cooperation with the local Indios.

In any other household, with as large a group of families as were there, a week of feeding a group this big would find the cooks scraping the bottom of the food barrels. Especially in November, when there were no fresh vegetables from the kitchen garden. Garciella smiled, thinking again of her food stored away.

Don Federico stuck his head in the kitchen and saw the bustle. He tried to exit before his wife saw him, but he was not quick enough for that.

"Federico, I saw you. Obviously, if you are here, it's because the younger men don't need your advice. Tell me how the talks have gone. Are we any nearer an accord than we were yesterday? If this isn't decided soon, we will have some of these people all winter. It has already snowed in the higher villages. It won't be long before we have snow as well."

Federico Bernal sighed and stepped back into the kitchen. "I don't know what to tell you anymore, Garciella. Sometimes I think we are right on the doorstep of an agreement, and sometimes I think we will never be able to even talk to each other in a polite manner. Maybe I am too close to it to know."

Garciella patted his hand and gave him a glass of wine. "That's all right. I will ask Father Philip later. He will know how close we are. Perhaps he is ready to send them home now. Don't you worry, when I find out, Federico, you will be the first to know."

Federico smiled, and kissed her hand. "What would I do without such a wife?"

Garciella snorted and took her hand back. "You would not be Alcalde of the village, and you would starve, then die alone without children."

He laughed, gulped his wine, and set the glass down. "You are probably right."

Near La Bajada Hill
November 1634

Don Raum Santiago Angel de Bances did not feel very titled or privileged at this moment. Yesterday, the old shaman had unwrapped his arm from the splint, and Raum had been surprised to see his arm so thin and pale. It would take some time before he could hold a lance properly. But he no longer had bandages. He was declared healed.

He was wrapped in a bear skin that had been given to him by Te'n-ot jaka, and had a water skin. A sack full of an odd mixture of ground corn and berries and fat was on his back. The food was unappetizing to look at but surprisingly tasty and filling. And he had a couple of pieces of dried meat. That was what the village could spare. They had saved his life; their responsibility to the gods was finished. Now it was his job to get to shelter before the snows.

Te'n-ot jaka had told him, as had Pov'op'u, that Don Federico was having a council meeting this week. The village of San Felipe had sent someone to the talks, and Te'n-ot jaka and his wives stayed here to supervise the last of the harvest, what they could gather. Food was going to be short, with the corn fields burned during the conflict.

Right now, Raum was struggling up a hill, following a deer trail through the rabbit brush and juniper trees. The sun was out again, skittering between large cloud masses. The snow that had accumulated about an inch a couple of days ago was melted, leaving the ground muddy. The path was very narrow and had never seen wagon wheels. The trail moved from a mixture of volcanic black stone and lighter sand to slick clay. There didn't seem to be much of what he thought of as soil up here.

He had to stop frequently just to catch his breath, and the bone in his arm, while mended, ached almost all the time. He had been walking for two days, and the previous night, he had sat by a tiny fire and shivered through the darkness. So today he was exhausted. Tonight, he really had to find a place to sleep.

Everything seemed pretty quiet around him. He could hear a couple of squirrels quarreling up slope, and he spotted a small herd of deer drowsing under cover in the daylight. It wasn't much daylight, the sun gradually disappeared, leaving everything clouded and grey, and there was a steady north wind that cut cold to the bone.

He didn't know what had happened to his cuirass or morion helmet. His sword was missing, as well as his pistol. He still had his boots and shirt, and a good sturdy dagger at his belt. So when heard movement behind him on the hill, he ducked into cover and pulled the bear skin around him to complete the camouflage.

He was expecting to see a local hunter, or maybe a bear or bobcat. What he saw was out of place on this northern mountain. He saw a Nahuatl shaman. He had seen one in Mexico City before his trip up here to the Interior. This man had the iconic shaved head with feathers, and carried the unique macuahuitl, edged with wicked obsidian teeth. In this cold wind, he was wearing more than the loin cloth and feathered cloak Raum had seen before. He was wearing leggings of deerskin, and some sort of dark cloak. And he seemed to be carrying something relatively heavy, and that threw off his balance from time to time, but the shaman didn't make any effort to shift the sack, or redistribute the weight.

Crouched where he was, about one hundred yards away, Raum's trained warrior eye noticed little things. The shaman moved smoothly through the brush without breaking twigs or dislodging small stones. He seemed large and well-muscled, and displayed none of the telltale signs of fear or cowardice. This was not the kind of leader that would sit in the lodge and send out young men to die. This would be a formidable foe.

The man turned his head in Raum's direction, and Raum stared at the ground. It was obvious he had sensed Raum watching him, and the young Spaniard didn't want to let the shaman look into his eyes.

They both froze for a moment, both controlled their breathing, both listened. The forest had gone silent, not even the crickets or squirrels made any noise.

Finally, the Nahuatl man moved on. He was going south, moving as quickly as the terrain would allow. Raum crouched until the man was out of sight, and then stayed in place for some time more, thinking.

It was unusual to see someone from the jungles of the south moving through the high desert like a native. He had been told when arriving in Mexico City that the Franciscan missionaries had stopped the pagan practices of human sacrifice and cannibalism. He was certain that some of that statement was made up to bolster the position of the Church in the colonies. But he had never seen evidence of the Nahuatl in this territory.

So, instead of continuing on to Bernalillo, Raum decided to follow this priest, and see if he was up to mischief.

✳ ✳ ✳

Raum had encountered the Nahuatl shaman in the mid-morning and continued stealthy pursuit through the day. The man was not headed for any settlements that Raum knew about and was avoiding roads, even game trails. He was cutting almost straight west from La Bajada. Raum tried to visualize what was in this direction, but couldn't remember. So he continued to follow.

The sun began to set early, showing that winter was in the wings. Raum began to think about a warm place to sleep and wondered how he would continue to track the southerner if he didn't stop.

But with the lack of sleep the night before, Raum knew he would not be able to continue through the night. He was hopeful that the rain or snow that was threatening would hold off tonight. He found a large juniper tree where the outer branches arched down to the ground, creating a shelter underneath. He crawled into the tree-cave, hollowed out a sleeping spot in the fallen foliage and dead grass, wrapped the bearskin around him, and fell asleep as the dusk deepened to full darkness.

He slept for a time and woke in the darkness. He could smell dampness and knew that the dew had settled, so it was close to morning.

The air outside his bearskin was chill, and he could see his breath. He came out of the warmth for just a bit to relieve himself and then crawled back into the robe. The warm was comforting. He had another handful of the corn and berries he carried and fell back to sleep.

It was full light when he next awoke. He knew he should have been up earlier to try to find sign of where the shaman had gone. But he just didn't have the energy. He was stiff and sore from sleeping in the cold on the ground. He stood up and stretched to get his muscles moving again. He wished he dared to build a fire and have something hot for breakfast, but there just wasn't time. He needed to know where the Nahuatl had gone.

The land looked very different in the daylight. The gray clouds were gone, and the sun was at his back as he moved west looking for signs. He found a site similar to where he had slept and could see that the shaman had burrowed under a tree, then come out in the morning.

That was good news: that meant that his quarry was not too far ahead. The shaman had crawled out in the darkness, maybe before the dew had settled, because he left almost no footprint. But Raum was able to follow the track.

He followed it for two more days, always stopping when he was exhausted, and then pushing on as soon as he was able. By now, he thought very little of his arm that had been broken. It had stopped twinging with pain and now was only noticeable when he tried to lift things. The arm was just not as strong as it had been before. He would have to work and train to get it back up to fighting strength.

By now, it was obvious that the shaman knew paths that would avoid most people. They were climbing up and down the legs of the Jemez mountains, crossing that way instead of going around. The priest still carried the sack, and it seemed as heavy as before. So it was not the man's travel food, which would get lighter as he went. Raum remained curious about the bundle.

Raum was still feeling exhausted. His fighting stamina had really suffered with his fever. Today, the priest ahead of him was gaining because Raum was running on little sleep, and his food bag was almost empty. This late in the year, there was little he could find to eat on the way. He began to resent the staying power of the Nahuatl.

He pushed himself to the top of the ridge in front of him and looked across the small valley. Yes, there was the shaman, climbing the hill on the far side.

The time had come for Raum to make his way to Bernalillo. He could see that the priest wasn't going to any settlement that Raum knew about. He would go to Bernalillo, see what the situation was there, and get more food for travel. Briefly, he wished for Fausto, the fine white stallion Governor General Ceballos had sent him, but he was not even sure if the horse survived the battle.

So he followed the valley down until he reached a small stream, and he followed that until it reached the Rio Grande. From there, he headed south, knowing that eventually he would come to the village of Bernalillo.

Cavern of Tocatl Coztic, Jemez mountains
Late November

Quimtchin stood at the entrance of the cave. Much work had been done to the entrance. Now one did not have to crawl through; it was high enough that a small person like Quimtchin had only to bow his head in reverence and pass through the portal. Someone taller, like Teopixqui, had to bend farther, but could go through on his feet.

Inside, the floor had been smoothed, and Teopixqui himself had carved the tree of death and the image of the scorpion, the demon that

Teopixqui worshiped. Now the large cave was a throne room, with a blood altar down a hall and galleries for worshipers to witness and scream themselves into ecstasy.

But today, Quimtchin wrung his hands. He was still hump-backed, and now his skull was misshapen from the crack it received some years ago. But he was still living, and that was an achievement for anyone that associated with someone like Teopixqui.

He was nervous because the master had said he would be gone for a fortnight, and it was sixteen days now since Teopixqui left. How long was he to wait before deciding that someone had killed the Nahuatl priest, and he was safe to return to his comfortable jungle in the south? This was the question that he pondered every day since the master left.

Quimtchin turned and shuffled through the throne room, and moving the curtain behind the throne. This was his room at the back. It was a way that servants could move through the space and not be noticed. It led to his own little cell where, occasionally, he was allowed to rest and sleep.

Teopixqui had gone on an exploration to find men and women willing to leave the confines of the villages and experience the freedom of worshiping something that the black robes despised. Not many came, but there were one or two in every village. Eventually, they would grow and destroy everything the Ironskins had built in this country. Or so Teopixqui believed.

Quimtchin was not sure what he believed any more. He had grown up kneeling and praying with the black robes and learning catechism. He had been kidnapped one day as he was slow to reach home. Teopixqui had snatched him off the trail home, and he had never returned. He didn't know if his mother and father still lived. He didn't really miss them, but his little sister came to his thoughts frequently.

There were children here, most of whom had been kidnapped by Teopixqui in the same manner. They were kept caged in a chamber down below, except when they were working as slaves somewhere in the temple complex.

Quimtchin arrived in his small space. He would have peace and quiet until Teopixqui returned. And day and night the small man worried both that the priest would return and that he wouldn't. Both were terrifying.

by Kevin H. and Karen C. Evans

CHAPTER 15

Father Philip's Scriptorium, Bernalillo
Early December 1634

Raymundo peeked into the scriptorium and saw Father Philip bent over, studying a letter by the light of a candle. The boy was tall for his family, almost as tall as Father Philip. Approaching his fifteenth year, he had been working for Father Philip since the Jesuit arrived in Santa Fe. "Father? I have been sent to fetch you."

Father Philip looked up. "Is there a problem? A crisis? I was just rereading some of my mail. It doesn't look like we'll get much for a long time."

Raymundo stood with his hands behind his back, waiting for Father Philip to stop talking. "No, there is no problem, but Don Federico would like your opinion on a matter. He is waiting for you in the dining room of the hacienda. We have put the riding saddle on your burro, and he is waiting at the door of the church."

Father Philip smiled. "That is very kind of you, Raymundo. I know you asked me to address you by your given name, but I've forgotten it again. What is it?"

"It's Baji-delier, Father."

Father Philip stopped. "Really? That doesn't sound anything like what I remember. Baji-delier. Does it mean something?"

Baji-delier blushed slightly. "It means whirlwind. My mother despaired of ever getting me to sit still. The priest in the parish in Santa Fe thought it was hard for him to say, so he baptized me as Raymundo. But I like the name my mother chose, if you don't mind."

Father Philip nodded. "Yes. Things are changing here, we must be open to the changes. I will call you Baji. Is that acceptable?"

Baji-delier smiled. "Well, it's a start."

By now, they were out the door. In the past couple of years, Baji-delier had come to realize what a kind person Father Philip was and had come to love him. Now, when many men were angry about the missionaries and their war on the old gods, Baji-delier was happy to stay and help Father Philip. It was like he had a father again.

They came out into the courtyard, and Father Philip stopped to look at the sky. Baji-delier was used to this behavior; Father Philip looked at the sky every time he stepped outside. Today had been warm for November, but at least it wasn't windy right now. It was late afternoon, and the sun was low, coloring everything in the courtyard a rich yellow gold. There were few clouds in the sky, and the cottonwood trees along the river had leaves of the same yellow gold. Father Philip took a deep breath and sighed. "Now, Baji, where did you say my burro was?

"Over here, Father." The boy pointed to a little group of people near the large church doors. Baji followed the priest, watching his face for the surprise.

As they approached, the crowd opened up, and Father Philip glimpsed a ragged individual who seemed somewhat familiar. He was dirty, wrapped in a bearskin rug, and had a scruffy beard.

Father Philip grinned and ran forward. "Raum, my boy! You're alive. Our prayers are answered. Have you been walking? We sent searchers out after the battle, but we didn't find you. Where have you been?"

Baji-delier noticed the Alcalde, Federico Bernal, hurrying through the gate. He was laughing and reaching to shake the Teniente's hand. "Good to see you, boy. We were hoping you still lived."

Father Philip frowned as he saw de Bances tense up. "Are you all right, son?"

Raum grinned and pushed his hair out of his eyes. "Yes, father. it's just that the last time I was in a crowd of people like this, they were all trying to kill me."

Father Philip took Raum's hand and started up the stairs to the church. "That's all right, Why don't we sit down here in the chapel, and you can tell the Alcalde and me what happened.

Raum visibly relaxed. "Thank you, Father. Being indoors would suit me fine. But first, where can I clean up and get something to eat?"

Don Federico said, "Wait, Father. The Teniente is right. We need to feed him after his ordeal. Why don't you all come up to the hacienda, and Garciella can give him some dinner. We'll feed you and Raymundo as well."

Raum grinned. "That sounds like an excellent idea to me. It has been a long time since I ate good Spanish food."

✳ ✳ ✳

Twenty minutes later, Father Philip sat at the large dining table, across from Teniente de Bances. Don Federico sat at his left, at the head of the table. Father Philip said, "Don Raum, we are so curious as to what happened to you. Fausto was spotted very soon after the caravan of refugees left here. But we had no clue you had survived. I have heard rumors of your exploits to keep the column safe. Your bravery is not a question. But where have you been for almost two months?"

Raum broke a hunk of bread off the loaf Doña Garciella had set next to his bowl of stew. "I woke up in San Felipe, and Te'n-ot jaka supervised my recovery. He is very kind, and doesn't seem to resent my people like so many others do."

Don Federico said, "We're not sure what happened that night, but we know the caravan had passed us on the way to Isleta, and you were assigned to command the defense of the rear. Did something happen?"

Raum took a huge bite of bread and chewed for a moment. "I remember that I spotted some suspicious activity, and rode to check it out, leaving the command of the squad to Sergeant Ruiz. When I saw the size of the attack prepared, I seized the opportunity and charged them, blowing my horn to warn my men. The Indios swarmed around me. When it looked like I wouldn't survive, I sent Fausto away. I don't remember much after that."

Don Federico sighed. "We're glad you're here now. It is comforting to have a trained soldier with us."

Raum dug into his stew. "To tell you the truth, I was surprised to learn that there were any Spaniards still here. I thought everyone had evacuated."

Father Philip broke himself off a piece of bread. "Everyone who had taken shelter in Santa Fe certainly left. But there are several others who either got here late or felt more secure on their own land."

Don Federico sipped some wine. "From our efforts to find who is left, I think we have maybe twenty families, and that means about about one hundred and fifty Spaniards. We have contact with the nearby Pueblo villages and are on good terms with the Apache, and to a lesser extent, the Navajo. The Utes sent a representative to our council meeting, but I still don't know if they are friend or enemies. I would like to make friends with all of them and mutually protect our territory. But I still haven't found the one thing that will bring them together. I had thought it would be the revolt, but it doesn't seem to have worked."

They all sat quietly as de Bances continued to eat. They still had a lot to think about. Raum sat back and asked, "Do you know if there are any Nauhuatl around?"

Don Federico frowned. "What's that?"

Father Philip said, "Isn't that the tribe of Indios that lived in Mexico City? The ones Cortez conquered?"

Raum shrugged and got another piece of bread. "I don't know the history; I just saw a Nauhuatl shaman while I was in Mexico City. Tall, with lots of feathers, wearing a loincloth, and a feather cloak?"

Don Federico shrugged as well. "I was born here, never been to Mexico City. My wife was born down there, she would know. Why do you ask, Teniente?"

Raum swallowed some wine. "I think I saw one in the mountains, on my way here."

Father Philip looked worried. "I didn't think there were many left. If you listen to the Franciscans, the pagan temples have been cleansed and the sinful priests exterminated. I have never seen one in this territory."

Raum said, "Well, there's one now. I saw him near La Bajada. He was alone and carrying a sack of something large on his back. I followed him for two days. He was headed up into those mountains north of Bernalillo. Are there any villages up there that you know about? Because as far as I know, it's a mountainous and fairly empty area."

Don Federico got up and rummaged in a drawer of the cabinet, and came back to the table with a crude map. It was not very detailed, but showed Bernalillo and Santa Fe, the Rio Grande, and the Camino Real del Norte. He spread it out, and they all studied it for a moment.

Raum said, "I can't say for sure, but I think I saw him go into a canyon right about here." He pointed at an area north of Bernalillo and east of Jemez.

Don Federico nodded. "I will bring it up at the council after Christmas. Maybe one of our neighbors has seen something. I just wish it was easier to get them to understand that we are stronger together than we are separately."

Father Philip finished his stew. "I think that we don't have an accord yet because the revolt was ignited by hate and resentment. We need to find something we all love that we are all willing to protect. That will bring us together."

Santa Ana Pueblo
December 1634

Eduardo Bernal was busy. It was only days after he'd returned from duty as mailman to El Paso. He was proud of the way he got the letters into the mail going south. He'd dressed as a peasant with a large sombrero and put on an attitude of abject humility, then approached the Teniente in charge of the mail. "Kind sir, is it possible for me to send word to my mother? I hope she still lives in Mexico City, and the priest helped me write to her. I have a little money."

The Teniente frowned and sniffed, as the serape Eduardo was wearing had been a horse blanket and smelled quite a bit. "How much money?"

Eduardo pulled a small pouch from his shirt and shook out several copper pieces. "I know it is not much, Kind Sir, but it is all I have."

The Teniente took four coppers, and said, "This will do. Where's your letter?"

Eduardo held up a sack; the Teniente sighed and grabbed it. He didn't look inside. Eduardo smiled as he thought of Father Philip's letter, headed for Spain.

And now, there was much to do. The trip only took three weeks down and four weeks back. Now he was wanting to help his father quell some of the agitation in the area.

Since the evacuation of most of his neighbors, he had thought that the persecution of the indigenous people would stop. But the fact was that there was more than before. Now, they had no Father President to fear, and they could indulge themselves in heaping their hatred on the heads of the Indios that lived near their villages.

In his "secret" identity as Ka-ansh, he was out almost every night, freeing slaves and making a nuisance of himself. His identity was a secret from most of the Spaniards, but it was known to a few of his friends in the Santa Ana Pueblo. They were his co-conspirators. Eduardo's father, the Alcalde of Bernalillo, had always been tolerant of the neighboring pueblo. Some of the boys Eduardo had grown up with lived there.

He snuck out of the village gates to meet his crew. Oji-ok'u was the first one to greet him. "Ka-ansh, we have a task for you. One of the young men from the Navajos has come to tell us that the Ironskins living near Isleta are locking up their Indios at night. They were not allowed to come up to Sandia for a wedding celebration, and the groom is the uncle of some of them. We have family obligations to carry out, and it can't happen when they are locked in a barn all night."

Eduardo rubbed his chin. He was seventeen years old and hoping that his beard was coming in. None of his Indio friends could grow a beard. He felt it would add to his reputation and maybe impress the girls. "To get to Isleta, we would have to ride for a good part of the night. But it may be worth it. I can tell my mother tomorrow that I'm coming down with a cold or something. Let's do it." He ran to saddle his horse; the rest of the boys already had two horses for the five of them. They were all wiry and so doubled up on horseback. Eduardo pulled Oji-ok'u up with him, and they rode off.

Cavern of Tocatl Coztic, Jemez Mountains
December 1634

It was after dark when Teopixqui came through the door to the cave. He snorted irritably as he noticed nobody there to greet him. It also meant no guard to keep the curious out. "Quimtchin," he shouted. "Where are you, you lazy flea-bitten dog?"

He heard a noise in the space behind the throne, and a disheveled old man came out of the space. "Master, is that you? I had begun to think that you were dead and that I would starve in these mountains, having never seen the jungles of my birth."

Teopixqui dumped the sack to the floor, and sighed. "Shut up, Quimtchin. I have no need of your maunderings. Come and take charge of this child. I want a drink and a bath. These people have no glimmering idea of hygiene, and the Spaniards are the worst of the lot."

"Is the child Spanish, then?" Quimtchin was already untying the sack.

"No, he's from a village north of Santa Fe. The Spaniards in this area are too gaunt to take any of their children. The mothers are still traumatized from the war and evacuation. They stay closer than mother hens to their sickly chicks. This one is from the pueblo of Pojoaque, and although I think he's five or six, his mother never taught him not to wander away from people. So he's here with us now."

Quimtchin pulled the boy out of the sack by his hair. There was no response. "Is he drugged, Master?"

"Of course he's drugged. I walked for four days to get him here, and I couldn't have him kicking me all that way. If he comes out of it, it will be in a couple of hours. He will be thirsty, and maybe a little hungry if he's not nauseated. Don't bother me with the details. And leave him here while you prepare my bath."

Quimtchin dumped the child on the ground and pushed himself up off the floor. "It will be done, Master."

by Kevin H. and Karen C. Evans

CHAPTER 16

Bernalillo Chapel
January 1635

Father Philip watched men filing into the chapel, and worried. Next to him, in vestments for a mass, stood Father Tómas. And the men coming in weren't the usual Bernalillo congregation. It was a collection of all the Spanish families left in the territory. If any other Spaniards were here, they were army deserters, and they had no idea how many of those there were.

Don Federico had invited the families all for Christmas, and the spare rooms and outbuildings were crammed full of women and children. After the mass, they were planning another meeting to talk about how they were doing getting along with the Indios.

Father Tómas signaled the altar boy and began the ceremony. Father Philip took his seat and let himself enjoy the mass. No matter how anxious he felt, the sweet familiar mass always strengthened his faith and bolstered his resolve to do better. That alone was a blessing.

As they finished, instead of filing out of the chapel with the women and children, the men sat down again. Don Federico stood. "Friends and neighbors, you all know why we are meeting today. I will have a meeting later with the Indios in the pueblos, all those who are willing to come and talk. If possible, I want to meet with the Navajo, Ute, and Apache tribes as well.

"I am sure you have heard the rumors, and even the accusations, that your favorite enemy, be it Pueblo, Apache, or Navajo, are abducting children to use as slaves. I have heard several versions of the same thing.

"And some of you came here to rally others into another war. Many of us are concerned with the disappearance of people in our communities. I need to know just how many have been lost and what the circumstances were."

For a moment, the men looked at each other, waiting for someone else to start. Then Diego Cedillo, the young man from the Cedillo hacienda, stood up. "Don Federico, I am neither the oldest nor yet the wisest of this assembly, but before we came this winter, one of the families near our village lost a son. He was about fourteen years old and very devoted to his mother. She had sent him off to help gather the sheep, and he never returned. Men searched the rest of that day and a couple days after, but we couldn't take too much time; we were preparing the sheep for the winter, and we needed to get it done before the first snow, which, as you know, came early. The young man's mother still weeps for him and has a candle burning at all times in the chapel."

Then they all began to have something to say. One after another stood and related the loss of a girl or boy between the ages of twelve and sixteen. Some were younger, like a six-year- old girl some months ago or a grandfather only a couple of weeks ago. In all cases, the person disappeared while walking alone somewhere, and when the men searched, they didn't find the person or a body. Nothing but occasional signs of a struggle.

Eduardo, and his friend Oji-ok'u stood in the back, watching the proceedings. Oji-ok'u leaned over and whispered to his friend, and immediately, Eduardo raised his arm and caught his father's eye. "Father, this is not unique to the haciendas and villages of the Spaniards. Hear Oji-ok'u. Similar things have happened here in Santa Ana."

Don Federico nodded. "Come here to me, Oji-ok'u. I have heard your report, but tell these men what you told me."

The boy walked to the front, and it was evident that he was uncomfortable, especially with some of the stares and sneers from the congregation. But he stood next to Don Federico and spoke in Spanish. "We too have suffered a loss. During the harvest moon, the youngest daughter of our chief, Vi'vif was with a group of women collecting dried reeds for baskets. She had only six summers. When the women were finished and headed back to the pueblo, she didn't answer when they called, nobody had seen when she left. They hurried back to the pueblo, and men went out to search, but there was not much time before darkness. The next morning, the hunting party went to search and found the mark of a struggle in the soft mud near the river. There were no more of her footprints but those of a man left that place. They tracked him until he came to a cliff of a mesa and the tracks disappeared, as if he flew away. She has not been seen since."

Don Federico put his hand on Oji-ok'u's shoulder and nodded. The young man returned to the back with Eduardo. The Alcalde continued. "You can see that this is not limited to the Spanish settlements. The pueblos and the Apache and Navajo villages have suffered losses as well. But the Keres blame the Navajo, the Spanish blame the Apache, the Towa blame the Tewa. If we are to find out what is happening, old hatreds and resentments need to be put aside."

Father Philip felt the men in the room become uncomfortable. It's true that nobody likes to be told they are imperfect, and these men were no exception. There were several about to take to their feet and argue with Don Federico.

So Father Philip stood up to speak instead. "Brothers, it is not important at this time to assign blame. This may be the first time some of us are aware that things have been happening, and it looks like it has been going on since before our friend, Teniente de Bances, returned from San Felipe. I have estimated from stories told me in the last couple of months that there have been as few as twenty, and possibly as many as fifty, abductions since the war. What are we to do?"

Don Baltazar Lujan, from San Ildefonso village, stood up, angry. "Why are you telling us about the Indios? Why should we believe anything they tell us? They are the ones that attacked Santa Fe and drove the Governor General Ceballos to evacuate with most of our people. Those of us who got left behind are not here to hold the hand of whatever poor sot can't count their own children when out in the wilderness. I want to know when we are going to send an armed force to the Navajo and force them to give back the captives they have taken? Everyone knows they are the most notorious slavers in the territory."

Don Federico stood up, and put on a smile that would hopefully calm the acid tone of Don Baltazar. "Sir, we don't have proof that any of the captives are in the hands of the Navajo, and even if they were, which village would you attack, and which force would you send? We have a handful of soldiers who were severely wounded and are still recovering. If there is to be a force, it must come from our own households. Are you ready to send your sons and old men into the teeth of a warlike tribe like the Navajo?"

Silence fell on the group as they emotionally accepted the fact that life in Nuevo Mexico had changed profoundly.

Later that night, Don Federico, Doña Garciella, and Father Philip sat in the hacienda sitting room, with a small fire on the grate, and mulled wine to sip. It hadn't snowed significantly, but tonight the wind was whipping through the trees, and the temperatures had dipped to freezing. Father Philip said, "Well, we had the meeting of our Spanish brethren, and it didn't go as well as I would have liked. What do you think, Don Federico?"

Don Federico was quiet for a moment. "I think we have been lucky so far that there haven't been bloody encounters ever since Ceballos led the caravan out of sight. Many of the Spaniards hate the Indios. And the Indios themselves are not cohesive, with so many languages and traditions among the Pueblos, and the bloodthirsty training the Apache and Navajo get. I think it's a miracle that we've only had some mysterious abductions."

Doña Garciella finished her wine and stood up. "I think you are both missing something important."

Father Philip looked puzzled. "Really? What?"

She put her fists on her hips and turned full force on the Jesuit. "We have heard of abductions from every major settlement in the area. Right? Every settlement except this one. There are some out there that are already thinking we are responsible for the abductions because one has not happened here. Just what are you going to do about that?"

She turned in a flurry of skirts and petticoats and went to bed.

Don Federico frowned. "Do you think she's right? Do you think it's someone here in Bernalillo?"

Father Philip shook his head. "I don't, and this is why. Remember the report we got from the Teniente? He followed a man for a day and a half before turning away and coming here. That means that one of the abductors was going away from here."

Don Federico nodded, and rang a little bell. When Baji-delier appeared, he said, "Could you please invite Don Raum to join us for some mulled wine?"

Father Philip raised an eyebrow. "What are you going to do?"

Don Federico smiled. "I'm going to have him conduct a search of the area where he last saw the man. We need to do what we can before the snow gets deep. It may already be too late, and we'll have to wait for the spring. But any information we get now will help. And besides, if I'm seen doing something, the gossip hounds will go bay at someone else for a while."

CHAPTER 17

Jemez Mountains
January 1635

T eniente Raum Santiago Angel de Bances turned his horse, Fausto, around and looked to the end of his column. And using the term column was more than generous to the straggling civilians on horseback he had to work with. Still, it was good to be in the saddle again, especially since Don Federico had presented him with Fausto, the fine fighting stallion that had once belonged to the Governor General.

They had been out of Bernalillo for three days, camping last night in the foothills of the Jemez mountains. When the other Spaniards heard that Raum was going to search for the lost children, they all wanted him to wait until they could come along. So he didn't leave until the last week of January. By now, snow was heavy on the tops of all the mountains visible from Bernalillo, and there was little hope that they could find the same canyon he had seen last fall. But at least they were doing something.

In the time since he had arrived in Bernalillo, he had ridden up to Santa Fe, and looked through the armory of the palacio. The Indios living there didn't really care about the Morion and cuirass that he found. But there was no gunpowder left, and all the firearms had "mysteriously" disappeared.

Not to be deterred, he'd ridden back to the mesa, the location of the battle he had fought to protect the end of the caravan. There he found rags and broken spear hafts. But no bodies and no muskets. He did find a sword that may likely have been his, so at least he had that.

And then, just last week, as they had been preparing for this expedition, Father Philip appeared with a pistol, a powder horn, and a musket. These were just what Raum had been searching for. "Father, where did you get all this?"

Father Philip tried to look innocent. "I thought you knew, I, uh, inherited them. From a dear friend. Who shall remain nameless at this point. Go ahead, Don Raum. Use them, and keep yourself and all the others safe from whatever evil you are hunting."

So now, three days into the expedition, Raum was as armed as any soldier of Spain should be. Several other men from the Spanish settlements were also armed. It was interesting to see weapons appear out of nowhere when they had been thinking that there were no other firearms in the territory. In all they had seven muskets and fifteen pistols, and one of his riders had a lance. Raum was certain that the nineteen year old boy carrying that lance had no idea how to use it well, but he had given the young man a quick and dirty rundown of the weapon.

His thoughts were broken when Marcos Cháves, who lived near Sandia, came up beside him. Marcos had ridden ahead, looking for any sign that there were people up this canyon. "What did you find up there, Marcos?"

The boy shook his head. "As you come around that bend up there, there's snow on the ground. I'd say it's been there two or three days. And there are no footprints in the snow except for deer, rabbit, and coyote. I think I heard a bobcat in the woods as I went, but I'm not sure. I don't think a person has walked up there for at least a week. Are you sure this is the canyon?"

Raum shook his head. "No, I was on foot, eating sparingly, and still a little confused after my recovery. Everything looks different now. I know it was up here somewhere, but I'm not sure which canyon it was."

Marcos cocked his eye at the sun, which was starting to settle close to the shoulder of the mountain to their left. "We have maybe two more hours of daylight. What do you want to do?"

Raum looked at the line of horses. It still straggled and would never have the precision of a trained military unit. "Pass the word. We're going back to the mouth of this canyon to camp, and we'll try a new one in the morning."

Cavern of Tocatl Coztic, Jemez Mountains
January 1635

High priest Teopixqui had been alone in the throne room, breathing deep of the smoke from the brazier. He had recently discovered the prophetic qualities of certain mushrooms known to the people in this place. This was the third time he had immersed himself in the intoxicating haze.

It was beginning to fade when he heard a rustle of clothing and shallow breathing from the space behind his throne. "Who is it interrupting my communion?"

Mazhiia of the Apache stepped into the chamber and prostrated himself. "Serene One, I have news. The sentries have spotted a mob in the canyon to the east."

Teopixqui moved the brazier to the side and focused on Mazhiia, still face down on the ground. "What do you mean by mob? Are they angry or shouting?"

Mazhiia sat on his heels to speak. "No, Serene One, they are following one man and may be organized. He is a Spaniard, with a beard, and he is wearing armor and riding a horse. Following him is a mixed group of young men, Ironskins, Pueblos, and Apaches. One of the sentries said he saw some Navajos, but it is approaching dusk, and nobody else believed him."

The priest was silent for a long moment, and Mazhiia waited patiently. A part of Teopixqui wanted to wait and see how long the other man's patience would last, but there wasn't time to play. He stood up. "How many of our agents are here?"

Mazhiia fell back to full prostration. "Only three, Serene One. We expected the bulk of them back two days ago but have not heard from them yet."

Teopixqui untied his feather cloak and left it draped on the throne. "That's fine. I think with three I can discourage this mob, as you call it. Follow me."

Instead of heading to the opening of the cave, Teopixqui turned and went to the altar room, deeper in the cave. Mazhiia, Pinang-oi-yws, and Tse-bit-a followed the high priest through a curtained door at the back of the altar room and found themselves in a narrow passage that ran around the end of the altar room. Teopixqui saw their questioning looks and handed Mazhiia a pitcher clay bottle of water. In fact, there was a bottle for each of them. "Bring these. We go to petition the great Tocatl Coztic to intervene with the Ironskins."

He moved another curtain, and they were out of the passage into the depths of the cave, where no others were allowed. There was a pool of some kind in the center of the cavern, and they could all feel the heat from the heart of the mountain.

Teopixqui skirted the pool and went to the back of the cave. He seemed able to see in the darkness, but the others held their torches high. At the very end of the cavern, there was a large crack in the floor, and there Teopixqui stopped. He had his agents gather on either side of the crack, with him at the end of it. He started singing a death chant to the demon of the Earth.

The other three men knelt down and chanted a counterpoint to Teopixqui's song. After some time, the high priest stopped and pulled mushrooms from his pouch. These he passed to the men chanting, and each one put the dried fungus in his mouth and chewed, then continued chanting.

After that, it was difficult for the observers to tell what was real and what was not. But they felt the chant coming to a climax. At that moment, Teopixqui stopped and picked up the water bottle, and poured its contents into the crack. The water steamed and hissed. Teopixqui broke the bottle, and threw the shards into the crack as well, and finished his chant.

They waited, afraid to breathe for a moment, and then felt a rumble from deep under their feet. Teopixqui grinned as the floor shook, and the torchlight glinted off his sharpened teeth. He said, "He is pleased. We must go."

Canyon of the Scorpion
January 1635

Raum was in the saddle again. It was mid-morning when the scouts spotted a path leading up the canyon. It was not a deer path because it didn't hug the ridge. And besides, Marcos spotted human footprints in the soft sand at the bottom of the arroyo.

Raum asked, "Were they adult or child prints? And can you tell how many feet have used this path?"

Marcos shook his head. "No telling, but the footprints happened after that rain we had a couple of weeks ago. So it isn't anything ancient."

The report was interrupted by a deep rumble. At first, Raum thought it was distant thunder, but it went on too long. Smoke rose above the western range of mountains, and then the ground began to shake.

The horses spooked and bucked their riders off before they ran madly down the canyon and out of sight. By the time the rumble stopped, the search and rescue posse was jumbled and confused. Several of the men had panicked with the horses and run after them. And the riders went in search of their horses, as they were rare and not worth losing.

Raum sighed. He still sat on his horse, Fausto. The horse didn't spook for a mere earthquake. But it looked as if he was the only one who didn't. Raum started shouting orders but noticed that there was nobody near him listening. The fear was too compelling, and the command structure collapsed.

Bernalillo Chapel
January 1635

When the earthquake hit, many people were milling in the courtyard, because mass was over but it wasn't lunchtime yet. The noise was astounding, and it shook the adobe brick buildings. The tower on the chapel swayed, and if there had been a bell there, it would have rung the alarm.

Horses screamed, babies cried, dogs barked, men shouted, and women wept. It was chaos. Father Philip, who had spent time in Rome, was more familiar with this kind of event. But none of the locals or the other Spaniards had any warning that the earth itself could be so unsteady.

Don Federico found Father Philip in the plaza, looking up at the clear blue sky and quietly fingering through his long rosary. "Father, what is this new disaster?"

Father Philip turned and regarded the Alcalde. "It is an earthquake, Don Federico. Have you not ever experienced one? Well, don't worry, at least until the aftershocks. This one doesn't seem to be as strong as the one they had near Rome in my youth. It may even be over by now. Do you want to bring them into the chapel? If you want, I can talk to the people and try to ease some of the fearfulness. Don't worry, this is not the end of days."

Don Federico nodded. There was still worry on his brow, but the man was a born leader. His face cleared as he moved to someone who had been hurt by falling debris. Father Philip was glad to serve with someone of such heroic character.

✳ ✳ ✳

The Epiphany was over and the holiday season finished as the winter became more serious. Teniente Raum returned with the boys of the Spaniards, and others filtered off as they got packed up. Many took food with them for the winter months, all from Doña Garciella's larders.

There were still resentments and hatreds that the season of Christmas didn't erase. And while nobody had been killed in the earthquake, some were injured. For those traveling home, nobody knew what they would find when they arrived.

Worst of all, the kidnapped children had not been recovered. Many blamed the Teniente because he didn't perform some kind of miracle. As the village emptied, Father Philip despaired of ever having a comfortable version of peace again.

by Kevin H. and Karen C. Evans

CHAPTER 18

Mesa near Bernalillo
April 1635

T he first hints of spring sent fingers of green grass and leaves throughout the Bosque, the forested area along the Rio Grande. On the fine white stallion, named Fausto, saddled and loaded for an expedition, Teniente Raum de Bances stopped and looked out over the land. This was a great vista. From here, he could not only see the village of Bernalillo but also the pueblo of San Felipe and the winter camp of one of the Navajo bands. The swath of cottonwood trees along the riverbed were still bare and gray. But elsewhere, the spring sap was turning the ends of the willows red. Birds were returning, and the ground was damp and rich.

Raum found out that springtime in Nuevo Mexico was not like other places. Instead of numerous soft soaking showers, they got snow and lightening, or wind. Springtime meant the wind. Nobody really liked it, they just hung on for warmer weather and green trees.

All winter, whenever he could, Raum had ridden out of the village of Bernalillo and explored the mountains north and west of them. He knew that somewhere in there he would eventually find the lair of those evil kidnappers. But so far, he hadn't found it.

Luckily, when the weather was foul, there were fewer kidnappings. But the numbers were steadily rising. And many still didn't believe that the depredations were not caused by their hated neighbors.

Besides searching all the little blind canyons for a hidden cave, Raum was also assessing the warlike behavior of the locals. The Jicarilla Apache band had moved south to warmer lands for the winter, as had the southern Utes. He watched for their return and for any new threat that could pop up in this place.

Fausto shifted underneath him and made a rumble in his chest. Raum was alerted and stared at the bush and trees near him. His horse knew there was an enemy close by.

The arrow came from somewhere behind him, and he didn't see it until it struck the saddle near his right thigh. It was almost silent; all he heard was the thunk of the arrowhead hitting the wood of the saddle, quivering like an aspen leaf. He touched his heel to the withers of his horse, and the two burst into action. Raum pulled his sword because he liked the feel of the weapon in his hand and he didn't have a target to shoot at.

As one, the man and horse wheeled around and headed for the rock outcropping that was Raum's best guess as the hiding place of the shooter. He could feel Fausto's eagerness as they charged the rocks. There was a rustle in the grass, and six warriors stood up to face the charging stallion.

They had shaven heads and were painted black and red, which was garish and bright, but the paint had succeeded in one purpose: to break up the shapes that a human eye could construct into a man. Two were armed with bows, and the others carried clubs with wicked antler points. And one had a spear with an iron spearhead. They would be fearsome opponents against one man.

But Raum was not just one man, he was an armed man on a trained war horse. Many foot soldiers had died under the hooves of such a horse. And Raum had also been blooded in battle. He felt no fear of these men, only adrenaline and anticipation. These Indios had no idea what kind of wasp nest they had just disturbed.

The shorter one, armed with a club, shouted, "Death!" in Spanish and charged toward Raum's left elbow. A split second later, the rest broke up and attempted to surround him. It was attempted, because instead of riding directly at them, Raum signaled with his knee, and Fausto wheeled to the right and flanked the line. Now Raum and Fausto had only one man to face at a time.

Before Raum could draw a bead on anything, Fausto reached out with his dinner-plate sized rear hoof and smashed the first man in the throat. The Indio crumpled, gasping and clawing at his collapsed windpipe. He was no longer a threat.

The remaining five men pulled back from directly in front of the horse and circled to the sides. Raum back slashed with his sword and caught one under his left arm. The sword cut into the ribs, and the man collapsed. The slash almost took the sword from Raum's hand, but the blade suddenly freed up as the angle of the cut opened the ribs enough for the blade to slip free.

Meanwhile, the attacker with the spear came up on Raum's right side. Raum couldn't see him because of Fausto's head. But Fausto saw. The horse got the man's arm in his teeth and clamped down hard. It was the man's left hand, but instead of attacking Raum the man began beating the horse's head with the haft of the spear.

As the sword freed from the torso of one, another attacker took a swing at Raum's head with an obsidian-studded club. The sharp points skidded off the morion helmet, and Raum kicked the man in the face. The Indio fell over, and the war horse wheeled again, stepping expertly on the man's chest.

As the attack began, the two men with bows backed up and watched for an opportunity to fire arrows. But it was moving very fast, and their own men were blocking shots at Raum. Then, apparently, a shot opened up, because Raum suddenly had two arrows into his buff coat. But they were not iron arrowheads, and they stuck between the chain mail underneath the heavy leather coat. Raum barely noticed them.

Then they were through the line, and Fausto wheeled to return. Already, it looked better. Only one man with a club remained standing, and the two archers. Raum decided that the arrow threat was a little greater, so he charged at them. That left the man with the club out of range.

As the archers realized they were the target, one turned and ran. The other got an arrow nocked but never sent it, as Raum pulled his pistol and fired. They were close, so the flame and the ball met the man at the same time. He fell with a hole in his chest and his eyebrows on fire.

The man with the club closed on Raum and Fausto, and they wheeled toward him. Raum slashed with the sword at the same time as Fausto kicked out with a front hoof. Both attacks were successful, and the man fell in a bloody heap. If anyone was counting, it would have been difficult to tell which was the killing blow.

And as suddenly as it started, it was over. Five men lay dead or dying on the ground. Raum considered riding after the archer but decided against it. The sun was close to the horizon, and it would be cold as soon as the sun was gone. It was time to return to Bernalillo.

Cavern of Tocatl Cavern of Tocatl Coztic, Jemez Mountains
April 1635

Teopixqui sat in the throne room, twirling his feather quirt. He was waiting for a report, as he had sent six men out to find and report on activity near Bernalillo. Since January, when they had watched the

Ironskins get lost and not find the cavern, he had been feeling pleased that he could not be found.

Now he was not so sure. The snows were starting to melt on the mountains, and soon it would be plowing and planting time. It would also be time for the Ironskins to hunt for the cave again. The priest thought it a better idea to get them before they got close.

There was a disturbance in the hallway outside the throne room, so he sat up. "Who is disturbing the great Tocatl? It is unseemly, this amount of noise."

One of the servants hurried in the door and threw himself on the ground, face down. "Serene One, it is the men you sent."

Teopixqui grinned, with his sharpened teeth gleaming in the torchlight. "By all means, send them in. I am eager to hear of the destruction of our enemies."

But instead of six men with trophies of their expedition, there was only one, still painted for war and carrying a bow. The man went to his knees, put his forehead on the floor, and stayed there, not speaking.

Teopixqui stood and looked towards the door. "Where are the rest of your brethren? Surely you have not returned alone."

The man spoke quietly. "I have, Serene One. The others are dead."

"I hope you killed them yourself because they were cowards and ran in the face of the enemy."

The man said nothing. Teopixqui's rage was massive, enough that he thought he would burst because of it. He strode to the man on the floor and placed his sandal on the man's neck. "Or it is that you are the coward and fled instead of carrying out your purpose?"

"Lord, I shot my arrows at the man, and I saw them hit, but it did nothing. How is that possible? And before I could shoot again, the others were destroyed. I came immediately to tell you of the white wizard. He is invincible, nothing can hurt him or his horse."

Teopixqui didn't like the frightened murmur that slithered through the throne room like a snake of fear. He glared around the corners of the room where lesser priests and slaves huddled. "You think he is a wizard? Or are you just saying that to save your own skin? I think it's time to release you from that obligation. Prepare him—we need a sacrifice today to ask Tocatl Coztic to forgive us for having a coward among us."

CHAPTER 19

Cocinas de Bernalillo
May 1635

T he Alcalde of Bernalillo was up to his knees in mud. He and most of the village of Bernalillo worked to protect the cocinas from the flood. They were building a thicker wall on the river's edge.

The spring runoff this year was at flood stage, and the river was rising. Along the entire length of the Rio Grande, people were frantically trying to get out of the way. The villages most at risk were those of the Pueblos. They had been farming along the edge of the great river for centuries. But usually they lived on top of the mesa. The Spaniards had forced many villages out of the heights and down to the flood plain. The Pueblos watched for signs in the spring runoff. Usually they could predict it very closely.

But not this year. The sun in April and May had been unusually hot, and the snow from the high slopes of the mountains all melted at once. Don Federico had gotten word just yesterday of a young man being caught in a narrow canyon by a flash flood that killed him. The tribe was still searching for his body.

Finally, it looked like they had a wall that would stand. It had been reinforced with saplings and brush. If the flood stayed at this level, they would survive and be able to plant corn and squash and beans.

Cavern of Tocatl Coztic, Jemez Mountains
June 1635

When they were children, the boys and girls of the Sandia pueblo all had to sit with the old shaman, Pot-cowagi-io, and listen to the stories of creation. It covered the older gods and the worlds before this world. They didn't dare make fun of the old man, because he had a walking stick that could find its way to the head of the boy or girl causing problems. Many of them suffered whacks to the back of the head before they figured out they needed to sit and listen.

One of the stories concerned a demon that the shaman called Litsoof. This demon loved darkness and evil and stayed in places that the sunlight could never reach. He was a giant, shaped like a scorpion, but much more intelligent. And he lived in a cave in the mountains near the hot springs. It was not close to the village, but they all knew where it was because their fathers took them to the canyon to make sure they knew. Every member of the pueblo was forbidden to go near that cave, and if they did, the consequences were dire.

Now, it was ten years after those lessons, and the boys were fourteen and fifteen summers. None of them wanted to be on the ridge overlooking the cave. It was twilight, about the hour the deer came out to graze.

Ok'uwa'enu said, "I don't think we should be here. We should go home."

Oji-ok'u agreed with him. "Ku'nfayte, this has gone too far. Let's just go home. We won't tell them anything; let them think we were brave enough to go into the cave."

But Ku'nfayte was a bully. He was bigger and stronger than the other youths, and he wanted to make them suffer. "Sure, Oji, the others won't know. But I will know you are a coward. Prove to me you are brave, and I won't punch you in the head tonight."

Unwillingly, Ok'uwa and Oji started down the slope. They moved slowly in the fading light. Ku'nfayte started pounding his fist into his other hand. "What are you waiting for? Do you really like it when I beat you up? Go show me if you're brave."

They had reached the flat bottom of the canyon, sandy with rabbit brush. Oji could see the petroglyph opposite him, warning them not to proceed. He took a step forward. The truth was, he was more afraid of Ku'nfayte than he was of the stories of Litsoof and the cave. He looked sideways at Ok'uwa and shrugged. "Ready?"

Ok'uwa nodded, and they turned uphill. Ku'nfayte stayed on the ridge, yelling into the darkness, as the others moved away. The boys did their best to ignore him.

When they disappeared from Ku'nfayte's sight. He called out their names. "Ok'uwa, Oji-ok'u, have you touched the back of the cave yet? Or has Litsoof taken you? Are you too afraid to answer?" He laughed derisively.

There was silence. It was odd. Ku'nfayte noticed that he could no longer hear crickets, or birds, or even the wind. Fear touched his neck and shoulder, then ran a cold finger down his spine.

He slid down the slope and headed uphill. It was now fully dark but cloudy, so not even moonlight touched the sand of the canyon. He shouted again. "Oji, answer me. I'm going to pound you when I catch you, and I run faster than either of you." Then he heard a scream. It was a scream like he had never heard before, and it ended in a wet gurgle.

Ku'nfayte could feel the hair rise along his arms, and down his back. His ears felt as if they were growing, as he stretched them to hear another sound or see anything in the blackness of the cave.

Silence. Darkness. Then a sound. It was horrible, a roar like the mountain itself was calling for his blood. His legs were carrying him away before his brain registered the noise. He was already moving as fast as his feet would go. The soft sand made movement difficult, and he felt like he was swimming in sand. His ribs began to hurt and his breathing was ragged. He thought that if he could reach the mouth of the canyon, he would escape.

But it wasn't enough. Something hit him hard in the back of the head. He didn't stop running. Then there was terrible pain, and he saw something sharp come through his chest. He collapsed on the ground.

Father Philip's Scriptorium, Bernalillo
June 1635

Eduardo Bernal, the son of the Alcalde of Bernalillo, came to the door of the scriptorium. "Father Philip, come quick. There has been a horrible attack!"

The priest looked up to see Eduardo, in the doorway, much agitated. Father Philip stood, wiping his fingers on a rag at his belt. "An attack? From the Apache or from the Navajo?"

Eduardo did all he could to hurry the priest along the corridor except pull on his sleeve. He had too much respect for Father Philip to treat him as a child. "Neither, Father. It isn't one of our boys. He is from the Sandia pueblo down the river."

Father Philip raised his cassock and ran behind the young man. They hurried across the village plaza and into the house behind the cantina. Abuelita Margareta Baca was bathing the forehead of a young man unknown to Father Philip. He couldn't have been more than fourteen, and he had deep lacerations on his face and chest. The priest could see there was more, as the boy was sweating as if with a fever.

"Margareta, what happened to this boy?"

The woman refused to look at the priest. She crossed herself, then went back to the cool rags in an effort to keep the fever at bay.

Father Philip turned back to Eduardo. "What do you know about this? Who brought him here to Abuelita Margareta? Why won't she tell me?"

Eduardo said, "Some men from Sandia brought him. He has been sick for two days, and they can do no more. Many feel that Abuelita Margareta can heal fevers."

The priest sat down beside Margareta. "Has he said anything?"

Margareta nodded. "Yes. He was raving about it. The thing that attacked him. I don't want to speak of it." She made the sign of the evil eye and went back to bathing the boy with a wet rag.

Father Philip sat down on a chair across from her and took her free hand. He noticed that she was shaking, and that surprised him. Abuelita Margareta was old, maybe in her sixties. She didn't know her age for sure. But as long as he had known her, she had been a rock of Christian faith. "Are you afraid? Because I am here to help."

A slow tear slipped down Margareta's face, and she nodded without looking at the priest or Eduardo. "Something I heard when I was a little girl. I was born near Mexico City, and we had a Nahuatl governess. When I was naughty, she would tell me stories of a great evil. She would not speak its name, but she would tell me that if I were not good, the demon would drag me away to a cave."

Father Philip squeezed her hand. "There are many stories told to naughty children, and yet, I have never seen a case where a child is dragged away by a demon. You have nothing to fear."

213

Margareta shook her head and began to sob. "I have heard other stories, Father. My friend, P'o-tsawa, from Sandia pueblo, is married to my cousin. She told me a similar story. When she was a child, they told her of Litsoof. She said it was evil, a giant."

Father Philip nodded. "Is that all?"

Margareta shook her had. "No. I didn't understand what this boy said, not all of it. They speak Tiwa at Sandia, and I don't know it. But he keeps saying, "Litsoof." It was as if he were trying to run from it in his dreams. He screamed and screamed." Margareta buried her face in her hands and sobbed.

Father Philip looked at Eduardo. "You know more of the Tiwa language than me. Do you know this word?"

Eduardo shook his head. "I have never heard it before."

Father Philip pulled up his rosary and began praying.

CHAPTER 20

Bernalillo Hacienda
Nighttime, July 1635

Eduardo was awakened by a tap on his window shutter. It was very dark out, and the heat of the day had subsided. He moved silently over to the casement and peeked out.

He saw his friend, Ok'uwa'enu, who had recently recovered from fever. "Oku, what are you doing here?"

The young native looked left and right before replying. "I came to warn you. The Jicarilla are dancing the war dance. They think that the white men have stolen their youths. They come to burn your village."

Eduardo said, "Where did you hear this?"

Oku looked for anyone else listening again, and whispered, "They came to our village last week and searched. They said two boys were stolen. But they didn't find them. My father sent me to watch them. I heard them singing and shouting. They will come at dawn."

Eduardo said, "I understand. I will tell my father."

When the drumming stopped, and the Apache ran screaming from the council fire, they only had a short distance to the village of Bernalillo. But the Ironskins were not surprised as the Apache had hoped. The village was barricaded, and torches lit the area outside the barrier. Don Federico and Teniente de Bances met the Indios with muskets pointed at them.

Don Federico nodded at Baji-delier, who had been known as Raymundo, and the boy shouted in Apache. "Stop. What do you want?"

Kuruk, shaman of the Jicarilla shouted back. "We are here to rescue our children. Open the gate, or die in fire."

A couple more muskets were shoved over the barricade. Baji shouted again." Your children are not here, and we lost a little girl yesterday in the reeds near the river. We found prints and signs of a struggle, but nothing we could follow. We are also victims. How do we know you're not trying to appear innocent of these kidnappings?"

The young men behind Kuruk growled and shouted at the accusation, but he held up his hand, and they relapsed into silence. "We have searched other villages, but not here. Where else can they be?

Don Federico stepped down from the barricade, opened the sallee port, and stepped out, unarmed. Teniente de Bances stepped out behind him, pistol in hand. Don Federico took his kerchief out of a pocket and waved it over his head, then stepped forward four paces. "Chief Kuruk, you have lived near us through the spring and into the summer. You have heard of others whose children were kidnapped. We have suffered losses, as have all people on the Rio Grande. If you want to search, please come forward with one other, and search. But please leave the warriors here at the barricade.

Kuruk frowned but then nodded. He pointed at Kogen-lii, and the two stepped forward. They were allowed to enter, and they stepped through the sallee port with Don Federico. The Teniente stayed outside the barricade and watched the Apache warriors, and the muzzles of muskets remained pointed at the war band.

It took some time, and the moon was westering before Kuruk and Kogen-lii stepped out of the sallee port. Kuruk held up his spear and shouted at the Apache band. "They are not here. We must go home."

✳ ✳ ✳

That night, Father Philip spent extra time in the chapel. The problem of abducted children and missing men had been addressed at the council meeting after Christmas, and for a time it appeared to ease off. In the deepest winter months there were no abductions, and in the spring only one or two from the whole territory. There were still resentments and finger pointings throughout the community, but Father Philip knew these human reactions would not be eradicated.

But now, in the heat of summer before the monsoons, children and youths, usually around the age of ten to fourteen, boys and girls, were disappearing again. The Tewa accused the Apache. The Navajo accused the Keres. The Apache accused the Spanish. But as they edged toward all-out war, no trace of children was found.

Today, he prayed for the children and for the people. There was a great evil loose in the land. It did not help that the summer was hot, and the rains didn't come in time to save the tender squash in the fields. And a mysterious illness was sweeping through the villages. Women, men, all were susceptible to the lung disease.

Finally, as he stood up from his prayers, he knew what to do. They needed to talk to everyone, to plan. He would call a meeting, a singing.

Bernalillo Cocinas
July 1635

They met near the Great River, north of Bernalillo. This was a wide place in the river with ample banks near good water. It had been a trading spot for time out of memory. The Navajo, the Jicarilla Apache, and leaders from two Tewa pueblos, a Keres pueblo, and two Tiwas met together. The Zuni refused to come for they were certain they were superior to anyone else. The Hopi were too far away and refused to come as they had not had any abductions.

Bitter rivals were sworn to temporary peace and camped on opposite sides of the river. Father Philip almost despaired of getting this contentious group together at all, and he knew it would only last a matter of days. He directed Baji-delier to build a bonfire in a place where everyone could gather around the fire in a circle.

Finally, they were able to begin. Father Philip, as the most neutral, was to address everyone first. He stood with Don Federico Bernal, the Alcalde of Bernalillo, Pimp'opi, elder of the Tewa from Nambe, and Kogen-lii, chief of the Apache. All others had agreed to listen to these elders before deciding.

Pimp'opi, stooped and grey, stood up to the bonfire. He raised a painted gourd, and with the rattle, chanted ancient words that no one else understood. Then his voice became the familiar singsong of the storyteller. "Long ago, when I was a boy, my grandfather told me of a time when the Hewendi, the Ancient Ones came to this earth. The ancestors of humans were living down below in a world under the earth. They weren't humans yet; they lived in darkness, behaving like bugs. Now there was a Great Spirit watching over everything; some people say he was the sun. He saw how things were down under the earth, so he sent his messenger, Spider Old Woman, to talk to them. She told them that the Sun Spirit wished better for them than what they had, and that she would lead them to another world. When they came out on the surface of the earth, that's when they became humans. This we all know. But my grandfather told me the rest of the story. There is another, that lived with the humans under the earth. When Spider Old Woman led the humans to the world above, Tsisdvna, the Dark One, would not go. He didn't want to leave his darkness. He didn't want to answer to the Sun. We have been taught not to speak of the Dark One, because it could summon him in the night, his domain. That is the end."

Then Kogen-lii stood before the fire, and raised a wand made from the leg of a deer. "Hidatsa and White Painted Woman came to the earth and married. They had thirty children, but the man was ashamed of having so many so he hid half of them under the ground. Those hidden children became demons. That is why we are taught to avoid the darkness in deep caves."

The crowd was silent, then they started murmuring. Father Philip stood up next to the fire. "Not all of you may know, but we have a young man here that Abuelita Margareta nursed back to health. He was brought here by his Tiwa brothers. Ok'uwa'enu, come and tell what happened to you and Oji-ok'u."

A young man, in his fifteenth year, stood from the crowd and came into the light of the fire. He had a large scar on one side of his face, and he walked with a limp. Before speaking, he shot a guilty look at his pueblo elder, Pimp'opi. "We were up fishing in the creek, near the cave of the old bear. It was almost dark, and we were preparing to go home when we heard sounds in the canyon. Ku'nfayte laughed at Oji and me because we were afraid of the noise. I told Ku'n that we were forbidden to go in the cave. It is a place of hot spring. But Ku'nfayte laughed and called us worms. He said real men would go in the cave, and not be afraid of a few bats and snakes." The young man stopped talking, like his throat was choked up. There were no tears, but his eyes were limpid in the firelight.

When he got control of his voice, he went on. "Oji and I went in, expecting to be carried away by demons at any moment. It was unpleasant. Ku'nfayte stayed at the mouth of the canyon, calling us names, and laughing at our fears. We made a small torch, but it didn't show us very much. We came to what we thought was the cave, but it was a wall of dead brush hiding a turning of the canyon. It went back much farther. The air stank of sulfur and death, and we were choking. Oji was ahead of me with the torch. He ducked under a low entrance to the cave, and I heard him gasp. Then he turned and started running. I asked him why, but all he said was, "Run!"

So I ran. I was ahead of Oji-ok'u, and I could hear footsteps coming behind him. I heard shouts, but I didn't understand them. And until we came to the turn in the canyon, it was very dark, and we stumbled. Then we turned and saw Ku'nfayte on the ridge above the canyon. I felt as if they were right behind us, and I heard Oji cry out. Then we were out, running down the arroyo. Ku'n saw us running, shouted that we were little girls. Then he heard our pursuers, and he started running as well. He didn't catch us, and when we reached the lip of the arroyo, we looked back. He was lying in a pool of blood, dead in the sand. Oji and I hurried home, but he was also wounded, with deep scratches. He is still in a fever. That is the end."

There were shouts and rumbles in the crowd, and some accused others of lying, of having men in the cave.

Then Don Federico stood up. He was the highest ranked civilian left after the rest of the Spaniards evacuated after the war. He had a land grant and was the mayor of the little village of Bernalillo. Most of the men there respected Don Federico because he was fair to soldiers, natives, and his own people, and treated all as equals. As he stepped toward the fire, all others quieted to hear his words.

Don Federico stood with his back to the fire and looked over the assembled men. "I have listened to the account of Ok'uwa'enu, and I believe him. There is more to that cave than ancient stories and tales to tell naughty children. We have a great evil among us." He stopped speaking, and let everyone think about that.

When the rumble of voices got louder, Don Federico continued. "This is not a threat of our neighbors. This is something that your forefathers warned you of long ago. This is an evil from ancient times. Father Philip, last year, you received writings from the future, from a town in Germany. I know you have read them again and again. Is there anything in them that can help us here? Is there a part that tells of the destruction of a monster?"

Father Philip stood next to Don Federico and addressed the group. "Don Federico, I have searched but have not found any reference to an ancient evil. When I resided in Rome, long ago, I knew of a group that was kept secret. I only knew because my cousin was recruited by this brotherhood. They were dedicated to fighting and killing monsters and demons that attacked the church. But none of them are here with us, and I don't know how we could contact them. We must face this challenge by ourselves."

Don Federico nodded as Father Philip stepped out of the firelight and sat down. "That means that we need a plan. I propose that we have an expedition of men, from all of our groups, who can go into this cave together and destroy what they find there."

The crowd murmured again, and everyone was talking. Then, near the back, a young man stood up. It was Teniente Raum Santiago Angel de Bances. He walked toward the fire. Don Federico acknowledged him. "Don Raum, we recognize your strength of will and your training. What have you to say?"

221

The Teniente stepped into the light of the fire and turned to look at the gathering. "Don Federico, I volunteer to lead this expedition. I am young, but I am the only officer you have left. I understand tactics and have command experience. I call for others to volunteer to protect us from this Evil."

Before Don Federico could respond, others stood as well. All were young warriors, strong and savage. Ok'uwa'enu stood as well. "I will go back to the cave. I will show you what my friend Oji and I found. I want to help destroy what attacked us. I want to help find the missing children."

A cheer went up from the Tiwa people there, and as other young men moved to the front of the gathering, their people shouted as well, until there were thirty young men near the fire, and all the people in the river valley were shouting.

Carlos Tapia and Pepe Montoya had attended the meeting by the river for a good laugh. They were not at all interested in the reasons that the Indios were trying to kill each other. They were more interested in where they could find more alcohol. Father Tómas kept too sharp an eye on the sacramental wine, and they were fond of the mescal they got from the locals.

Now, the two miscreants were in a shed by the river where they stored things they had stolen. Carlos and Pepe had come to the point in their lives that they no longer wanted to do anything difficult or strenuous. There were moments that they appeared to be working, but it was never the case. They worked at minimum, and then, only to earn enough for more mescal and more women.

They were watching the sunrise after a particularly riotous night. "Hey, Pepe, I heard a rumor, but there was one word I didn't know. Did you learn any new words from that woman you were with all last week? You must have talked to her a little."

Pepe was picking at his teeth with his dagger. He looked at his partner and grinned. "I learned some words, but Carlos, she was a Navajo."

Carlos ran his fingers through his thinning black hair. "Well, what did you learn? Maybe the rumor I heard was in Navajo."

Pepe grinned and put his knife away. "We didn't spend a lot of time talking, and I don't know much Navajo. But she was whispering something to me about Litsoof. Isn't that what that kid over at Abuelita Margareta's said, you know, when he's raving from the fever? Litsoof?"

Carlos leaned a little closer. "That's the word! What do you think it means?"

Pepe shrugged. "As far as I can tell, it is something yellow."

Carlos laughed long and loud. Pepe watched him, forgetting about his teeth for the moment. Finally, he said, "What's so funny about yellow?"

Carlos was trying to dance in the small shed. "Pepe, if what I heard is true, we can go back to Spain as rich men. I was buying something from a couple of the men from out of the Jemez village, and they told me that they have legends of a scorpion, a really big one."

Pepe frowned. "How big? Like this stone?" he picked up a river rock, about the size of the palm of his hand.

Carlos squatted on his haunches to look his partner straight in the eye. "No, bigger. They said it was the size of a horse. And made of solid gold."

Pepe snorted, and went back to cleaning his teeth. "Size of a horse? There's not that much gold in this whole country. If there were, you know Cortez would be up here hunting for it."

Carlos shook his head. "I know they were probably exaggerating, but what if it was the size of a dog? That's still a lot of gold. They said it was solid, too, not hollow. Gold all the way through."

Pepe put his knife away, and his eye had that gleam he got when he had an idea. "Hey, you know those men that volunteered to go kill the monster? We could go with them, and when they are battling it we could look around for the gold."

CHAPTER 21

Cavern of Tocatl Coztic, Jemez Mountains
July 1635

Deep in the cave of Tocatl Coztic, in the stinking heat of a sulfur hot-spring, Posuwa-i knelt and bowed before a golden image of a scorpion. "Oh great Colōtl-cōzauhqui, destroyer of man and beast, Lord of the darkness. We grovel at the foot of your awesome power."

As Posuwa-i rose to his feet, he heard a snort behind him. Pinang-oi-yws stood next to the linen curtain that separated the image of Colōtl-cōzauhqui from the view of the altar. Pinang was from Acoma and didn't even speak in Tewa. Posuaw-i could hardly stand staying in the same room with the fool. He frowned at the jeering face of his fellow priest.

Pinang-oi-yws laughed at Posuwa-i. "You don't believe all this garbage, do you? This nonsense of a 'Lord of Darkness' is laughable."

Posuwa-i tried to pass his associate to enter the altar room, but Pinang-oi-yws grabbed his arm. "Do not ignore me. You know what I mean. Do you believe everything that the stinking foreigner has told you?"

Posuwa-i pulled lose and glared at Pinang. "Of course I do. When the priest Teopixqui came among us and taught us of the terrible power of the darkness, I believed him, and I still do. You are a hypocrite, for I have heard you profess belief, and yet here you stand, laughing and jeering in the very presence of the Lord of Darkness. I hope you are the next to be sacrificed."

Pinang-oi-yws snorted again. "You really have bought every whimsy that the old Nahuatl charlatan has told you, haven't you? Of course I professed belief when he came among us. After the white men lost the war and left, it was time for those with vision and superior minds to take control. This cult of the Golden Scorpion is the perfect disguise for us. We will be in control before the elders of the villages even know what is among them, and then those of us with the brains to see what is really happening will step up and rule over these fools."

Posuwa-i moved the curtain and walked away from Pinang-oi-yws. He vowed in his heart to stay away from the heretic.

Down in the cavern, beneath the altar, the cave of cages remained. Otfuwa Potiitsii was in one of the cages. She was the daughter of a shaman, and he had trained her in many of the practices. After all, she was already fifteen summers and a woman. Soon she would marry and raise warriors. So as she lay in the cholla cactus cage, she refused to give in to tears, or give up hope. Otfuwa didn't expect to be rescued. She planned to rescue herself.

The last time someone had come by with food, she had looked at the walls of her cage and seen that one of the sides was weak. It was lashed to a floor piece, but in the light she saw that the lashing was loose in that corner.

The next two days, she worked at those lashings by touch with her fingernails and with her teeth. Little by little, they loosened. And little by little, Otfuwa was closer to freedom. It would not be long.

Bernalillo Plaza
July 1635

The young warriors gathered in Bernalillo and prepared to confront whatever had infested the cave. It was in the mountains near Walatowa, one of the Jemez villages. There were many hot springs and caves up past the village. So they would need Ok'uwa'enu to show them the one where Ku'nfayte died.

Now, it was only days before they were to go. They waited for a favorable moon to please the Zia shaman, Nan-so-ge-unge. There were about twenty-five volunteers in all, some natives, some Spanish settlers, and even a couple of soldiers that had deserted the long column that evacuated to The Pass last summer. Teniente Raum was worried about some of the volunteers. He took the matter up with Father Philip. "Father, I don't think we should allow Carlos and Pepe to come with us. They are deserters and would just as likely kill us as be of any help."

Father Philip frowned. He was not the parish priest for Bernalillo, but many considered him to be the Father President of their community. He had a scriptorium here where he could study and write letters. Today was warm, and he longed for a breeze through his south-facing window. "May I call you Don Raum?" The Teniente nodded.

Father Philip pointed to a chair, but the young officer took no notice. So Father Philip stood. "Why exactly do you have these feelings of misgivings about Carlos and Pepe? I have talked to them, and while both of them may have some problem with sloth and drunkenness, they both have worked hard in the village for their keep. When they volunteered, I was encouraged that it was a sign that they can rise above the baser instincts and learn a more Godly way."

Teniente de Bances snorted; then his voice, which had started out respectful, became loud. "Father, you have a kindly heart, but those two drunken gamblers are not going on this expedition for saintly reasons. I don't know what the reason is, but I will find out, and then I will have them thrown out of the village, exiled. I do not trust them." Then he turned smartly on his heel and stomped out of the scriptorium.

Father Tómas peeked through the door after the young officer stomped away. "Father Philip, are you all right? I don't think that the young Teniente should have been shouting."

Father Philip put his hand on his colleague's shoulder. "You are probably right, Father. But I think that Teniente de Bances has a lot on his mind right now, so I am willing to forgive him. What do you know of Carlos and Pepe? I have not seen them in the confessional."

✳ ✳ ✳

The day came that all was prepared. Before the march began, Teniente de Bances watched as mothers cried and fathers laughed, sending their young men out. It was different for him, he had no family here. He was unsure if his father still lived, in faraway Spain. A little part of him began longing for his boyhood home. but he shut down the thought before it got started. He felt his choices in Spain were severely limited. So this was home now.

They left in the morning, with dawn still painting the eastern sky. It was not as early as Don Raum would have liked, but at least they were moving.

The first part of the journey was very routine. Raum rode a horse that had been found lame in a blind canyon. He had not wanted to risk Fausto, given to him by the fleeing Governor Ceballos. This gelding was young enough, and still wasn't accustomed to Raum's commands. But it was good to be in the saddle again.

They had a small burro carrying supplies and bed-rolls. Raum knew it would take some time to get back up in the hills far enough for this to be a mystery to these people. And he was not looking forward to supervising what some were thinking was going to be a summer picnic. He had a rumble in his gut and an ache in his healing shoulder and arm that told him this was going to be so much more. There was something out there, and it was evil.

* * *

The first day shook out all the kinks. Ok'uwa'enu was enjoying this trip. It wasn't like the hunting trips they were able to go with. Teniente de Bances wanted more discipline.

They were in for a four- or five-day trek. For the first couple of hours, a hoard of girls kept up with the group, laughing and flirting with the young men. Ok'uwa'enu watched the Teniente ride up and down the 'column' and tried to keep them together. But the natives had never moved in a disciplined manner, and the former soldiers, Carlos and Pepe, were not models of behavior either.

But as the day heated up, the visitors quit the pursuit and returned home. By mid-afternoon, it was just the volunteers, weapons, one horseman, and one burro. Ok'uwa'enu looked at the sun, edging toward the western horizon, They weren't in the mountains yet, but they loomed ahead. The closer hills were covered in cholla cactus and juniper trees, but the ones behind were blue, covered with pine trees.

Ok'uwa'enu, who know precisely where they were going, walked near the front of the column. The Teniente rode up next to him and then stepped down off his horse to give it a rest. "Well, we're finally on the way," he said.

Ok'uwa'enu smiled. They had become friends while both were recovering from injuries. "Yes, but with the blessings old Nan-so-ge-unge gave us, we should prosper."

"Ok'u, because of our late start, we aren't going to get even as far as Zia tonight. Do you know of any good camping spots ahead?"

Ok'uwa'enu looked ahead for a moment. "We need to camp on top of that mesa, the sky feels like rain, and this is an arroyo. I will go ahead and find a spot. It's a good thing we have plenty of water."

The Teniente nodded. "It has been so long without rain, I have a hard time imagining it."

Ok'uwa'enu jogged ahead of the line. The dust hung in clouds around his feet, and dried grass rattled in the constant wind. Ahead, the mesa rose over his head forty or fifty feet. It would not be easy to climb to the top; they would have to use one of the smaller canyons.

Mountains near Zia
July 1635

Teniente de Bances chose sentries, then settled down with his bedroll. He was not going to sleep; he had misgivings about this whole expedition. Little by little, the camp settled and went to sleep, with only one small fire burning near the watch post.

They were on a high ridge, in a zone between the Ponderosa pine of the higher altitude and the juniper near most Pueblos. So this was an area with a rare Ponderosa, a lot of scrub pinion pine, and some cedar and juniper. The ground had little grass, but the sand was comfortable for sleeping.

Don Raum reclined on his saddle and watched the darkness. He could hear crickets and the flutter of bats chasing mosquitoes and flies, and he heard a pack of coyotes in the distance. The moon was above them as they settled for the night, and Raum watched the moon cross the sky and settle in the west.

And there was still something in the air he couldn't identify. When the fifteen-year-old sentry from Jemez fell asleep, Raum kept watch. And in the cold and dark, before the sun touched the Sandia mountains in the east, he heard something. He heard footsteps.

Raum put his hand on his sword and waited. He heard it on the left and on the right, they were almost surrounded. Surreptitiously, he picked up a small round pebble and tossed it at the dozing sentry. The rock hit the young man's thigh, and he jumped up with a start. But everything was silent, and there were no more footsteps. Raum listened as the sky turned gray. There would be no attack tonight.

by Kevin H. and Karen C. Evans

CHAPTER 22

Jemez Mountains
August 1635

They traveled for the next five days and now walked through tall Ponderosa pine and smaller fir trees. Now Teniente de Bances' troop was straggled all along a stream in a steep canyon. It was broad daylight, and yet Raum was certain that he was being watched.

He turned his horse and ambled back to the end of the line where Ok'uwa'enu was walking next to the burro. The little beast was nervous, and Ok'u was trying to soothe it. "Now, be still, Pepito. You are not in danger with all these strong men around you."

Raum de Bances laughed, and Ok'uwa'enu turned quickly. It was obvious that Ok'u didn't know anyone could hear him. "Ok'u, I can see why Pepito has been so docile this trip: he has a good friend along."

The young native's face showed relief. "Yes, Teniente. I have always had a way with animals. They listen to my voice and know my heart."

Raum swung out of the saddle. "Don't worry about the other boys teasing you, Ok'u. I know the same thing. If I speak kindly with my horse, he is much more willing to obey."

They walked along in silence for a moment, each leading an animal. Then Raum whispered, "Don't look around, but I think we are being watched. Up there, on the ridge to the left." Then he laughed and slapped Ok'uwa'enu on the back as if he had told a joke.

Ok'u caught on quickly, and laughed as well. Then he whispered. "Yes, I saw a couple of faces above the rocks. We must move on with caution."

Raum laughed again and stepped up into the saddle. He leaned over like he was adjusting the bridle and whispered again. "Stay back here, and keep your eyes open. I'll ride ahead and see where they plan to attack us, probably a narrower place in the canyon."

Then he rode to the front and called a halt to rest and drink water. When the line settled onto the banks of the stream, Raum got off his horse and handed the reins to Carlos. At the same time, he whispered to the soldier, "Keep your eyes open, we may come under attack."

Carlos blinked, but before he could respond, the Teniente was gone up the stream. Carlos turned to Pepe. "Teniente says we are about to be attacked." And of course, that news was whispered down the troop.

Raum didn't care, he knew they would whisper and speculate while he was gone. It would keep them occupied and make the observers nervous.

It wasn't too much farther along when Raum saw the likely location of an ambush. The stream came around a gigantic boulder, and after that blind turn there was a waterfall, about four feet high. Raum muttered, "This is where I would set up to ambush someone."

He turned and was about to head back to his company, when he saw something out of the corner of his eye and ducked instinctively. Then he threw himself on the ground as an arrow buried itself in the tree stump near where his head had been.

There was a moment of silence, no birdsong or wind. The Teniente scrambled to his feet and ran down the bank of the stream. And then there was a hoard of screaming assailants behind him. He didn't take the time to look behind him, but threw himself through the brush and boulders towards his men. "Take cover, we are under attack!" And with that shout, he threw himself behind a bush and pulled his pistol. Then he took the opportunity to look around.

Most of the company was huddled behind bushes or rocks, facing upstream. He couldn't count the number of assailants, but it was more than ten. Some of the young men were stringing bows and readying arrows, but a couple stood in the open, unsure of where to go. They were the first casualties.

Raum spotted an archer crouching behind a rock and waited until the man stood up to fire. Then the Teniente pulled the trigger and sent a ball of flame full of lead towards the man's chest. He exploded in a shower of blood. Raum hunkered down by the boulder and reloaded his pistol.

Others in his party were shooting as well. And attackers were running into the clearing next to the stream with spears and hatchets. Raum shoved the loaded pistol into his sash, pulled his sword. "For Spain," he shouted, and threw himself into the melee. Those near the front of the column followed him, shouting.

✳ ✳ ✳

As always happens in any kind of a battle, suddenly there was no more enemy. Raum looked up and saw several bodies around him, and the only ones standing were his own party. It was exhilarating, but at the same time disturbing.

He turned and saw Ok'uwa'enu walking toward the stream with Pepito, leading the burro to get a drink. Others were coming toward him or groaning in pain from injuries. Raum knew what needed to be done and began issuing orders. "Ok'u, get that burro settled, then go check on the wounded. Okinga, you and Marcos check all the wounded and tell me who is missing. Has anyone seen Carlos and Pepe?"

His calm voice and clear direction was what some of these boys needed. Not many of them had faced a real battle and seen their friends wounded or killed, and they were dealing with the shock of it all.

The wounded were gathered in an open meadow, and they set up a small camp with a fire. Wounds were bound, and a small meal was prepared. Raum watched as some of the men dragged the five dead bodies of their attackers to the side of the meadow. They lost two and had two others seriously wounded, plus five with less serious wounds. Really, it was not too bad for a first encounter.

He walked over to look at the dead attackers. It was unusual, in that they were not all one thing. There were two pueblo men, two Apaches, and a Navajo. Raum had never heard of a group like this, composed of members from enemy groups. It was like someone had collected a group much like his own, which he had thought was unique.

He wondered at that, and knelt down to examine the bodies more closely. The first one was Apache by his dress and paint. He had nothing around his neck, but he had a pouch at his waist. Raum dumped it out on the ground and moved things around with his finger. There was some pollen, a carved turtle that was probably this man's vision creature, and a metal scorpion, about the size of a Real, the royal coin of Spain. Raum picked it up, and it was heavier than he had expected. It was a dull silver color, but was not silver or lead.

Curious, the Teniente went to the next man, a pueblo dweller. In the pouch at his waist Raum found another scorpion, almost identical to the first. And by the time he had finished with all the enemy dead, he had five scorpions.

Then he noticed Okinga and Ok'uwa'enu were standing nearby, waiting. He turned to Ok'u. "Do you need to tell me something?"

Ok'uwa'enu nodded. "We have counted everyone, and we are missing three. Nobody has seen Tush'yat, and we haven't found Carlos and Pepe."

The loss of the two deserters didn't surprise the Teniente. In fact, he had wondered to himself why they had stuck so long. But to hear that one of the Apache men was gone was disturbing. "Are you certain? He could have been wounded and crawled away. How far did you search?"

Okinga said, "Ok'u and I walked into the trees on all sides of this meadow. We saw the spot where Tush'yat fell. He only had a minor wound, to his leg. We saw sign in the grass that he was dragged away by two other men."

Raum looked around the meadow, and drew them away out of hearing. "I want you to keep this quiet, for the moment. Who in our party is the best tracker?"

Okinga looked over Raum's shoulder, because he didn't like to look anyone in the eye. "After Tush'yat, I guess it's me."

The Teniente nodded. "Good. You two follow the trail and let me know. Don't go out of sight of each other; we may still have enemies out there we don't know about."

The two young men nodded and left, and Raum went to examine his own dead.

* * *

The two young men were gone until late. Sentries were posted, and the only ones awake were the sentry and the Teniente. Ok'u and Okinga slipped back into camp and knelt near Raum. He sat up. "What did you find?"

Ok'u said, "Okinga followed the trail, even in the darkness. There is much moon tonight. We traced the drag marks to the next canyon, but there we lost it. The moon set, and there were only rocks, where they leave no mark."

Raum said, "Can you find this place again? I think that's exactly where we're going."

Both boys nodded, so Raum pulled the five scorpions out of his pouch. "Have you ever seen anything like this?"

Both young men leaned close to see what the Teniente held, then jumped back, startled. Ok'u was fumbling for a talisman in his pouch, and Okinga whispered something as they both scooted back away from Raum.

This surprised the Teniente. "What's wrong? What are these things?"

Ok'uwa'enu kept his head down as he answered, not looking at the objects in Raum's hand. "They are forbidden. We have been taught as children not to look at or touch those. You must ask a shaman. We will not speak of it."

Cavern of Tocatl Coztic, Jemez Mountains
August 1635

The throne room in the cave of Tocatl Coztic held, of course, an elaborate throne, usually occupied by Teopixqui, the high priest. He took all his meals there, breathing deep of the burning mineral smells that rose up out of the earth or the scented smoke from his brazier. He had his pet jaguar at his feet, with a golden collar, and his huge bodyguard, Diego Gutierrez, behind his left elbow. Gutierrez had deserted from Santa Fe almost five years earlier. Now Diego was never far from the high priest, day or night.

It was here that Pinang-oi-yws found Teopixqui and bowed himself to the ground. "O Serene One, we have returned."

The Serene high priest looked idly at the man on the floor. "I can see that. Did you destroy them? Did you take captives?"

Pinang-oi-yws didn't raise himself from the floor. "Serene One, we have one captive, but the rest of the expedition was not successful. They are not destroyed."

The Serene high priest threw his goblet against the far wall, showering Pinang-oi-yws in chocolate and spices. "Fools! What happened? Why couldn't you kill or capture all of them?"

Pinang-oi-yws raised up, and his face was a mask of fear. He tried backing out of the reach of the enraged priest, but the cavern wall was behind him. The Serene One was on him quickly, beating him with a staff. "The Lord of Darkness will have you all. He will feast upon your liver. And you shall watch him as you scream into oblivion."

Pinang-oi-yws struggled to escape. "Serene One, it was not our fault. They have some kind of wizard with them. One of the long-beards. He cast a spell on us and discovered our plan. He fought like a puma and killed five of your faithful servants himself. It is he you should attack. Without him, they will fail."

Unknown canyon, Jemez Mountains
August 1635

As darkness settled over the mountains, Carlos and Pepe peeped from behind a rock. "Pepe, it's a good thing you saw those men drag away one of our Indios. Otherwise, we would never have been able to find them in this part of the mountain. See, even from here, the entrance is hidden from sight."

Pepe was sitting on a boulder, sipping beer from his canteen. "I don't know, Carlos. There were a lot of them. How are we going to get in and steal any gold with all those men in there? It sounds like too much of a risk to me."

Carlos reached over and snagged the canteen and took a long pull. "I see what you mean. We don't want that." They sat and swapped the canteen back and forth until it was empty. It was already dark, and they were drunk, so it seemed like a good time to bed down for the night.

Carlos was already asleep, when Pepe sat bolt upright. "Carlos?" he asked in a loud whisper.

Carlos didn't open his eyes. "Go to sleep, Pepe."

"Wait, I have a great idea. We will sneak in after we see everyone leave. Then we will have the whole place to ourselves."

Carlos leaned up on his elbow. "Pepe, that's the first good idea you've ever had."

Pepe took that as a slur, and grabbed Carlos and tried to get him in a wrestling lock. They tussled until they both forgot the slight and fell asleep.

CHAPTER 23

Jemez Mountains
August 1635

Ok'uwa'enu sat on watch duty, very late. But he didn't have trouble staying awake because fear sat at his elbow. He didn't grow up in a pine forest, and there were strange shapes and strange sounds in the darkness. He kept expecting to see a red-eyed attacker come flying at him from the darkness. The watch fire had burned down to red coals in white ash, so he got up and put another piece of wood on the fire.

Finally, dawn arrived, and he could see that in the daylight, all of the monsters and attackers that he'd imagined turned into stumps and rocks. At sunrise, he said his prayers and washed his face. Then he went to check on Pepito.

That is where the Teniente found him. "Ok'u, I have decided that we need to get the wounded out of here. What's the nearest village?"

Ok'uwa'enu thought for a moment, then said, "I think that Winat'api'iwe is nearby, but I will check with Pan'ri'koti."

Raum nodded and went to saddle his horse. It only took about twenty minutes to get the wounded ready to move. One of the seriously wounded was on the Teniente's horse, and the other was dragged behind on a lashed carrying sling.

The walk to the village was more arduous than Ok'uwa'enu was expecting, because the mountain here was covered by large boulders, sharp volcanic gravel, and shrub. And just as they would think they were making good time, their path would be cut by deep canyons where they would have to find a safe way down and back up for the horse. So, although they only had to go three or four miles 'as the dove flies,' it took most of the day. By the time they arrived, in Winat'api'iwe, they were all bone weary, and the wounded were pale and non-responsive.

After they had been settled and checked over by the shaman, the chief of the village and other elders came to the Teniente and sat in council around the fire. Raum took the opportunity to show them the scorpions taken from the dead men. "What can you tell me about these? When I asked some of the men with me, they were frightened and told me I must ask the shaman."

The elders of the village examined the metal scorpions, but none would touch them. And for some time, nobody said anything. The chief sat smoking a long pipe.

Finally, in the sonorous voice of a storyteller, the shaman began. "Long ago, when the mountains were small, there was an evil spirit. We do not know his name, for we were told never to speak it lest he could hear us. This evil spirit is a spirit of pain and torture and delights in blood and suffering. He did much damage with the birds and the fish, but when he came to coyote's den, Father Coyote had much magic and dispelled the evil."

The shaman stopped and pointed at the metal scorpions Raum had sitting on a cloth in front of him, then continued the story. "So the spirit wanted a body like Coyote had. Then he could not be dispelled. He chose this creature for his form on the Earth. He poured his spirit into the body of the insect, and it responded to the depth of his evil. It became larger than any of his species. He became larger than Coyote. He became a force to be feared. But he did not know the power of the sun, and he felt weakness in his body in the sunlight. He loved the night, but he wanted to be powerful always. So he sought out the deep places of the Earth and called others like him to follow.

"From that time, men with the same black hearts found their way to him. And they are sent out to do his bidding in the light of the sun. These men that attacked you were from the cave of the evil spirit."

The shaman stopped speaking, and Raum nodded, then rolled the scorpions up in the red cloth and stashed it in his shirt. He was left to wonder if the shaman's story was an allegory or if they were really going up against a scorpion the size of Pepito.

✳ ✳ ✳

In the morning, Teniente de Bances got up before dawn with a headache from whatever was in the drink they gave him. He didn't remember it tasting like strong alcohol, but the blinding headache was reminiscent of the rum he'd had in the Carib on the way to Nuevo Mexico del Norte. He drained his canteen and walked toward the stream to refill it and wash his face. The sky was a clear blue, and the only sound was of waking birds. The breeze was cool and pleasant on his head, and the pain eased.

As he returned to the village, he met Eduardo Griegos. And that surprised him. Eduardo, at eighteen, had been kept in Bernalillo. "Eduardo, what are you doing here? How did you find us?"

Eduardo grinned. "Múh-shidáá, the shaman of the Apache, came to us with a girl. She is Jemez, and how she got all the way to the Jicarilla village is not known. When they found her, she was feverish and delirious. She had wounds on her wrists and ankles and small cuts along her ribs. But most of all, she spoke about an evil spirit and a cave."

Raum's eyes got wide. "A cave? Does she know where it is?"

Eduardo laughed. "Yes, that's the rest of the story. She led us here late last night. She says it is very near."

The Teniente was already hurrying back to his equipment. "Where is she? I need to talk to her. Does she speak Spanish? What does she know?"

Eduardo had to run to keep up. "She is in the chief woman's quarters. She's not irrational any more. She speaks a little Spanish, and I speak a little Keres. We get along all right. I had to come along because she was frightened of all the other men."

Teniente de Bances turned and grabbed Eduardo's elbow. "Then you must come with me; I want to speak with her. And you must keep her from being so frightened."

They came into the center of the village, and Eduardo led the Teniente to a group of women. "Otfuwa Potiitsii, come meet the Teniente."

A young woman, between sixteen and twenty, stepped up to Eduardo. She was beautiful, with thick black hair and eyes like polished onyx. There was fear in those eyes as she turned them in the direction Eduardo pointed.

At that moment, Teniente Raum de Bances was captivated. Not only was she the most beautiful woman he had ever seen, she seemed somehow familiar. He only saw her eyes for a second, then she dropped her chin and looked modestly at the ground.

So Raum squatted down in the way most of the Indios did when they wanted to talk. He looked at Eduardo and said, "Ask her to tell me what she knows, but don't upset her.

I will know if you ignore me."

Eduardo seemed a little disturbed by the look in Raum's eye. But he spoke a couple of words to Otfuwa. Raum couldn't take his eyes off her. The angle of her jaw and the soft planes of her face sucked his attention from his mission.

Teniente closed his eyes, and shook his head. What was the matter with him? Never before had the thought of a girl drawn so much of his attention. So he didn't look at her, he looked at Eduardo.

The sound of Otfuwa's voice threatened to destroy Raum completely. It was soft like velvet but as light and colorful as silk. Raum started breathing through his mouth in an attempt to wrench his mind from this girl. He knew that if he got close enough to smell her, he would be lost.

Eduardo listened and then said, "She says she was kidnapped from her village. She doesn't remember that, but she woke up in a cave. She couldn't see anyone else, but she could hear voices. Some were men, and she could hear whimpers of women or children."

Raum smoothed his goatee. It was a recent whim to grow it, and he was not used to it, so he would stroke it when he was deep in thought. He was not aware that he did so exactly has his father had done. "Ask her how she escaped."

Eduardo nodded, and passed the question to her with a few words and actions. It took a moment or two, but she spoke again. Eduardo said, "I think she said she chewed her ties." He stopped again and asked, and Otfuwa nodded, and mimed chewing at her wrist. "Yes, she did with her teeth."

Raum stood up from where he crouched and nodded. "That is enough. We need to get on our way."

Eduardo nodded, and spoke to Otfuwa, and she nodded as well. "She says she will come with you."

Raum frowned, but nodded. "Eduardo, you are responsible for her. You must protect her as we travel."

Eduardo nodded and put his arm around Otfuwa's shoulder. "Don't worry, Teniente. She will be safe." The hale and healthy of the troop packed up and left the village in less than thirty minutes.

Cavern of Tocatl Coztic, Jemez Mountains
August 1635

The scouts returned to the cave of Tocatl Coztic before sunrise. And Pinang-oi-yws stood in the entrance, waiting for them. "What have you found? Where did they go?"

Mazhiia, the chief scout, tried to brush past the man in the doorway. Pinang-oi-yws grabbed his arm. "Do not trifle with me, Mazhiia. What did you find?"

Mazhiia looked at Pinang as if he were sheep dung. "You take on airs of importance that you do not deserve. Take your hand from me immediately, you Keres swine." The two men glared at each other for a moment, then Pinang-oi-yws dropped his hand.

That was when the Serene One, Teopixqui, with his huge shadow Diego, came to the entrance. "Mazhiia, what have you found?"

Mazhiia and all the scouts dropped to the ground in obeisance, with Pinang-oi-yws dropping a second later. Mazhiia intoned the chant of welcome to the Serene One. "Great is your power, and the cries of suffering echo around you."

The high priest touched Mazhiia and motioned for him to rise. From his knees, Mazhiia reported, "Serene One, they returned to the village of Winat'api'iwe with their wounded. They were there still when we returned."

The Serene One flicked his feather wand at an imaginary fly. "Did they receive reinforcements? Do they have muskets or cannons?"

"No, Serene One, only some old men, who arrived near midnight. They will be no threat."

The high priest backhanded Mazhiia and laughed. "What do you know of threat, fool? Old men? Like a shaman? You have no idea what they can do."

Mazhiia recovered, and threw himself to the ground again. "Forgive me, Serene One. There were three old men, two young men, and a woman."

The high priest whirled, and started toward his throne room. "Bring a captive, we will need all the power of the Lord of Darkness to repel their attack." He stopped and gestured to Pinang-oi-yws. You, poser. I know your heart. Bring the knives and you will perform for me. Mazhiia, go back out, with your men, and keep an eye on them. Send reports every hour. Do not fail me."

Unknown canyon, Jemez Mountains
August 1635

Pepe woke up with the sun in his eyes. He had to struggle for a memory of where he was or what had happened the night before. He stretched and saw Carlos sprawled near him, sleeping with a rock for his pillow. Pepe couldn't resist, and he kicked Carlos awake.

Carlos jumped up with a knife in his hand. Pepe laughed and rolled on the ground. "You should have seen the look on your face, Carlos."

Carlos put his knife away and wiped his face on his sleeve. "You are a real clown, Pepe. One of these mornings you are going to wake up with your throat cut and laugh yourself to death."

Pepe stood up and started to gather his things. "You would have laughed if it had been old Nacho that I kicked, now wouldn't you? He was so arrogant."

His gambit worked, and Carlos smiled. "I would have kicked old Nacho myself, just to see him jump."

They packed up their campsite. It wasn't much: the beer was gone and so was their food. Carlos eased over to a boulder and peeked over at the entrance of the cave. "Pepe, look."

Pepe peeked over the edge, and saw about twenty men leaving the cave. "Carlos, did you know there were that many in there?"

Carlos shook his head. "No, but I'm glad that we didn't sneak in there last night."

Pepe snorted. "You were too drunk last night."

That was too much for Carlos. He had a hangover, and sometimes he really hated his partner. He swung a roundhouse aimed right at Pepe's head, and they fell to the ground wrestling.

The ground rumbled, and they heard a roar, as if the heart of the mountain had a throat. They froze on the ground with Carlos' hands around Pepe's neck. The rumble stopped, and there was silence. Even the wind and the birds were holding their breath. Pepe whispered, "Carlos, what was that?"

Carlos let go of his partner and eased back up to his observation spot. "Pepe, when I was young, we lived in Italy, and the ground rumbled like that. The old ones said it was the mountain re-awakening."

It was still very quiet. They watched the entrance for a long time. Finally, Pepe sniffed. "Carlos do you smell that? Sulfur."

Carlos stood up. "The men left. If we are going to find any gold, we should go now, before the mountain decides to belch and everybody is killed."

Jemez Mountains, near Cavern of Tocatl Coztic
August 1635

Teniente de Bances rode his horse at the rear of the line to keep anyone from straggling so far behind. He felt strongly that, today of all days, they would need to be closer together to give themselves safety in numbers. Also, he was struggling against his own thoughts. Never had he been this distracted over a mere girl. He was having trouble concentrating. He looked up to where Eduardo and the offending female were walking and saw Eduardo hold the girl's hand to help her over the roots of a large tree. He had to force his eyes down at his saddle. He liked Eduardo as a friend and respected the role the young man played in dealing with the threat of more kidnappings. But he had trouble wrestling the green-eyed beast of jealousy.

The trail was difficult, and it helped that he had to pay attention to the ground. He had to trust his horse to find footing. They were climbing a steep slope of broken stones and scrubby trees.

Ok'uwa'enu stepped next to Raum's horse and looked up at the Teniente. He was silent for a moment, then said, "She is beautiful. I was not expecting them to bring a woman on this dangerous mission."

Raum was gritting his teeth in the effort to not turn and look at her again. "I agree with you, it is foolishness. She will only slow us down and be a weakness in our fight. They could have gotten her to tell the way. I do not understand why those elders brought her all the way out here. It is too dangerous."

Ok'u looked back at the girl, and at Eduardo, holding her hand. "Teniente, can I tell you something?"

Raum was diverted, and looked down on the young Indio walking beside his stirrup. "Yes, Ok'uwa'enu, we are friends. You can tell me anything."

Ok'u frowned. "It is not a worthy thought, but it burns in my heart to see her with that boy. She is beautiful and of my people. She deserves a man, not a," he hesitated, then continued, "a village boy. Especially one of your people."

Raum had to catch the laugh before it exploded out of his chest. He had been raised to think of the indigenous people as less than himself, and yet here he was drawn so strongly to Otfuwa. And he knew that laughter would destroy the trust that Ok'u had in him.

He turned it into a cough. "I agree with you, Ok'uwa'enu. Like people should be together, and it is offensive for them to mix. I must have a word with Eduardo later." Then he watched Ok'u from the corner of his eye. The young man nodded and moved to the front of the column. Raum thought, "I will have to watch myself with that one, after this. He sees too much."

Nearby in the Jemez Mountains
August 1635

The acolytes of the Lord of Darkness moved silently through the brush. Mazhiia had trained his guerrillas well. They were quiet and deadly. They came to the rim of the mesa, and only Mazhiia peeked over, in the shadow of a tree.

The column of men surrounding a girl had stopped for water. They were by the side of a tiny spring, filling their canteens. The heat of the day made them move slowly. And this made Mazhiia smile.

He could see no sentries watching; everyone was focused on the cool water. He gave his men hand signals, and they moved down two arroyos, one on each side of the party at the spring. Mazhiia smiled again, and his eyes glittered in the shade.

CHAPTER 24

Jemez Mountains
August 1635

D on Raum de Bances felt the prickling on the back of his neck and surreptitiously scanned the perimeter. As he knew he would, he saw movement uphill from their location. Inwardly he cursed, knowing that he had not set sentries when they stopped to rest. His preoccupation with the girl had played havoc with his awareness.

He leaned over as if to pick up a pebble, but he whispered to Ok'uwa'enu. "We are being watched. Don't frighten anyone, but be prepared."

Ok'u acknowledged, and stretched and yawned, looking at the horizon himself. The Teniente stood and idly tossed the pebble into a bush near Eduardo. When the boy looked up to see where the pebble came from, Raum gestured slightly with his jaw and casually checked the primer of his pistol in the sash at his waist.

There was a blood-curdling scream directly up the canyon from Raum, and it seemed as if the forest opened up and spat out ravening attackers. They were frightening to look at, painted in black and red war paint. Their hair was mixed with some red substance, and looked as if they had all been dipped in blood. All were screaming and throwing javelins. One spear killed an Apache man of the search party instantly.

Eduardo hustled Otfuwa Potiitsii back into the hollow created by the water from the spring, then stood in front of her and pulled out his father's sword, which he had been trained to use. Raum glimpsed Ok'u wielding his war club expertly, and then his attention was diverted as a huge Indio hurtled from a giant boulder by his side. The man was shouting some kind of chant and brought some kind of tube to his lips.

Raum ducked to the side before he knew what he was avoiding. The man blew into the tube, and a small feathered dart flew towards him. By the time the dart hit the boulder behind him, Raum was not there. He dove to the ground, pulled his pistol, and fired.

The ball hit the huge Indio dead center, almost over the heart. The red-painted Indio didn't seem to notice and didn't halt his maddened rush. It was as if the pain meant nothing to him. Raum dropped the pistol, pulled his sword, and settled his stance. At least he was on a relatively level piece of ground.

The Indio lost his blowpipe and pulled a deadly-looking war club. It was vaguely sword-shaped, but had stones jutting along the blade like jagged teeth, all of something shiny like volcanic glass. The Indio came at him, and Raum fended off the blade, slashing for the man's elbow. When he nicked his arm, Raum knew that this attacker had never been trained in swordplay. The man's attack strategy was to use his powerful shoulders and arms and force his attack on a weaker subject.

But the Teniente had been trained by the sword-master of Toledo. Raum placed his sword high and put his dagger in his left hand. He automatically dropped into a guard position. It was as if the world slowed to a trickle, and everything was red. With his dagger pointed forward as a guard, he put his sword up behind his shoulder and waited for his attacker to make a move.

The Indio watched intently and was still chanting something. He stood up on his toes, then charged in where Raum crouched.

Raum caught the war club with his dagger, and he was thankful that he was wearing his heavy leather buff coat, because even with the block, the long club grazed his shoulder but did no damage. Raum took the opening to stand up straight, and the sword came off his shoulder in a dropping snap.

The Indio was not wearing much except paint and a loincloth. So Raum's sword left a bleeding gash diagonal from his shoulder to just under his ribs. The cut started bleeding, and still it didn't slow the Indio's attack, so Raum brought his sword around for another blow, this time to the man's neck and shoulder.

Now the man's blood was spraying, and still the Indio came in on the attack. The man grabbed his club with both hands and pulled back for another strike. He threw all his power into the blow but was a little off-balance.

Raum sidestepped the blow, and as the Indio hurtled past, Raum delivered the final stroke to the back of the man's shoulders.

The Indio fell to the ground in a puddle of his own blood. Raum turned his attention to the rest of the melee. To his surprise, there wasn't much for him to worry about. He saw bodies scattered in the visible area and five or six attackers running into the forest.

The heat of battle was still hot on the Teniente's brow. He glanced at his forces. The attack had been quick and brutal, with at least eight on the ground. He didn't take time to see if they were dead or alive; he still had more than ten ready to fight. "We must be close. Those who can fight, follow me. The rest of you see to the other wounded."

Without looking back, he started up the slope in the same direction as the fleeing Indios. As he climbed the hill, he reloaded his wheel-lock, settled his sword in the scabbard, and drank from his canteen. His mind raced as he planned strategy for the next encounter.

Cavern of Tocatl Coztic, Jemez Mountains
August 1635

Carlos and Pepe stepped around the bush-screened retaining wall, and, for the first time, saw the size of the cave. They could smell the sulfur, and an odd sickly-sweet smell that made Pepe uncomfortable. "Carlos, I don't like this. We shouldn't enter this place; it is evil."

Carlos grinned. "So, next time you are near a priest, go to confession. But for now, I want to see their gold."

They stood for a moment, listening. When they didn't hear footsteps or voices, Pepe shrugged and stepped into the cave. Carlos looked at the entrance and saw a pot full of torches, so he picked one up and lit it. "Come on, Pepe. You saw them all leave. There's nobody left."

Pepe said nothing but was content to let Carlos go first. Maybe the evil Indios would kill him first. They walked down about thirty feet, and the cave seemed to come to a halt until Carlos saw an opening on the left side.

They didn't have to squeeze through as Pepe had thought, but it turned at such a sharp angle that it appeared to disappear.

Carlos and Pepe came into a large gallery, lighted with torches along both sides. No one was there, so they walked confidently down the center of the court. At the end, they could see a large chair covered with a feathered cloak and draped with strings of jewels.

Carlos stared at the jewels as if they were a beautiful woman. Pepe grabbed the torch as it tumbled from Carlos' nerveless fingers. Then he stood and watched as the man knelt almost reverently and fingered the amethyst and topaz.

"Carlos, if you're going to take them, come on. They will be back any second." Pepe was nervous. There was something here, like some deep sound just out of his hearing, and it made him uncomfortable.

Carlos didn't respond, so Pepe nudged him with his toe. "Carlos . . ."

When Carlos snapped to his feet and shoved a dagger under his nose, Pepe's voice trailed off to silence. Carlos said, "I will come when I'm ready. I don't answer to a little sneak like you."

Pepe backed away. In all the years, and misadventures they had shared, he had never seen Carlos like this. "Sorry, hermano. I'll just go over here now."

Carlos had turned away and didn't seem to hear the end of the sentence. He had gone back to the allure of the jewels.

Pepe took the torch and started looking for other ways out of the court. As he walked near the wall, he found that the doors were deceptive, hidden by tapestries or cleverly hidden in the shadow of two torches. Some of the ways were locked or smelled of death or vermin. He didn't want to go down those ways.

Finally, he came to a lit hallway and went down it. There was something inviting that kept him walking. He began to recognize that there were paintings of men and scorpions on the wall. But when he focused on them, it was difficult for him to tell what the paintings encompassed. It was as if he could recognize them from the corner of his eye, but when he turned his attention to them the contents began to swim and blur.

Then Pepe became aware of noises. He had thought that they were in an empty cave, that all the men who usually lived here were gone. But he heard guttural chanting that sent shivers up his spine.

The scream stopped him dead in his tracks. It was the kind of sound that clutched at your heart and threatened to empty your stomach all over your boots. He dropped the torch and considered the possibility that he would have to turn and run. He was not sure he could make his feet move. He felt as if he would not be able to scream, either.

It was not until his back hit a wall that he noticed his feet were shuffling backwards, away from the noise. And it was almost exactly at that moment that Carlos grabbed his arm. Pepe's scream almost matched the other, if not in timbre, at least in heartfelt terror.

Carlos pulled Pepe and hissed in his ear. "Shut up or they will come and investigate the noise."

Pepe put his hand over his own mouth to silence the whimpers that were still seeping out of his lips. He turned and looked at Carlos.

The other man was already moving down the passage, toward a door. "Come see what I found. I think it's the treasury."

The thoughts of gold and jewels somehow pushed the fear out of Pepe's mind. His heart was still certain that they would be eaten by something horrific at any moment, but he endeavored to ignore it and followed Carlos.

He found his partner up to his knees in scorpion figurines, all made of gold. Pepe became hypnotized with the dance of torch light on the gold.

CHAPTER 25

Canyon of Tocatl Coztic
August 1635

eniente de Bances lead the charge up the hill, and those behind him were pumped as full of adrenaline as their leader. The Indios in red and black paint fled with no thought of subtlety or secrecy. And Raum knew exactly how to use that to his advantage. They pursued almost on the heels of the frightened attackers and so were able to see them disappear.

Raum halted and took stock of his forces. He had fifteen young men, Spanish and Indio, who were trained warriors, and none had serious wounds. He didn't know all of them well, but was pleased to see that Ok'uwa'enu was unscathed. Raum was impressed with the youth's courage and abilities. His heart sank, though, when he saw Eduardo, and trailing behind him was the girl, Otfuwa Potiitsii. He shook his head and pushed the thought out of his mind. It was not his concern at this moment whether the girl survived the coming encounter.

He peeked over a small hillock and saw that nobody was around, so he stood and signaled for the others to follow.

They came around the bushes to the entrance of the cave. Raum checked his wheel-lock and shook it to make sure the mechanism was tight and the powder secure. Then he shoved the pistol into his sash and pulled his sword and dagger, and everyone else readied their weapons. Then the Teniente nodded, and they charged through the entrance of the cave, shouting and waving weapons.

They burst into a long anteroom and found about twelve men there, still looking pale and frightened. When they heard the shouting and saw the attackers following Raum, they froze for that critical second before grasping their clubs and spears.

And that was when the Teniente was upon them. He was savage with his dagger and sword, so caught up in battle that it was if his arm was independent of his thought. He slashed and chopped his way to the other end of the chamber, then turned to find that they had dispatched the followers of the Scorpion.

His energy was still high when he came to the end of the room and saw the narrowness of the exit, but he stopped. This would be the place that the denizens of this place would hold their defensive line. It was not a place to rush into blindly.

Canyon of the temple of Tocatl Coztic downhill from entrance

When the Teniente had chosen to chase their attackers, Eduardo was right behind him. This was his first real battle, and he had managed to kill the man that endeavored to kill the girl who crouched behind him. That was a marvelous feeling, like nothing else he had ever felt. Now for certain, Otfuwa would see him as a desirable adult.

He turned to the girl, and said, "Otfuwa, you stay here with the wounded. They will protect you, and I will go and help the Teniente." That was all. He didn't even stop to see if she understood or agreed. It seemed to obvious to him that nobody would want a helpless female in a battle situation. He hurried after the company.

Behind the Throne Room, Temple of Tocatl
Coztic
August 1635

Carlos was wading through the pile of golden scorpion figurines and stopped in the middle of the room. He had gold piled up past his knees, and he had been picking up the small pieces and pouring them over his head like water. Pepe watched from the door and was laughing and jeering, when Carlos stopped. The Spaniard was no longer laughing, and after a moment, neither was Pepe. Carlos looked closely at the little scorpion in his hand. "Pepe, look at this. There is something sticky on this gold."

Pepe could see Carlos' face and didn't want to step into the room with the scorpions. Carlos looked pasty and pale, even with his two-day growth of whiskers. And red splotches were appearing on his hands and face. Carlos didn't seem to notice yet. "It's sticky, and it smells bad. Pepe, what's wrong with you? Why aren't you coming in to see?"

Pepe was ready to wretch himself. The red patches were starting to seep and then to bleed. Carlos seemed unaware that something was eating through his skin. Then Carlos began to shudder. "Pepe, what's happening to me? Help me!"

Pepe couldn't move from his place by the door. It was as if he had been nailed in place. He watched as his friend began to convulse and then fall on the floor with foam pouring from his mouth. As he fell, a new avalanche of golden scorpions shifted and began covering his shaking body with gold. And to Pepe, in the wavering torch light, it looked as if the shadow of a giant scorpion stood hovering over the gurgling form that had once been his friend. He saw the shadow of the tail raise up, as if to deliver the coup de grace.

That was when Pepe gained control of his feet, and he started running. By now, he couldn't tell where the exit was, but it didn't matter; he wanted to be somewhere far away from here.

Sacrifice altar, temple of Tocatl Coztic

The inner sanctuary was in the heart of the mountain, and the high priest was deep in his sacrificial trance. Pinang-oi-yws stood at the head of the altar, ready to hand Teopixqui, the Serene high priest, anything he may need. Diego Gutierrez stood at the other side of Teopixqui and glared at Pinang. They were almost to the climax of the ceremony, and Pinang knew that there could be no interruption. The drugged ecstasy of the acolytes made them unaware of their surroundings.

The drummers and other acolytes were swaying and chanting, almost as overcome as the high priest. The only one in the chamber who was not swallowed up in the madness was Pinang. He was nervous that he would make a mistake. The last man who didn't perform his duties perfectly died on the spot. He tried hard to concentrate, to feel the rhythm of the drums, to throw himself heart and soul into the heat of the ceremony.

But something was irritating a part of his mind, and he couldn't focus. Something was working to get his attention. Something was wrong. Pinang closed his eyes, and turned his head slightly, for a better angle at the irritating noise. He could hear slight screams, but that was generally true.

Then he heard it. The sound of sword and club. There was a battle in the temple! What was he going to do? Should he interrupt the ceremony that was in full blast now, and would be for the next hour or so, or should he let it play out, and hope that the Serene high priest didn't notice?

And then it was too late. The curtain at the back of the altar room was torn off its rail and thrown to the floor, and there stood the very sorcerer who had disrupted their previous raid, wearing a beard and morion.

At the Mouth of the Temple of Tocatl Coztic
August 1635

Otfuwa Potiitsii waited until Eduardo was out of sight over the hill before she moved. The men who were wounded paid no attention as she slipped out of camp to the top of the hill. From there, she could see Eduardo hurrying after the Teniente and his men. For a moment, she turned and looked back at the scene behind her, blood, death, and wounded men seeing after each other. That was not the place for her. She was the daughter of chieftains and shamans. She would not sit by as a docile child. This was an evil place, and she would go and chan, and call down the wrath of the gods.

So she made sure both of her knives were secure, one at her waist and one in her boot.

And then she ran after Eduardo.

✳ ✳ ✳

Teniente de Bances strode through the corridors of the cave complex like a destroying angel. No acolyte could stand before him. He saw a curtain at the end of the room, and he tore it down.

What he saw sickened him at first. There was some kind of altar, with acolytes around the sides, chanting and drumming, swaying in some kind of ecstasy. Tied down on the altar was a young man, dressed in rags. He had many small cuts all up and down his arms and legs. Blood ran down the surface of the altar to a bucket at the end.

By Kevin H. and Karen C. Evans

When the captive spotted Raum in his good buff coat and helmet, the man struggled to escape his bonds at his wrists and ankles, but to no avail. Raum barely glanced at him, then strode into the room, sword raised. The melee came into the altar room, and there was no more time for thinking. Raum was like a machine, cutting, stabbing, kicking, killing by instinct. And the men of his party, armed with war club spears, were inspired by him and rushed in as well.

Temple of Tocatl Coztic
Altar room

Teopixqui, the Serene High Priest of Tocatl Coztic, came out of his trance to see the great wizard of the white men, in a steel Morion, wreaking havoc on his weaker vessels. He ignored that for a moment, slit the throat of the captive, and took a handful of the spraying blood and drank it, hot and sticky. He could feel the power of the scorpion thrilling throughout his body. He threw the stone knife at the wizard and grabbed for his ceremonial war club, the macuahuitl that hung from his belt.

Teopixqui didn't bother to look at Pinang or Diego. Either they would live or die, and neither possibility was important to the high priest. By now, the warrior in the helmet had killed his way to the high priest and took a swipe with his steel sword. The high priest stepped in with his macuahuitl and took his best shot at the man's face and neck. The obsidian edges left bleeding lines on the wizard's face, but the man stepped away too soon for the club to break any bones. Now the fight was on in earnest.

✳ ✳ ✳

When Pinang-oi-yws saw the high priest occupied with the white wizard, he stepped to another curtain and hurried out of the room. He was

262

certain that there would come a moment in the melee that Diego would try to kill him. And if not the Spaniard, the high priest would take the opportunity to offer him to the Lord of Darkness.

If any of them survived, he might be labeled as a coward, but he didn't worry about that now. He came to a new corridor and ran as if the dogs of hell were on his heels. And in all likelihood, they were.

Temple of Tocatl Coztic
Near Throne Room

Eduardo had not kept up with the Teniente as he had wanted to, because just as he was about to charge in with the rest, he stepped on a large pebble and turned his ankle. The adrenaline was surging strongly in his veins so he barely noticed the pain, but the injury did slow him. By the time he got into the body of the cave, the corridor was empty, and he couldn't tell where everyone had gone. He stopped for a moment, listening, and could hear shouts and the clash of weapons, but the echoes of the cavern made it difficult to tell where the noise came from.

He turned left towards what he thought of as the loudest fighting. He was wrong, but it probably saved his life. He was moved along a corridor, heard a noise, and turned in time to see

Otfuwa Potiitsii slip into the corridor behind him. He felt anger and frustration that she didn't stay where he had told her. It was probably true what his father told him, that women and cats will do as they please. He pushed his worry from his mind and headed for the noise.

When he turned around, he almost ran into an Indio carrying an ornate dagger. The man was hurrying toward the entrance and almost ran into Eduardo as well. The two saw each other, and Eduardo took an inexpert swipe at the man with his father's sword. The sword missed the man's head, skipped off the shoulder, and nicked the man's arm near the wrist. That began to bleed, and the man raised his dagger to attack Eduardo.

The young Spaniard was in for it all. He found that his feet arranged themselves. All the things his father had taught him came together, and his body knew what to do without him thinking about it. He grasped the long handle of his sword with both hands and charged at his enemy. It did not occur to him that this man, though about the same height, outweighed him by maybe thirty pounds. Today, Eduardo was a giant.

Temple of Tocatl Coztic
Altar room

Diego Gutierrez saw the Serene high priest, Teopixqui, cast a spell on the Teniente in the Morion and was suddenly afraid that de Bances would recognize him. Diego had been at the palacio just before the rebellion of the Pueblos, on a mission from Teopixqui, and had glimpsed Raum as the Teniente was first reporting for duty.

Suddenly, the betrayal of his Spanish roots burned in his gut and made him doubt the choices he'd made ten years ago. It was a momentary thought, but in that moment, his target, Pinang-oi-yws, had slipped away. Diego was unsure whether he should follow the coward Pinang or jump to protect Teopixqui. And that was another moment of hesitation. The huge altar was between him and the high priest. Other attackers followed the Teniente into the altar room.

Diego picked up his six-foot halberd and charged the young men attacking. Not making a choice was making a choice. And at least this was something tangible he could do; he pushed thoughts of anything else from his mind. Shouting, he charged the Spanish attackers.

CHAPTER 26

Temple of Tocatl Coztic
Near entrance

Otfuwa Potiitsii saw Eduardo engage with the large man. He was very tall for an Indio, and something in her memory struggled to place the man's face, but she could bring no association to mind. Otfuwa, who also wanted to avoid the heavy fighting, had been in these corridors before. She headed for the captive cave. Today, her name was not Otfuwa Potiitsii, but Vengeance.

Temple of Tocatl Coztic
Lost in dark corridors

Pepe didn't halt his headlong flight but ran blindly through the chambers and corridors. Wherever he heard sounds of fighting, he headed a different way, so in all actuality, he was bouncing back and forth like a rubber ball.

Then he found himself back at the ornate chair, which was covered with a feathered cloak. Again, the jewels there caught his attention, and he stopped running. He snuck over to the chair and began stuffing jewels into his pants, which were tucked into his boots, so they were like one big pocket. He was so occupied with the baubles that he didn't hear anyone come into the room.

Temple of Tocatl Coztic
At the entrance

Ok'uwa'enu was not a stranger to violence. He was tall for a Pueblo, and well muscled. Although he was only in his fifteenth winter, he fought alongside the men of his village. Twice the Apache had attacked, to plunder or to seek revenge for some imagined slight. He had blooded his club just last spring. So today, when Teniente de Bances had charged up the hill after the fleeing men, Ok'u was one of the first to follow.

Inside the cave, all the young Indios, who had been raised with stories of this kind of evil, felt a strange power in the air. But Ok'u pushed that from his mind. He followed the Teniente into the corridors.

It wasn't long before they had no time to think. They were attacked again and again by men in groups of three or four, and the Teniente didn't hesitate to attack.

For Ok'u, it felt good to wreak some vengeance for his friend, Oji-ok'u. He had received word from Otfuwa that Oji had died from the poisons in his system, and Ok'u was ready to kill those responsible.

Temple of Tocatl Coztic
Altar room

Raum de Bances had been running and fighting and had not met much opposition to his running and fighting style. Until now. This high priest, with the wicked toothed club, was a canny opponent. And yet, Raum was thrilled with the challenge. At last, here was someone worthy of all his skill.

The Teniente grinned like a madman as he caught a blow from the club with his dagger and feinted for the man's head. The sword was deflected off the high priest's headdress, and Raum drove in with the dagger in his left hand. Destreza, the fight training he had received as a youth, was serving well today.

Temple of Tocatl Coztic
Entrance

Pinang's day went from bad to worse. He felt he was almost within sight of the exit cave when he ran into this young white man. The lad was pale and appeared to Pinang to be frightened, with a sheen of sweat on his face.

When the youth took a stance with his Spanish steel sword, held in both hands over his head, it almost brought Pinang to laugh out loud. Somehow the boy reminded him of a six-year-old with a stick. He reached to his belt to grab his vicious war club, then felt a moment of pure panic when he found that it was not on a lanyard at his waist. All he had in the way of weapons was his ceremonial dagger, still grasped in his left hand.

Pinang took a deep breath, then charged the ridiculous little figure in front of him.

Temple of Tocatl Coztic
Back corridors

Otfuwa Potiitsii had explored many of the passages of this cave complex after she had escaped from her cage. She moved confidently through some of the back ways that few used. She came into a large, poorly lit cavern, with wooden cages lining one wall and supplies or other sundries lining the other. She went from box to box, cutting through the thongs that lashed the doors shut on the cages. Slowly, the captives came out and blinked at her. One of the girls asked, "Otfuwa, is that you? Why did you come back? What are we going to do? We will never get past the men at the entrance."

Otfuwa watched the freed captives slowly crawl from their cages, and then she moved to the entrance of this cavern and looked past the edge, listening. There was no noise of pursuit, and she could still hear shouts and fighting in other parts of the complex.

Otfuwa whispered, "Yes, Vi'vif. It is I. I came back with help. We have men from all the villages, as well as some Spanish. They are fighting the evil ones now. We can go for the entrance, and nobody will stop us."

She looked over the group that had crawled out of the cages and realized she was the oldest. There were eleven in all, seven girls and four boys, about twelve years old. None of them were in the best of health. Some were sick from the bad food and water, and a couple had been drugged in anticipation of taking them to the altar room. "Ke'twpuje, you help those two boys, Naakii and the other one, as we go. Giusewa, you bring up the rear. Find a stone or something for a weapon. We will never go back into those cages; we're going home."

She looked them over one more time, then led the way out of the captive cave.

Temple of Tocatl Coztic
Altar room

Teniente de Bances was toe-to-toe with an opponent like none he had ever encountered. This man was every bit as trained with his weapon as Raum was with his own. Nothing else mattered to these two, and they battled, each trying to find or create a weakness in the other.

268

The men that came in with Raum succeeded in killing all the acolytes they met, but they didn't know if they should try to help the Teniente or go find another fight.

Raum was starting to feel the strain of battle. After all, he had fought outside where they'd stopped for water, then ran uphill and fought his way through the cave complex to this point. He was starting to feel a slight twinge in his side as his lungs struggled to keep up with his fight. And when he looked into the eyes of the high priest, he could see the glaze of drugs burning in the other man's blood. There was no fatigue or hesitation in the attacks. Raum had to do something to change the balance of the fight.

He started moving backward, towards his men, and he was thrilled when he saw the high priest staying engaged, moving forward to keep up with Raum. It should be possible to signal one of them to take a shot at the high priest. But as far as he could tell, no one was looking his way.

The high priest took the opportunity when Raum's attention was slightly diverted to push the attack. He pulled a small dagger from his waist and slashed at Raum's arm.

The movement caught Raum off guard and left a slice along his forearm, Raum ignored it and feinted for the high priest's body, then snapped up into a head shot. He was lucky, because although he had not aimed it well, the sword nicked the priest's ear.

The high priest took a step back, felt his ear, and came away with his hand covered in blood. His eyes glittered as he licked the blood from his fingers and stepped in to attack again.

Temple of Tocatl Coztic
Entrance

Eduardo was starting to realize that this man fighting him was older and more experienced and that he was bigger and stronger than Eduardo. At first, he had been elated to see that the man carried only a dagger. He had thought to make swift work of this evil Indio.

But that was not what happened. Eduardo realized that there were some things his father had told him that he had not listened to closely enough. The man was vicious in his attacks, leaving nothing to chance. Eduardo found himself backed into a corner, defending his life with every stroke. And he was beginning to tire. Already, his arms felt as if they were on fire and weighed more than the heavy sword he wielded.

Temple of Tocatl Coztic
Corridor outside altar room

Ok'u delivered a deadly blow to the back of the head of a man trying to stab his cousin, Okinga. The man fell, and Okinga followed another trying to escape the altar room. Ok'u ran to follow him, then felt as if someone was behind him, and he turned.

The shadow of a huge man fell over him, and he looked up to the tallest Ironskin he had ever seen. And not only was this man tall, but he was massive, as if his mother's bread oven had stood up off the ground and come to kill him.

Ok'u gripped his club and tried to consider how he was going to kill this man. It would be difficult, because the moving mountain seemed to be made all of muscle. This man was carrying a tall thing that looked like a spear or javelin, except for the blade on the front of it, something the white men called an 'ax'.

He saw that the mountain of a man was looking at him and smiling. That angered Ok'uwa'enu, and he gripped his club and shouted one of the curses he had learned from his grandfather, meant to frighten demons and evil men. Then he charged the giant.

Temple of Tocatl Coztic
Dim corridors in back of cave

Otfuwa led the captives toward the entrance and didn't encounter anyone until she reached the throne room of the high priest. She had only been through this way once, and then she had hidden behind a curtain for hours until the room was empty so she could escape.

Unfortunately, it was not empty now. She peeked into the room and found a fat Spaniard stuffing jewels into his pants. She must have unknowingly made some kind of noise as she stepped into the room, because the man jumped as if he had been stung, and he pulled a sword and pointed it toward her.

Otfuwa froze as he glared at her, but then he put the sword back in its scabbard. "Oh, it's that little Indio girl who came along on our expedition. Are you here alone, child? Perhaps Tio Pepe will take care of you."

She didn't like this man. She wouldn't acknowledge that she understood Spanish, but she suspected that it wouldn't matter. He had always smelled of drink and filth from the first time she had laid eyes on him, and she'd had a deep dislike of him ever since then. She wondered where his comrade was but didn't ask.

Otfuwa looked over her shoulder at the captives behind her, but the line straggled out of sight in the darkness. She thought that if she could go around this evil man, they could get the rest out.

So she tried to slip by the man, but he was too fast for her. His large hand closed on her forearm, and he dragged her closer to himself. She glimpsed Okinga at the curtain she had stepped through. The girl hunkered down on the floor and signaled for the rest of the captives to do the same.

Then Otfuwa couldn't worry about the captives, because she had her own problems. The Ironskin wrapped his other arm around her shoulders and was fondling her hair and neck. She could smell his fetid breath on her as he examined her up and down. "No reason for you to leave so quickly now, is there? You are a pretty one, even if you are only an Indio."

The man tried to pull her against his chest, and she twisted her wrist from his grasp. That brought a look of disgust from him, and he grinned with a wicked light in his eye. "Hey now, you don't have to be afraid of old Tio Pepe. I'll treat you real nice, you just watch." He tried to grab her again, but she was backing away with a dagger in her hand.

Otfuwa didn't speak a lot of Spanish, but she understood a good amount. She also knew instinctively that this man meant to harm her. She waved her long dagger at him and started edging toward the door at the entrance of the cave.

Pepe didn't like being threatened by anyone, especially by a girl he wanted as badly as he suddenly wanted this one. He took three large steps and reached over to grab her knife out of her hand. Then, before she could run, he grabbed a handful of hair on the back of her head and pulled her close to him again. This time, he gathered her wrists in one hand and let go of her hair so he could fondle her breast.

Otfuwa glanced over to where she had left the captives. They were all so young and suffering from abuse. Ke'twpuje was at the doorway but didn't seem to want to come and help her. The other girl had dark circles around her eyes, and looked as if she only had strength enough to escape the cave. Otfuwa wriggled, trying to get away from the Spaniard, but he pulled her close again and slapped her. "Stop struggling, this won't take long. You girls are already giving it to the young bucks, right? Why can't Pepe get a little of you as well?"

Otfuwa had no idea what he was saying, but he was holding her wrists in a vice-like grip, and his breath was disgusting on her neck. She was on her own for this struggle.

*   *   *

Vi'vif, daughter to the chief of Santa Ana, admired Otfuwa's courage and decided that she could not let a Jemez girl be the only one to show courage. She was near the back of the group of freed captives, and she heard a noise. She inched back from the group and hid herself in a shadow.

What she saw surprised her. It was the old servant of the high priest. He was old and pitiful, with a hump on his back and nothing to wear in this damp cave but a loin cloth. But today he was skulking along the corridor, not looking at her or the other captives. He seemed to be hurrying and looking over his shoulder.

Vi'vif felt on the ground until her fingers closed on a fragment of sharp stone. Now she had a weapon. This enemy could come closer, and she would not panic. Her heart was beating faster, but somehow, everything slowed to a crawl.

*   *   *

Quimtchin hurried along the passage. He had been to the captives' cave and found it empty. He had seen the Ironskin wizard fighting with Teopixqui. He was fighting two fears. What if the white wizard won and killed Teopixqui? What if he didn't kill the priest, and Teopixqui beat him for losing the captives. Quimtchin had decided that it was time for him to run away.

He was running along a passage, looking over his shoulder in case the white wizard killed Teopixqui and would come for him next. He didn't see the girl in front of him until too late.

Temple of Tocatl Coztic
In entrance corridor

Eduardo felt so fatigued that he was ready to die. A small part of his mind wished he could remember the last rites, but his memory of that was blank. He stood with the sword over his head, protecting himself from the flaying blows of the enraged Indio.

Then the cave shook as if it were a dog, shaking off water after swimming in the river. It knocked the Indio from his feet. But because Eduardo had been driven into a corner, he was able to stay upright.

Before the Indio had recovered, Eduardo had run over and placed his sword at the man's throat. And yet, in that instant, Eduardo hesitated, finding that he couldn't just run through the man's throat with his sword.

The Indio looked into Eduardo's eyes and laughed. Then he ripped the sword from Eduardo's grasp and threw it across the cave. Eduardo started to run, and he could hear the Indio's laugh echoing behind him in the darkness. The Indio was already on his feet, reaching for Eduardo's arm. Eduardo lost hope.

CHAPTER 27

Temple of Tocatl Coztic
Altar room

Teniente Raum was in a fight for his life. He could tell that he was tiring, and the cut on his hand from the tooth of that stone sword was sending such shooting pains up his arm that it was hard to concentrate on the battle. He wondered fleetingly if the blade had been poisoned, but if it had, there was nothing he could do at the moment. Raum continued to fight.

His focus had narrowed now to the point that he only saw his opponent and vague impressions of the room around him. He did notice the room moving oddly, but he wrote it off as fatigue. This opponent never seemed to tire.

Temple of Tocatl Coztic
Corridor at entrance of altar room

Diego saw the young man with a war club and decided that he wasn't going to kill this one, but capture him for the sacrifice. He knew that the fire he saw in this one's eyes would feed the Lord of Darkness well.

He was a little surprised when this one chanted an old curse and came running at him. That didn't happen very often; usually they ran away from in fear.

Diego licked his lips in anticipation of a good fight and stepped up with his poleaxe.

Temple of Tocatl Coztic
Throne Room

Otfuwa understood very little of what this nasty man was mumbling against her skin, but she intensely disliked him. She writhed again, attempting to loose his hand from her wrists, but that only brought two swift blows from his fist.

She went limp, hoping that would distract or deter him, but nothing seemed to slow him down. Otfuwa breathed in shallow puffs as she considered what her next move would be.

She made her decision when the man threw her onto the floor and began pawing at the hem of her dress. A fire of anger and disgust burst out in the center of her being, and she was willing to die to kill this man and stop him from doing anything disgusting again.

She waited for him to get positioned just as she wanted, then drove her knee sharply between his legs. He grunted and rolled off her, then rolled on the floor, mumbling in Spanish that she didn't understand. She didn't need to understand. She ran and picked up her large dagger she had dropped on the floor and walked back to where he was still moaning.

She dropped to her knees with the dagger in her right hand and grabbed the beard on his chin to force his head up. But before she could pull the blade across his throat, his hand caught her wrist again and forced the dagger from her hand. There was nothing she could do; he was so much stronger than her.

Now the man was up off the floor. He kicked her dagger to the center of the room and then held both her hands against the floor by her head. Otfuwa prayed in her heart to any gods that would hear her.

Through the rock underneath her, Otfuwa felt and then heard a deep rumble, as if the entire mountain was coming to life in answer to her prayer. And then the entire room seemed to tip sideways and shake. She knew the gods had answered. She pushed against the man with her feet and kicked him in the stomach. With the shaking of the room, he had become unsteady. He fell to the floor and tried to rise again.

By now, pieces of the ceiling were falling, and Otfuwa grabbed a rock that almost hit her. She rolled to her feet, and grasped this stone in both hands, then brought it down full force on the back of the man's head.

She felt his skull crack, and the man fell as if he had been shot. She pulled the small knife from her boot and deftly slit the man's throat, then left him in a pool of his own blood.

She ran over, and scrabbled in the fallen rock until she found her large dagger, then went back to the entrance of the room. The captives were huddled there with their heads covered. All eleven of them were together. Otfuwa held up her large dagger and shouted, still thrilled that her attacker was dead and she lived.

"Come, children. The gods have answered my prayers! Stand up, we must hurry before their wrath closes us into this mountain."

The captives caught her enthusiasm and stood as well, then followed her at a run towards the entrance.

Temple of Tocatl Coztic
Lost in dark corridors

Eduardo ran through the shaking corridors, and the huge Indio was close behind. For a little while, he took left or right turns somewhat at random, so had no idea where he was when he came to a turn in the corridor and saw a horrific scene. There was an altar with a dead man bathed in blood and dead acolytes and soldiers littering the floor. For a moment, he didn't see anyone living until he noticed the Teniente circling with someone in bloodstained robes. The Indio had a war club, and Raum was fighting with his sword and dagger.

Eduardo watched for just a second, then remembered that the Indio was still behind him. He picked a club from the floor and turned to see where the man had gone.

That was the moment that the mountain shook again, and this time there was a huge roar as if from a gigantic throat. He looked into the eyes of his opponent and realized that he saw fear for the first time.

That inspired Eduardo. His mind cleared, and he remembered the words of his father. "Technique is not the important thing. What is important is facing your opponent without fear. Strike true, and you will prevail."

He realized that he wasn't afraid. He found new strength, and so, instead of hiding against a wall and shaking, he strode toward his opponent with confidence. His arms no longer burned, and his breathing slowed.

The huge man frowned at Eduardo's new-found courage and started backing up. He was muttering something and kept stealing furtive glances toward the Teniente. But Eduardo wasn't falling for some kind of trick, he never took his eyes off the Indio. He knew he had this.

Eduardo took the club in both his hands, raised it over his head, and then grinned. That was too much for the Indio, and the big man turned and ran back the way they had come in. Eduardo ran after him, hot to finish the fight.

Temple of Tocatl Coztic
At entrance of altar room

Ok'uwa'enu didn't stay in one place but was constantly moving. He realized that his only hope of surviving the encounter against this giant was to be agile. He noticed that he had faster footwork. And that was especially true when the room shook from side to side. Pieces of the ceiling fell around them, and Ok'uwa was able to dodge all but the smallest pieces.

The big Spaniard did move slowly, but he was by no means stupid. His eyes glittered with wily intelligence and guile. He waited until Ok'u stepped back, almost falling when his foot hit the hand of a dead man. That was the moment when the giant released his blow with the big ax. And if Ok'uwa'enu had been slower, it would have cleaved his skull in half. As it was, he got a glancing blow from the shaft of the long ax that left a contusion on one shoulder.

By that time, there were not as many others around them fighting, as they had either been killed or had run away. And Ok'uwa'enu began to feel that the outcome was not as sure as he had thought.

Temple of Tocatl Coztic
In dark corridors

Eduardo ran to follow the Indio, but when he turned the corner, the Indio had vanished. It was as if the empty corridor had swallowed him whole. It was difficult to see for certain because the earth tremors had knocked torches from the wall. So Eduardo walked the length of the corridor, searching. The floor shook again, and this time Eduardo lost his feet and fell.

He still couldn't see the huge Indio, but his hand felt something cold. So he reached into the shadow, and drew back a sword. Not only was it a sword, it was his father's sword. Encouraged, he went to search the other end of the corridor.

The quakes were coming more frequently, and Eduardo began to wonder if he should try to get back to the entrance before the whole thing came down on his head. Then he saw a curtain twitch, and he knew he had the man. The coward was hiding in a darkened room waiting for Eduardo to tire and leave. Eduardo tore down the curtain, and saw the man in the back of the room. The boy couldn't tell if the Indio still had a weapon, but it no longer mattered. He strode forward with his sword held high. And the Indio rose to his feet, holding a wicked war club. Maybe, thought Eduardo, the man had come in here to retrieve it.

Eduardo looked the larger man in the eye, and then winked. He remembered his father telling him that many Indios were surprised at that kind of control of the eye muscles.

The amazing thing is that the wink worked. The Indio was focused on Eduardo's face, so the boy kept his head level and delivered a perfect blow. The sword contacted the Indio's body just under the left arm, from upper left to lower right, severing the spine and killing the Indio.

He cleaned his father's sword on the Indio's robe and ran back to see if the Teniente needed help.

✳ ✳ ✳

Vi'vif raised the sharp stone over her head, and when the old Indio running in the passage came close, she brought the rock down on the man. She had been aiming at his head, but when he saw her moving, he jumped, and her sharp rock hit the man in the neck. But it was more than she expected, when blood appeared, then sprayed the side of the cave.

Now, she didn't hesitate. She stepped up to the man and beat his head with the rock over and over. It was a moment before she realized that he was no longer struggling to stand. She stood up and saw the bloody mess his head had become, and her hand began to shake. Her stomach clenched, and if she had eaten that day, she might have lost it.

But Vi'vif clenched her teeth, dropped the rock, and ran to catch up with the other children escaping from the cave.

* * *

Quimtchin didn't see the girl, but he saw something moving by his head. He was not as spry at avoiding a blow as he had been in his youth. The sharp rock caught him under the chin. He tried to back away from the attack, but the blood made his feet slip, and he fell to the floor. The last thing he saw was a small woman or girl attack him with a rock. He knew he would never see the jungle again.

Temple of Tocatl Coztic
Altar room

Raum became aware for the first time that it was the room that was shaking and not himself. He saw the statue of the Golden Scorpion at the head of the altar shiver and dance on its resting place. And Raum had to wipe his eyes, because for a moment it looked as if the statue was alive. But since he didn't see it again, it was probably the smoke and dust that caused it.

But the distraction of the statue looked like the beginning of the end for the Teniente. Already his left hand was stiff and swollen around the scratches from the war club. And when he glanced away from the high priest and towards the statue, the Indio took the opportunity to bring a blow against Raum's head.

He would never know if it was skill or luck, but Raum saw the blow and moved, so the club didn't crush his Morion into his head, but instead landed on his left shoulder. At first he brushed the attack off as ineffective, until he found that he couldn't move his left hand. He watched as the poniard fell from his nerveless fingers. And then the pain hit him, and he fell to his knees.

As his eyesight was fading and he was losing his hold on consciousness, he thought he saw an angel step up to him and help him to his feet. Raum tried to prepare his soul to enter heaven, but his mind was leaden and not very responsive.

Something was placed at his lips, and he drank by instinct. Then he realized that it wasn't water, but brandy. The liquid burned down his throat, but worked well to clear the confusion from his mind. Raum looked up to see Eduardo at his side.

"Teniente, come. The quaking is worse. We can't stay here." Eduardo was attempting to get Raum to his feet.

The Teniente was still a little fuddled. He said, "Where is the Indio priest? What happened to him?"

Eduardo struggled with the Teniente, who was not standing and not cooperating. "What priest? There's nobody living in here. We must go."

The Teniente struggled to his feet, but leaned heavily on Eduardo. "We can't leave yet, the evil is still here. The Golden Scorpion. It must be destroyed."

Eduardo wasn't listening. Raum thought that perhaps the confusion in his mind was also in his tongue and the Eduardo didn't understand. Raum mustered a deeper effort. "We can't leave without destroying the evil."

Eduardo said, "Teniente, if we don't leave now, we will be destroyed with the evil; the mountain is shaking. This cave is going to collapse. Can you walk on your own, or do I need to carry you?" As Eduardo spoke, he hustled Teniente de Bances out of the altar room, down the corridor, towards the entry.

Temple of Tocatl Coztic
Corridor near altar room

Ok'uwa'enu was backed, step by step, by the giant Spaniard. He could keep out of the way of the large ax but not get in close enough to do real damage with his war club. And he was tired. It was hard to get a deep breath with the dust and smoke. He stepped through a door and found himself in the altar room. There were no living inhabitants.

Then he felt the altar at his back, and the giant laughed. He picked up his big ax and placed it against Ok'uwa'enu's chest.

The cave shook again, and a crack opened up in the floor. Both the young Indio and the giant Spaniard looked down. There was another rumble, and a jet of hot water shot up through the crack, directly into the giant. He fell over, screaming from the scalding jet. Ok'uwa'enu scrambled up off the floor and onto the bloody altar until the geyser finished.

By the time he was able to crawl down to the floor, the giant was dead. There was nobody left to fight. Ok'uwa was on his way out of the altar room when the movement of the Golden Scorpion caught his attention. Although the room itself was not shaking at the moment, the Scorpion was dancing and bouncing on the shelf where he sat.

He peered at the statue, trying to see why it was moving, and he saw ruby eyes glittering in a strange light. *Could the statue really be alive?* He couldn't quite tell.

by Kevin H. and Karen C. Evans

CHAPTER 28

Temple of Tocatl Coztic
Corridors of the cave

Eduardo finally got Raum moving. Before they left, he picked up the Teniente's sword and poniard. Steel was still rare in this wilderness, and he didn't like the thought of leaving it behind. The hallway was shaking, and the air was filled with dust and smoke.

Finally, the Teniente spoke again. "Eduardo, I can't seem to remember. Did I kill the high priest?"

Eduardo kept going. "No, Teniente. I didn't see him. He must have gone before I arrived."

Raum stopped and could not be moved farther. "Not dead? Take me back. I am charged with finishing this evil. That's an order, Eduardo."

Eduardo reluctantly turned around, and they headed back toward the altar room. And before they reached it, suddenly, as if he had risen up out of the floor of the hallway, stood the high priest.

Raum pushed Eduardo behind him and fumbled for a sword. The high priest laughed and picked up his war club. And just to demonstrate how uninjured he was, he made a show of swinging it around his head, laughing.

Raum watched in silence, then pulled his wheel-lock pistol from his sash and fired it toward the high priest's head. They were only six or seven feet apart.

The ball hit the Indio dead in the forehead, and he toppled over like a tree from the ax. Blood was pouring out a perfectly round hole in his forehead, and anyone could tell he was no longer a threat.

Eduardo and the Teniente stepped to the door of the altar room. That was when they saw Ok'uwa'enu. Raum felt as if he had not seen the Indio boy for a year, even though they had come into the cave together this afternoon. Ok'uwa was standing mesmerized in front of the Scorpion statue, as if it was talking and he was the only one who could hear. Raum shouted, "Ok'uwa, it's time to go. Leave that filthy thing here."

The boy didn't move. Raum leaned against the wall, and Eduardo went over and touched Ok'uwa's elbow. "Are you all right, my friend?"

Still, Ok'uwa didn't answer. Eduardo grabbed his arm and shook him, and the boy turned, dazed. Eduardo again said, "Are you all right?"

Ok'uwa blinked and then slowly nodded. "The Lord of Darkness is calling me. I don't want to go, but he is calling."

Raum came over, and with his good hand, slapped the boy across the face. "Snap out of it, Ok'uwa'enu. We must leave. The Dark Lord will have to be content with destruction."

Ok'uwa grabbed Raum's arm before he could be slapped again. "No, I must stay. I must destroy the Lord of Darkness before he finds others like these. It is my destiny." He pointed at the bodies of acolytes and the high priest on the floor. As Raum looked, he realized that although the high priest was Aztec, the others were local Indios, with one huge Spaniard dead near the altar.

The room shook again, and there was a rumble under the cracked flooring, just like there was before the giant was killed. "Teniente, Eduardo, my friends, you must go now. You will be killed. Go."

He pushed them from the altar room, then ran to the other end and wrestled the Golden Scorpion from its ledge. Eduardo was about to go to him again, but Raum stopped him. "Eduardo, let him go. This is something he must do. We have to go. We will see if we find any others alive. And perhaps, he will succeed and join us."

Eduardo nodded and put the Teniente's arm over his shoulder and hustled him out of the altar room, toward the entrance of the cave. Even as they turned the corner, they heard the geyser again and heard Ok'uwa'enu shouting in his native tongue.

Canyon of Tocatl Coztic
August 1635

Eduardo half-carried Raum out of the cave. They stopped in the sand at the bottom of the canyon, and he let the Teniente sit down on the sand. He was pleased to find that there were three other men from their party who had survived the battle and gotten out ahead of them. Even more surprising, Otfuwa had managed to free captives and was nursing the ill among them.

It was almost dawn, and Eduardo could not believe that he had been underground for almost a day. He found a comfortable spot for the Teniente and built a good fire. There were several more tremors, and finally the roof on the entrance cave collapsed, shooting out a cloud of dust.

They spent the rest of the day resting. Eduardo found a pack of supplies, and about dusk, little Pepito, the burro, came wandering into camp. He seemed pleased to have found humans again. There were less than twenty of them from the force that had numbered close to fifty. All were just glad to be out in the open air, alive.

That night was a rather pleasant time, with food, fire, and the comfortable feeling of safety that they hadn't felt in all the trip up the mountain to this place. Of the twenty men and boys that followed Teniente Raum into the cave yesterday, there were five left. And seventeen escaped captives. Eduardo felt so much cleaner sleeping where he could see stars.

At dawn, the next day, Teniente de Bances ordered them to pack up, help the three who were not very mobile, and head for Winat'api'iwe.

CHAPTER 29

**Village of Bernalillo
August 1635**

The trip back to Bernalillo was uneventful. When they came to the village gates, little Jose, Eduardo's younger brother, was first to see them, and ran shouting into Eduardo's arms. His shouts brought the rest of the village, and soon, Eduardo felt as if he were an island in the middle of a sea of people.

There was joy and tears as Eduardo recounted everyone with some highlights of his journey. And when Don Federico Bernal came running out to the plaza where they were all gathered, Eduardo found tears in his eyes at the relief he saw in his father and mother.

Father Philip came out to the plaza as well, and the mood was so buoyant that it was difficult to feel sad. Don Federico declared a feast day the first of September, and everyone got back to normal.

As the days went on, Eduardo found it difficult to give up hope of Ok'uwa'enu's surviving the earthquake that closed the cave. He wanted to go back and dig down, to see if Ok'uwa was still alive. But both Teniente Raum, as local commanding officer, and his father, Don Federico, vetoed that idea. It was almost impossible that Ok'uwa was alive.

Beyond that, the gathered shamans of the Pueblos, as well as the Apache, the Ute, and the Navajo, felt that it was only the heroic sacrifice of Ok'uwa'enu that saved all the others. They even performed a memorial dance for his spirit and warned all that the cave in the mountains was permanently stained with evil.

Cocinas of Bernalillo
September 1635

The celebration feast was successful. It also marked the time when they came together, a year previously, and agreed to share food and help each other survive. Now, Spaniard, Navajo, Apache, and Pueblo all felt part of the community. Father Philip sat at his table for the feast, outside near the cocinas, and looked over the crowd. There were still animosities and hatreds. Perhaps those would remain as long as this generation of people lasted, Father Philip didn't know. But here they were at a feast together, and there had been no threats of murder.

As the meal reached the late afternoon, Don Federico stood up on a small raised platform that had been built for him. He rang a small bell for attention, and when all eyes were turned to him, he began his speech. He and Father Philip had worked on it just this morning. "My fellow citizens of these Territories Al Dentro, I welcome you to our celebration of the destruction of the Cult of the Golden Scorpion. We come together today, united in our joy at the return of some of our loved ones and mourning for those who will not return but are with our ancestors."

There was some murmuring at this and sniffles from several women in the crowd. Don Federico continued. "We felt it was time to establish some leadership. I don't want any to feel that they are unrepresented. So, I want to hold an election."

He gestured, and from behind the platform, Eduardo and his friends, about six of them, came and placed a large empty cauldron on the ground in front of Don Federico. They also put two large baskets of small stones on the corners on either side of the Alcalde.

Don Federico said, "This election is for the heads of households or families. Each family can send one representative to vote. If you are the representative, you come to one of these buckets, and choose a small stone, either a black one, a red one, or a white one. You don't have to show it to anyone, but put it in the cauldron to represent your vote. The black stone is for Kogen-lii of the Apache. The red stone is for Okuwa-oky of the Pueblos. The white stone is for myself. You are choosing who you want to lead this group.

In each area of the feast, Father Philip watched as families and clans gathered to talk in their native tongue. Then, one by one, men stepped up to a basket, took a stone, hidden in his fist, and cast it into the cauldron.

At one point, someone stood up and waved an arm at Don Federico. It was a Navajo man, Ma-iit-soh. Don Federico stood up from where he'd been watching, and said, "What is it? You have a question?"

Ma-iit-soh said, "It is not the custom of our people to have the warriors make this kind of choice. We would send a woman to represent us."

Before Don Federico could speak, Father Philip stood. "I understand your concern, and I see no problem of her voting, as long as she is the selected representative of your clan."

Ma-iit-soh nodded and sat back down. In a moment, a woman stood. She was dressed very finely in a dark skirt and bright red woven shirt.

The back of her hair was done in the elegant squash blossom style, and she was wearing a treasury of silver and turquoise jewelry. She came forward, chose a stone from a basket, and cast it in the cauldron. She frowned at Father Philip, then at Don Federico, and sat back down.

By evening, all had voted. Father Philip, friend Blue-eyes, was trusted to count the stones. He did so in sight of everyone. He took out a stone, announced its color, and put it in the appropriate pile. There were many white stones.

Finally, Father Philip stood and said, "It is finished. There were a few votes for Kogen-lii and many more for Okuwa-oky. But the majority was white stones for Don Federico as governor.

The crowd broke into cheers and laughter. Don Federico was the governor. He stood up and said, "I accept your choice, and I will do my best on your behalf. Now, as my first act as governor, I propose that we choose the leader of our Catholic church. I propose that Father Philip be chosen as Bishop of Bernalillo.

The cheers and shouts were louder than they had been for the election of Governor. Father Philip stood up and tried to talk, but the noise would not stop. Finally, Governor Bernal stood up and signaled for silence.

Then Father Philip said, "I can't allow our governor to interfere with the operations of the Church, but I will serve as a leader if that's what is wanted."

The cheers were louder, if it was possible. It was embarrassing to Father Philip, but he stood next to Don Federico and said no more.

The next couple of days, in clumps and hoards, the people filtered out of Bernalillo to their own homes. There was still the last of the harvest to store, and some of the more nomadic folk were preparing to head for winter camp sites.

Father Philip's Scriptorium
October 1635

A couple of weeks after the exodus, Father Philip was surprised when Don Raum de Bances knocked on his door. Don Raum had been firmly established by Don Federico as commander of the few soldiers remaining in the territory. Father Philip stood up and cleaned off a chair. "Don Raum, what can I do for you? Sit down."

The young man sat down and stared at his hands in front of him. Father Philip was content to sit and wait for the young man to come to his purpose. Finally, Don Raum said, "Well, Father, things have changed since Governor General led the Spaniards out of the territory."

Father Philip said, "Yes, many things have changed. I'm now in charge of churches all over the territory, and you're in charge of our small force of soldiers. How many do you have now?"

Don Raum shrugged. "It's hard to tell. There are still stragglers arriving from who knows where. I'd say we have about twenty men, some swords and halberds, and only six muskets and two pistols. The supply of gunpowder is down to two barrels that Don Federico had hidden away before the bulk of the Spanish left."

Then he said nothing. Father Philip said, "Are you concerned that you don't have enough resources to protect us from attack?"

Don Raum was staring at the floor now. He shook his head and stroked his beard. Father Philip examined the young man. He still had his left arm in a sling and would probably always walk with a limp. The father could tell Raum had something on his mind. Father Philip let him sit for a moment, then asked, "Son, do you have a question, or is this a social call?"

Raum sat for a moment longer. "Father, what do you think of this business? I mean, the Indios worshiping an idol?"

Father Philip leaned back and steepled his fingers. "Are you speaking of the Aztec cult that we so recently resisted? Because they have been on my mind of late as well."

Raum looked at the Jesuit. "Father, I don't know about some of this. I think I have been possessed by a demon."

293

Father Philip's face showed none of the concern he felt. "What exactly do you mean, Teniente?"

Raum leaned back and stared at a blank wall, but Father Philip knew that he wasn't looking at the wall, he was seeing something far away. "In the past weeks, in my dreams, and now even in my waking hours, I can hear Ok'uwa'enu's voice, chanting as we ran from the cave. I dream that he is still there, that I need to go back and save him. And yet, there is something else. Something that is not Ok'uwa. Something that frightens me."

Father Philip looked closely at this young man. Even with all his accomplishments and his obvious courage and determination to do his duty, this man was still young, not yet thirty. But he had not slept well, as evidenced by the dark circles around his eyes. "Tell me, Raum, do you think you are a good man?"

The Teniente shook his head. "I have gone to confession and prayed for forgiveness. I lit a candle for each member of our troop who was lost, and I have even prayed for Carlos and Pepe, though they stole and cheated and fought against us. But I also find flaws in my character, such as sloth, and greed. And I have these dreams every nightand so metimes into my waking hours. Perhaps I am not a good man." De Bances leaned forward, and put his face in his hands, looking hopeless.

Father Philip put his hand on the Teniente's knee. "All good men doubt. All good men have moments when thcy wonder if they have faith. You are no different. And yet you worry that you are possessed of an evil spirit? Has it forced you to commit sin?"

Raum shook his head. "No, but I hear a whispering voice calling me to the cave. I fear that I have an evil heart, and the evil there is calling to me."

Father Philip put his hand on Raum's arm and waited until the young man looked up. When he did, the soldier's face was streaked with tears.

"Raum, a demon possessing you would not let you do good. It would not allow you to feel remorse or worry if you are good. It would not allow you to pray. It would consume your soul and leave you a dry husk. I think that the shamans, as deluded they may be for not following Our Lord," and Father Philip crossed himself, and touched his rosary, "they may have it right. That cave is an evil place, and we need to stay away as we would avoid all sin. You do not have an evil heart, but if you are still worried, go to the chapel and say your Hail Marys."

Don Raum stood up, and nodded. "Yes, Father, I will try."

Hacienda Bernalillo
October 1635

Eduardo did not go to talk to Father Tómas, but he also had bad dreams. He was not the only one. Most of those that had been captives, or anyone who had escaped before the cavern collapsed, woke up screaming in the night. Eduardo knew that the Teniente de Bances did not sleep well either. But every night, Eduardo hesitated going to bed. Sleep was not his ally as it had been before the expedition to the scorpion cave.

His dream was always the same. He would see himself, lit only by torchlight, helping Teniente Raum out of the cave while his friend, Ok'uwa'enu, stood watching. Then, when the Teniente was safe, Eduardo would turn back and watch the cave collapse and close. Ok'uwa'enu never came home.

Tonight was worse than ever. Eduardo had been sitting in the cantina until they threw him out so they could close. Then he went to the stable to sit with his burro. And Esteban, the stable master, had sent him away as well. "Go home, Eduardo. Get some sleep. Leave the horses and your burro to do the same."

When he reached his hacienda, Eduardo found his mother waiting for him. "Eduardo, why aren't you in bed yet? There are things we must do in the morning."

Eduardo ran his fingers through his hair and stared out the window. "Mother, you know why I can't go to bed. The ghosts won't let me sleep. I keep dreaming about Ok'uwa'enu."

Garciella put her hand on Eduardo's head, just like she had done when he was a little boy. "I know, son. That's why I made you some of this tea. It has herbs that will help you sleep. If you don't get some rest you'll fall ill, and the ghosts will reap your soul. Drink all of this. I put some honey in for you."

She handed him the cup with curls of steam decorating the top. Eduardo smelled chamomile and honey, and there was a bit of mint and something else less familiar. He sipped it under his mother's watchful eye, and finally set the empty cup on the table and stood up. "Good night, mother."

Garciella went up on tiptoes, and Eduardo bent his head a little so she could reach. She kissed his forehead and patted his chest. He put his arm around her and gave her a hug, then turned and headed for his bed.

The tea was very effective at getting him to sleep. Unfortunately, it couldn't keep him asleep. Before long, Eduardo was aware that the room was very cold. But it was summer, how could it be so cold?

Then he saw Ok'uwa at the foot of his bed. At least he hoped it was Ok'uwa'enu. Mostly it was a skeleton with red burning eyes. But it had Ok'uwa'enu's knife strapped on its waist and the sacred pouch that only Ok'uwa could wear. Eduardo sat up in bed.

The skeleton raised a hand and pointed directly at his heart. "Eduardo, you left my bones in that evil place. Now I'm cursed. I cannot rest. How can I go to my ancestors if my bones lie buried with the Scorpion and the evil men we killed here?"

Eduardo crossed himself. After all, it is very disturbing to see a ghost. He could tell he was dreaming, but it was so real that he wondered if he was seeing a vision. If so, he wished his soul had been shriven. "Ok'uwa, the Teniente prevented me from going back in. And when the roof of the cavern collapsed, he said that you wouldn't be able to . . ."

The ghost held up a bony finger. "The Teniente was not my friend as you were. He has his own conscience to answer to. You must decide." Then the ghost leaned toward Eduardo, and laughed. The laugh echoed in his bedroom.

Eduardo sat straight up in bed. Now he was awake. He could see that he had been dreaming and that there was no skeleton or ghost. There had been nothing that awakened his two younger brothers in the same bed. But he was shaking, and his stomach clenched, making him feel like he was going to wretch.

He climbed out of bed, dressed quickly, and went out to the kitchen. He gathered some bread and cheese, tied them up in a napkin, then hurried to the stables. Pepito was there and happy to see him. Eduardo slipped a simple loop over Pepito's head, a small blanket on the burro's back, and rode out to find the cave where Ok'uwa'enu had died.

* * *

Garciella tapped lightly on the door of the scriptorium, then stood and wrung her hands. What if Father Philip wasn't there? Or worse, what if he was, and she would have to try and explain her fears.

The door opened, and Father Philip stood, smiling. "Doña Garciella, come in and sit. Would you like some wine?"

Garciella stepped into the small room and sat in the chair held by Father Philip. "No, thank you. I just had some concerns. It's about my son, Eduardo. He hasn't been sleeping well, nightmares and such. And this morning, when I went to check on him, he was gone. I don't know what to do. Is it better to send out a search party and bring him home? What can I do to ease his mind?"

Father Philip sat at his desk and sighed. "He's gone? I will talk to Teniente de Bances; he's probably the most dependable. And both are suffering from their battle in the cursed cave. Maybe they can help each other.

Jemez Mountains, near the Cavern of Tocatl Coztic
October 1635

Of course, Eduardo had forgotten how far away the cave was. When he went out to meet the expedition, he had walked for three days to get to the village of Winat'api'iwe and then walked a couple more days. So he didn't arrive to the hidden cave for five days. By then, Pepito was not as thrilled to be with Eduardo. The small beast definitely didn't like to be in the vicinity of this cave. In fact, it had been a full day since he had seen any wildlife. It's not something one realizes until there is a lack. But there were no crows in the trees, no squirrels on the branches, and not even any flies or mosquitoes to pester or swarm around his head. It was silent.

Eduardo was not enjoying it much, either. As he traveled, the bad dreams had continued, and now, within sight of the cave entrance, Eduardo knew that he was under the compulsion of something more than the ghost of Ok'uwa'enu. The closer he got to the mouth of the cave, the more he didn't want to go in, and yet, he watched as his own feet walked him closer and closer. Eduardo wrestled with the compulsion, and it wavered a moment.

He was standing at the mouth of the entrance cave, struggling to run away. Then there was a ground tremor, and he stopped moving forward. Inside his head, Eduardo struggled as he had never fought before.

There was another shaking of the earth, and Eduardo heard an odd scrabbling. It sounded like something under all the rock in the cave was trying to dig its way out of the cave. He stood still, hardly breathing.

The sand and pebbles trickled down from a place about halfway up the pile of debris, and Eduardo squinted. Was there movement? Did he see something? Suddenly he could move, but instead of running, he moved forward. He stood in the mouth of the cave, peering all the way to the back.

There was something moving in the gravel like a trout negotiating a shallow stream. The rocks moved around it but didn't reveal the nature of the beast.

Eduardo took another step into the cave and was grabbed from behind. A hand was on his arm, pulling. "Eduardo, don't do it."

Eduardo turned and stared into the face of Teniente de Bances. The soldier had his arm in a death grip and was pulling him out of the cave. "Wait, did you see it? Teniente, let me look just for another moment."

Raum stopped pulling but did not let go of Eduardo's left arm. "What is there to see? Everyone who was here is dead. You know it: you killed some of them, and so did I. And so did the earthquake and cave collapse."

Eduardo held his head in his hands. "Do you hear him, Raum? Do you hear Ok'uwa? He won't let me sleep."

Teniente de Bances looked distressed. "I have heard him, Eduardo. But he is not here. His ghost is in your own head. Come home with me now. There is nothing we can do here."

Eduardo let out a long sigh. "There is one thing. I want to build a bonfire in there, and cleanse this cave."

by Kevin H. and Karen C. Evans

The sigh from Teniente de Bances was long and drawn out, as if he was blowing all the poisoned air from his lungs once and for all. "All right, Eduardo. Let's burn out the cave, and send their spirits to God's judgment."

Bernalillo Village
November 1635

Father Philip paced near the gate of the village while Baji-delier stood nearby, not sure how to help Friend Blue-eyes. They had come every evening for ten days, since he had sent the Teniente after Eduardo. There was just no way to tell what had happened. Baji said, "Father Blue-eyes, come back to the church. Either they will come home tonight, or they will not. Worrying by the gate will not . . ."

Marco, up on the wall, shouted. "It's them. I see the Teniente with Fausto, and he's walking beside Eduardo. They're home."

That caused a stir, as children ran home to tell their families. So before the young men were inside the gate, the village was on the road to meet them. Don Federico stood in front of everyone, smiling. His wife, Garciella stood next to him, frowning, with her arms folded across her chest.

Father Philip hurried out as de Bances stepped down from his saddle. "My boy, good to see you home again. I have prayed every day since you left. I see you resisted the dreams."

Teniente de Bances actually grinned, as nobody had seen him do since before the battle in the cave.

Don Federico hugged his son to his chest and wept. "Eduardo, why did you go? There is nothing there t0 find. All are dead, the good, the bad, the innocent, and the evil."

Eduardo stepped back from his father, and realized they both had tears. "I'm sorry I frightened mother. But I had to do something."

Don Federico looked deep into Eduardo's eyes and finally stepped back as well. He didn't find darkness there. "What did you do?"

Eduardo sighed and stretched. "The Teniente helped me, and we built a bonfire in the center of the cave. We burned out the cave to rid ourselves of the disease there. We watched until the coals were white. The ghosts are gone."

The Village of El Paso-
November 1634

Governor General Francisco de la Mora Ceballos sat in his office in a large house in the village of El Paso del Norte. He reflected on the past weeks. The suffering of the march had been so much more difficult than the battle of Santa Fe.

When he'd arrived in Socorro, he arrested Teniente Governor Carlos Francisco Gonzalez. Ceballos accused him of cowardice for not sending help to Santa Fe. It is true that they saved the storehouse of food from being burned and so insured the refugee column survival through the winter. And he evacuated the women and children from the rebellious Indios. It is true, he'd needed every able-bodied man to escort their column. So there were none to send north. Finally, after several days of testimony, Gonzalez was exonerated.

After that, there was a week of argument about whether or not they should stay in Socorro or go farther south. There were Indios with them. The entire pueblo of Isleta had evacuated with the Teniente Governor. These people worried that they would be harassed by the Apaches who lived nearby.

It was decided that in order to reach true safety, they would march to El Paso, and then build forces for a reconquest. But in order to do that, they had to take not only soldiers, but women and children, through the long dry miles across the valley known as the Journey of Death.

The preparations for the march south had consumed everybody for another week. And the less said about the miles between Socorro and El Paso, the better. It had been dry, and cold as the first storms of winter were now blowing across the valley.

Now Ceballos sat in a very civilized office in the town of El Paso, staring out a window. Standing nearby, Teniente Governor Carlos Francisco Gonzalez sipped a cup of wine. "Yes, Your Excellency. I agree we should have a solid place from which to start. We will need much of supplies and support from Mexico City, and that will take time. We need new weapons, and especially cannon. Our feet must be underneath us, and then we will punish these rebels."

Ceballos grinned. "I had my clerk copy the article from Father Philip that began this whole disaster. I was reading it just last night and learned something valuable. According to the letter from the Britannica, whatever that is, the pueblo revolt was successful, but Spain returned twelve years later. That gives us a goal and an opportunity to make a name for ourselves. We have twelve years to prepare, then we will return to Al Dentro and make those Indios pay for their mistakes."

Ceballos stood and stepped closer to Gonzalez. "A toast, then, to our eventual return. Let's drink to the reconquista. They will pay for what they have done." They drank the wine and laughed.

Printed in Poland
by Amazon Fulfillment
Poland Sp. z o.o., Wrocław

60555212R00175